PRAISE FOR

CITY OF PEACE

"Deeply spiritual writers often have difficulty with suspense. Not Henry Brinton. Faith's challenges are present along with its opportunities as the protagonist, Harley Camden, confronts both real and imagined assaults on his sensitivities. *City of Peace* is timely, compelling and entertaining—in hockey they call that the 'hat trick.'"

—**AL SIKES**, author of *Culture Leads Leaders Follow* and former Chair of the Federal Communications Commission under George H.W. Bush

"A tale of overcoming rage, unlearning religious prejudice, and finding the ground of community and forgiveness, Brinton's *City of Peace* speaks a needed pastoral word into our troubled, fractious time."

—**DAVID WILLIAMS**, author of *When the English Fall*

"The story of Harley is not just the story of one man, but also a story that many can relate to, one going from frustration and sadness into redemption, forgiveness and reconciliation. A must read."

—**SHAHID RAHMAN**, Executive Director, American Muslim Institution

"I have gotten to know Harley Camden and am all the better for it. In his stunning book *City of Peace*, Henry Brinton gives us unforgettable characters, an engaging and provocative story, and worthy revelations for us all."

—**PETER M. WALLACE**, author of *The Passionate Jesus* and producer/host of the Day1 radio program

"*City of Peace* allows us to see our religiously divided world through the eyes of a pastor in pain. Harley's grief opens him to receive comfort from unexpected places—shared meals with new neighbors, the sight of ospreys on the Potomac, and the needs of a young Muslim man. Such moments not only help heal Harley's grief, but equip him for the challenges of ministering in a community wracked by hate."

—**REV. RUTH EVERHART**, author of *Ruined (a memoir)*

"Terrorist murderers can change a loving man from the inside out when the victims are his wife and daughter. Henry Brinton's writing prowess is applied to the full extent of his storytelling power in this, his premiere novel, *City of Peace*, where he poignantly portrays the inner turmoil of a righteous and wounded soul, whose healing, and redemption, crosses the most unexpected of cultural and religious lines."

—**PETER PANAGORE**, bestselling author of *Heaven Is Beautiful: How Dying Taught Me That Death is Just The Beginning*

"A wonderful novel that reminds us of our shared humanity across faith and national origin through the personal struggle of a pastor trying to rebuild his life in the historic town of Occoquan in the suburbs of Washington D.C. Henry Brinton uses his own experiences to bring to life the complex dynamics of living in an extraordinarily diverse region and ultimately leaves us with the hope that diverse communities can be immensely enriching to all of us."

—**ÁNGEL CABRERA**, president, George Mason University

"What's a Presbyterian pastor doing writing a page-turning murder mystery? I'd say doing a dazzling job reaching readers who will appreciate a terrific mix of the spiritual and the thrilling."

—**MIKE MCCURRY**, former White House Press Secretary and Director, Center for Public Theology at Wesley Theological Seminary

"*City of Peace* is an enjoyable, well-written and face-paced story that illustrates how radical hospitality, especially in our current fractured political and social milieu, can restore individual and corporate peace to people who have suffered great personal loss and who have fears for future travails."

—**MIKE FROSOLONO**, author of *Beyond Duty, Comfort and Affliction,* and *Thoroughly Biased Opinions*

"After terrorists kill his family, a Methodist minister confronts his own prejudices when he takes over a struggling congregation. Unknown to him, his new home holds secrets that set him on an adventure as unwitting sleuth, confessor and witness. A compelling exploration of racism in a small town wrapped inside a murder mystery."

—**RICK PULLEN**, bestselling thriller author of *Naked Truth* and *Naked Ambition*

"A unique murder mystery with spiritual overtones, demonstrating how God can deliver good out of evil. You will find this timely book to be uplifting, an excellent and thought-provoking story."

—**JOHN J. JESSOP**, author of *Pleasuria: Take As Directed; Guardian Angel: Unforgiven; Guardian Angel: Indoctrination*

City of Peace
by Henry G. Brinton

Published by

◤ köehlerbooks™

210 60th Street
Virginia Beach, VA 23451
800−435−4811
www.koehlerbooks.com

City of Peace

A NOVEL

HENRY G. BRINTON

VIRGINIA BEACH
CAPE CHARLES

To Sadie, Sam, and Nancy Freeborne Brinton

Lovers of Occoquan

And to Eric and Carol Meyers

Diggers of Sepphoris

CHAPTER 1

Harley Camden was cleaning the deck of his powerboat when a Pakistani family appeared on the dock. His head was down as he scrubbed a number of mysterious black marks stubbornly adhering to the white fiberglass. The air was hot and heavy on the Fourth of July, and Harley grew frustrated by his lack of progress. Sweat flowed from beneath his red Washington Nationals baseball cap and dripped inside his sunglasses. He would need a second shower.

He had already cleaned up and dressed for the day, with no intention of working in the sun until he visited the boat and noticed the marks on the deck. He loved his boat—a twenty-three-footer with seating for thirteen and a powerful inboard-outboard engine—but hated the way that little maintenance projects called out to him like sirens.

"How much for a ride?" asked a voice from the dock. Harley looked up and saw a man with jet-black hair and a shirt with a computer company logo, standing in the middle of his family. A young girl with big brown eyes held tightly to his hand, looking expectantly at the boat bobbing by the dock. The man's wife gazed over his shoulder, smiling. An older man and woman dressed in colorful Pakistani shalwar kameez, probably the girl's grandparents, stood silently to the side, gazing stoically at the water. To Harley, they looked out of place beside the river. The flood of immigrants doing high-tech and service work was rapidly changing the Washington, DC suburbs. *More Muslims*, he thought. Restaurants and shops in his little Northern Virginia town, which had once had a largely white clientele, now drew a mix of Africans, Latinos, Asians and Middle Easterners—including Muslim women in headscarves.

Harley was a fifty-seven-year-old Methodist minister with a round face, thinning gray hair and a goatee, in decent shape from running but carrying about ten extra pounds. To the Pakistani family, he must have looked like a commoner who quit high school—most certainly not a graduate of the vaunted Duke University Divinity School. No, this sweaty fellow scrubbing stains on his boat must be a renegade, taking people on fishing trips and pleasure cruises on the Potomac River, enjoying a life of freedom in the outdoors while struggling with alcoholism and chronic basal cell carcinomas.

"Sorry, but this is not a charter boat," said Harley, wiping his hands on a dirty towel. The man smiled politely, but Harley could tell he was disappointed. "You might be able to arrange something down at Maxine's." Harley pointed down the town dock toward a large restaurant with kayaks and paddleboards for rent. The man nodded, picked up his daughter, and guided his wife and the grandparents toward Maxine's.

The sparkle on the river, herons swooping out of the sky, the lush green of the trees on the opposite bank, fishermen casting their lines under the Route 123 bridge—the entire scene was sleepy Virginia river town, duplicated in numerous places throughout the state. Harley had fallen in love with it, and suddenly realized that being a charter boat captain was not a bad idea—if the ministry business didn't work out. Still, the thought of taking a group of Muslims made him feel queasy.

Tossing his towel on the floating dock, Harley pulled the key out of the boat's ignition and checked all of the dock lines. He walked up a metal dock ramp and looked down the dock toward Maxine's and saw a large pontoon boat pulling in. No Pakistanis.

Harley walked between the rows of townhouses facing the water to his own place, which was on a street running parallel to the river. He lived in a community of twenty Victorian townhouses, patterned after the "Painted Ladies" of San Francisco, constructed with porches and bedecked with whimsical ornamentations. Ten of the townhouses faced the river and ten faced the street; each had a private dock. The rich folks lived on the river side and the poor folks lived on the street side, or so Harley liked to think. But the reality was that they were all pretty wealthy and were fortunate to have water access in a quaint historic town within a half hour of Washington.

As he walked up the wrought-iron steps to his house, 233 Mill Street, Harley reflected on the journey that had brought him to town. It was not a happy story. He had been the pastor of a growing Methodist church in Sterling, Virginia, a booming suburban city two counties north of his new home. As senior pastor of that congregation, he supervised two associate pastors, a youth director, a director of Christian education, a variety of musicians, and a number of office administrators—a large staff of church workers responsible for worship services and programs that ran seven days a week. At age fifty-six, Harley was at the peak of his career and proud of steering his church through the narrow passage between the Religious Right and the Secular Left, avoiding politics and preaching sermons that helped people to follow the path of Jesus. He led traditional services with organ music and hymns, as well as contemporary services with electric guitars and praise music, trying his best to offer a smorgasbord of spiritual nourishment. His efforts had seemed to be paying off, as church members heard his sermons and responded by doing what Jesus would do—feeding the hungry, sheltering the homeless, visiting prisoners, and welcoming strangers.

Then terrorists attacked the airport in Brussels. Harley's wife, Karen, and his college-age daughter, Jessica, were on a long-awaited spring break trip, which Harley couldn't join because he was swamped with preparations for Easter. He walked into a church staff meeting that Tuesday morning, hearing a news report about a bombing but not worrying about his family because he thought they were in London. When he finished the meeting, he happened to check their itinerary and saw that they were in Brussels. He called his wife's cell phone in a panic and got nothing but voicemail. Again and again he dialed the number, hoping that her battery had died or she had lost the phone. But soon Holy Week became the most unholy, revolving around a series of conversations with authorities and the growing realization that his wife and daughter had been killed. Harley ended up flying to Belgium and spending Good Friday in a morgue, identifying bodies.

The terrorists had carried nail bombs in large suitcases. The explosives sent shrapnel in high speeds in every direction. The officer who pulled back the white sheets and showed Harley the bodies tried to comfort him in broken English, telling him that Karen and Jessica had died instantly. A kind thought, but small comfort.

Harley had seen many dead bodies as a pastor, spending time with parishioners in hospital rooms and nursing homes as they took their last breaths. But nothing could prepare him for the sight of his wife and only child on stainless-steel tables in a foreign morgue. Although their cold skin had been scrubbed free of blood, he saw numerous punctures from nails all over their bodies. Jessica's hands were pierced in both palms, just like Jesus. He kissed them both, thankful that their faces were unscathed. Perhaps the bombs had detonated behind them. Or they had turned away to look at something in the airport. It didn't matter, and yet it did. He spent Saturday arranging for the return of their bodies to the United States and then caught an early flight home on Easter morning. The theme of the day was resurrection, which was what one of his associate pastors was proclaiming that morning in Sterling. It remained a distant and fuzzy concept as he stared out the window of the plane at a sea of clouds that contained no evidence of heaven. In a single act of brutal violence, Harley's family had been turned to dust and ashes.

The church staff and congregation were good to him, of course. They were kind and caring people. His colleagues covered his duties during bereavement leave and did a beautiful job with the funerals for Karen and Jessica. The congregation put on a lavish funeral reception and organized home-cooked meals for Harley every night for three months. People prayed, wrote cards, visited and ran errands. They were doing everything that they had been taught to do, showing the compassion of Jesus in their words and actions. But even though Harley appreciated this support and was comforted by it, his grief left him without energy or motivation. He had trouble getting out of bed in the morning and struggled to stay focused on his work in the church office. He seemed distracted in his meetings and counseling sessions with church members. When he finally returned to the pulpit, his sermons were listless. A once-inspirational lead pastor had become a drag on the church community.

What his parishioners could not see, and what he didn't dare to admit, was the rage eating him up. After the shock of the killings wore off, Harley's anger enveloped not just the murderous terrorists but all Muslims. Such racial and religious hatred were antithetical to what Jesus taught and his training at divinity school. His contempt distracted him when he tried to write sermons at church, made him short-tempered in lines at the grocery store, and took him to some very dark places when he was home alone at night. He started drinking alone in a recliner at the end of the day, quickly progressing from one drink a night to four. He would nod off in the recliner and be awakened by nightmares. His dreams became more real to him, the place where he could express his rage.

One dream mashed up the Brussels bombing and his seminary study of Dante's *Inferno*. It started with him spiraling down into darkness, flailing his arms and legs in a futile attempt to grab hold of something and stop his fall. He sensed that he was tumbling into hell, but for some reason the temperature became colder as he fell, not hotter. Finally, he plunged feetfirst into freezing water, and ice quickly closed around him so that he was trapped up to his waist. His legs were numb, he could move only his arms and head, and in the world of the dream he was convinced that he would be stuck in that dark ice pack forever. But Harley was not alone. His chest was pressed against

the back of a man in front of him—one of the terrorists who had killed
Harley's wife and daughter. Harley could not see the face of the man,
but he began to gnaw on the terrorist's head, chewing through his
scalp and skull and beginning to consume his brain. The terrorist and
the pastor were stuck in a frozen hell, locked together eternally by
their hatred for one another. When Harley woke, he felt immediate
relief that he was not trapped in eternal ice. But he felt no less angry.

After a year, the bishop had to step in. She was a tall woman in her
early sixties, with short gray hair and an attractive face. She visited
Harley in his office and talked with him about how he was feeling
and whether he was benefiting from grief counseling. He shrugged
and looked out the window, pausing for a few moments before saying
that grieving was a long process and he didn't know when he'd be
back to full strength. He did notice one positive change—he had
much less patience with the petty parish issues that used to consume
so much of his time.

"Yes, I've heard about that," said the bishop.

"Yeah," said Harley. "I used to spend a lot of time and energy
mediating church fights." He smiled for the first time in their meeting.
"Now, I'm quick to call people on their crap." He became animated
as he began to tell his story. "Disagreements about the color of paint
in the church parlor, whether a service begins with a praise song
or a hymn, whole wheat or white bread for Communion—I got
no time for it. Last week, the mother of a teenager came into my
office, angry that our youth director had been talking with middle
school students, including her precious daughter, about sexting. She
was horrified that a youth director would talk with thirteen-year-
olds about such a topic. I said, 'Look, I know for a fact that kids in
middle school are using their cell phones to send naked pictures of
themselves to each other. This kind of behavior is not going to stop
if we ignore it. I am giving our youth director my full support, and I
expect you to do the same.'"

The bishop took a deep breath. "Harley, I appreciate your candor,
but that kind of honesty doesn't always work. That woman called me
right after she spoke to you, and she is still upset."

"That's her problem, not mine."

"No, it's still your problem," insisted the bishop. "People deserve respect, even when you disagree with them."

"I'm just being honest," said Harley. "People need to hear the truth. You know, 'The truth will set you free.'"

That scripture had become one of Harley's favorites in recent months, along with Psalm 145, "The Lord watches over all who love him, but all the wicked he will destroy," and Revelation 16, "Go and pour out on the earth the seven bowls of the wrath of God."

The bishop struggled to find the right words. "I think I'm going to have to set you free, in a manner of speaking."

The blood drained from Harley's face as he began to think of what her next sentence might be. He had lifetime job security as a Methodist minister, but there were some pretty lousy places he could be sent for the last years of his career. His salary in Sterling was at the top of the pay scale, and he loved the large five-bedroom colonial that the church provided for him and his family. Sure, the house was too big now that Karen and Jessica were gone, but it was filled with their things and it helped him to feel close to them. He wanted to stay there if he possibly could and realized that this was probably his last chance to change the bishop's mind. He bit his lip and told himself to control the anger.

"Is this because of my sermon about the Islamic State?" he asked, point-blank. The bishop just sat there, absorbing the question. "How could I not address the barbarity of those cold-blooded killers, cutting off the heads of Coptic Christians in Libya? Yes, I know that we Christians have to work for peace. We're peacemakers, I get it. But the path to peace in the Middle East has got to include defeating the Islamic State. Anything else is just feel-good fantasy. I felt called by God to preach that sermon—the Sunday was, after all, close to the anniversary of those murders."

Everyone who heard the sermon knew how personal the issue was for him, and no one criticized his passion—especially since his preaching had become so listless after the deaths of his wife and daughter. But his graphic descriptions of the beheadings and calls for increased use of drone strikes against Islamic State commanders was a bit much for families with young children. One little girl had started crying in the middle of the sermon. A few mothers in the congregation questioned his judgment after the service, asking him to dismiss the children before talking about such topics. Harley showed little empathy. "That's the world we live in," he huffed.

The bishop had received a few complaints about that sermon. "I'm not here to talk about freedom of the pulpit, but instead to talk about your ability to serve a church as large as Sterling. You know, Harley, that you've got to be at your best to manage a congregation that large. Stuff is coming at you all the time, and you've got to be nimble and flexible—and respectful."

"How about truthful?" Harley asked, bitterly. "Is there any room for truth?"

"Sure there is," replied the bishop. "But truth has to be spoken in ways that people can hear. If you push people to get with your program, they are going to push back. If you talk about beheadings in a church service that is full of families with children, they are going to walk out and head down the street to a church with a more positive message. You know all this, Harley. You never would have made it to Sterling if you weren't diplomatic and thoughtful."

Harley looked out the window, gazing at the delicate cherry blossoms in the churchyard. He looked without seeing, feeling nothing but a slow-boiling rage. Yes, he was once an expert at diplomacy, but that was before the deaths of Karen and Jessica. Massaging the feelings of parishioners and carefully choosing his words now seemed like completely trivial pursuits. Dishonest, even. In a world in which terrorists slaughtered innocent air travelers and cut off the heads of Coptic Christians, what was the point of working hard to keep everyone happy? Speaking the truth about Islamic extremism was going to make people uncomfortable, but it was certainly more important than creating a bubble of happiness in an affluent Northern Virginia congregation. Of course, he knew that anger was not the most constructive of emotions—it could be so corrosive. But at times it was the only thing he could feel. Tender emotions such as joy and compassion were crushed by the weight of his grief, becoming flat as flowers pressed in the pages of a book. Only anger could stand up and assert itself, so Harley welcomed it. It was better than feeling nothing.

"Sterling needs a high-energy pastor with the ability to keep a lot of balls in the air without dropping more than one or two. You were that guy for five years, Harley, and I'm really grateful to you."

Here it comes, he thought. He had lost his family, and now he was going to lose his job. He felt a wave of panic as he thought of himself becoming another middle-aged loser, replaced by a younger man, a woman—or a minority.

"I could be that guy again. You know it. I just need a little more time. Time to heal."

"Unfortunately, Sterling can't wait," said the bishop. "The budget is in trouble because people are voting with their feet. Worship attendance is down, and you know how important metrics are in the church today. You are an excellent preacher, Harley, but your anger in the pulpit is not fitting our brand of 'open hearts, open minds, open doors.'"

Right about that, thought Harley. Now the bishop was going to show him an open door.

"Finally," the bishop stated with some reluctance, "your staff is in a leadership vacuum. They need firm guidance if they are to provide quality ministry, and you have not been giving it to them."

"Is this about Jack?" Harley interrupted.

Sterling had two associate pastors, Jack Stover and Emily Kim. Jack was a hyper-competitive young pastor who never missed a chance to grab a moment in the spotlight. Although he had offered words of comfort and support to Harley in his time of grief, Harley sensed that he was grumbling behind his back and undermining him at every turn. Emily had always been a true team player, but Jack wanted to be the star.

"Well, Jack has spoken to me," admitted the bishop, "but so have other staff members. They love you, Harley, but they need your full energy and attention. Remember how I said at a senior pastors' meeting that the greatest gift you can give your staff is the gift of clarity? Well, you are not giving them the clarity they need to do effective ministry and mission."

Clarity, schmarity. Harley gave a half-hearted nod. "Well, it may be that most of them love me, but I think that Jack is sharpening his knives. He has been looking for chinks in my armor for months now. I've always heard that associate pastors have a lust to kill the king, but I never believed it till I met Jack."

"Come on, Harley, he's not that bad," insisted the bishop.

"Oh really?" Harley smiled. "Then put him on your staff."

"Don't change the subject. I am here to talk about you."

"Tell me that you are not going to give Jack my job," said Harley.

"Of course not," replied the bishop. "There's no way that he is ready. He has a lot of gifts, but he will need many more years before he can handle a complex congregation like Sterling." She smiled wryly. "He might feel that he's equipped, but he's not."

Her words came as a relief. Maybe the bishop still knew what she was doing. He realized at that moment that he wasn't going to be able to change her mind, but he sensed that he could trust her.

"Okay, Your Honor, what's my sentence?"

The bishop laughed. "I'm not sending you to the gallows, Harley. Not even to prison. You are a good man, and you've got some promising years in front of you. I'm sending you to Occoquan."

"Occo-what?"

CHAPTER 2

Riverside Methodist Church in Occoquan had a black Jesus. Harley noticed it the first time he walked into the small sanctuary and looked up at the stained-glass window at the front of the church. At first, he thought that the glass was simply dirty, but as he moved closer he realized Jesus was designed to look more like a Palestinian Jew than an English Methodist. *That's probably historically accurate*, he thought, *and politically correct*. But then he looked closer and saw the date on the lower right corner of the window—1885. The dark-skinned Jesus had been installed in an era when most stained-glass images of him were decidedly Northern European white. This Jesus had a determined look as he calmed the waters of the Sea of Galilee. Harley quickly realized why. Riverside Methodist had been founded by a pastor named Bailey, a former slave, and for over a century it had been an African-American congregation called Emanuel Baptist Church.

Harley visited the church on his first trip to Occoquan, a small town perched on the southern shore of the Occoquan River. Driving south from Sterling, he took Route 123 through southern Fairfax County and passed the old Lorton prison, now repurposed as an arts center called the Workhouse. *The bishop said she wasn't sending me to prison*, he mused as he drove past, *but look—there it is.* A steep hill, heavily forested on both sides, dropped from the arts center to the Occoquan River. Harley was surprised by the simple beauty of the concrete bridge sweeping across the water into Prince William County, presenting drivers with a panoramic view of the Town of Occoquan to the west. He slowed his car as he approached the southern end of the bridge, and then turned on Commerce Street. Welcome to Historic Occoquan, Founded 1734.

Having just left the suburban sprawl of twenty-first-century Sterling, Harley felt like he was entering another world. Creeping west along Commerce Street, he saw Auntie's Pie Shop and Riverside Methodist Church across the street. He turned on Washington Street and eased his car into the parking lot of the church. Looking around, he saw the river, bridge, townhouses, and several blocks of shops and restaurants. He could explore the entire town by foot in less than an hour. The bishop had told him that Occoquan was an Indian word meaning "at the end of the water." *More like "at the end of my career,"* he thought.

The church was renamed Riverside Methodist Church in the late 1990s when the congregation of Emanuel Baptist had moved to a larger and more modern structure in Woodbridge. The church sat empty until 2001 when the Northern Virginia Board of Missions decided that the Occoquan area would be a great site for a new church, especially with the development being planned for the old Lorton prison site just north of the river. They purchased the little church and installed a series of pastors who helped to get Riverside started. Growth was slow through the church's first fifteen years, especially since so many people were looking for megachurches with praise bands and high-tech sights and sounds. Traditional worship in nineteenth-century buildings typically didn't draw large crowds.

Harley put a key in the front door of the church and was immediately assaulted by a wave of warm, musty air. "This is disgusting," he said aloud, waving a hand in front of his face. He walked through the small narthex and turned on the lights in the sanctuary. Rows of oak pews stood on either side of a center aisle covered with worn red carpet. The front of the church had a pulpit on the left and a lectern on the right, with a Communion table in the center, under the stained glass of the black Jesus. Harley walked down the aisle, trying to imagine himself leading worship in these dank quarters after years of presiding over services in a sleek modern building in Sterling. He spent a few minutes studying the stained-glass window, which the bishop had told him about, focusing on the stained-glass image of Jesus and the frightened disciples around him.

Harley felt a wave of mixed emotion as he contemplated the scene etched in glass. It was calming instead of the corrosive anger that had been burning him up. Part of him didn't want to let go of his rage because it felt so righteous. Without it, he was left with nothing but numbness and loneliness, a vast emptiness created by both the loss of Karen and Jessica and the loss of his position in Sterling. Running his fingers along the backs of the wooden pews, he imagined that the space had been the site of countless milestones over the course of a century and a quarter—dedications, baptisms, weddings, funerals. Anguished prayers had been said here, rousing sermons had been preached, lives had been changed. Generations of African Americans, in particular, had looked up at the Jesus in the stained glass and found strength to live with faith and dignity in a segregated society. A trickle of tenderness began to flow into the dry canyon that was Harley's heart. And yet, he didn't want to get sentimental. What had sentimentality ever done for him?

Looking around the old building and imagining the small congregation that would gather there, he realized that the church was going to be a lot of work. And this realization made him feel frustrated that he had been demoted at the very peak of his career. When he opened the door to his office, which was located next to the pulpit, he was shocked and disappointed. The office was hardly bigger than a broom closet, and the desk had a typewriter on it. Yes, a typewriter. In 2017.

At least the office also had a door to the outside, which Harley used to escape and gulp a breath of fresh air. He was suffocating, as much from his conflicting emotions as the stuffy little office. But the outside air was not as refreshing as he hoped it would be. It was a hot and sticky June day, and the air coming off the Occoquan River smelled like fish and decay. *What a dump!* he thought. Even the little white steeple on the roof needed scraping and painting. This was a place for a recent seminary graduate, not an accomplished pastor. Feeling insulted by the bishop's assignment, he wanted nothing more than to jump in his car and escape.

As he stood on the steps outside the office door, a man with a gray beard and a tie-dye T-shirt approached. "Hi there," he called out as he got close to the church building. "I'm Tim. Are you the new minister?" He stuck out his hand and Harley gave it a shake.

"Yes. I'm Harley Camden. The bishop has just assigned me to Riverside." He pulled out his car keys to signal he was leaving.

"That's good," said Tim with a smile. "I'm not a religious person, but I hated it when the church sat empty all those years. I really liked Reverend Jones, who was the pastor of Emanuel in the '60s and '70s. Good man. Really active in the Civil Rights movement."

The man was clearly not going to allow the minister to make a quick escape.

"So, you've been here a long time?" asked Harley.

"Oh yeah, my family and I, we go back a long way in Occoquan. My last name is Underwood. I'm a direct descendent of John Underwood."

Harley nodded, but had no idea who John Underwood was.

"You know, Underwood the traitor."

Harley nodded again, trying to mask his ignorance.

"You might not know it, but Occoquan was an abolitionist stronghold during the Civil War. My ancestor John was arrested for his antislavery views. In the 1860 presidential election, Abraham Lincoln received only fifty-five votes from all of Prince William County. Only fifty-five votes! They all came from Occoquan."

"Huh," said Harley. Perhaps Occoquan wasn't as musty as it seemed. He put his car keys in his pocket.

"Yeah, John was quite a rabble-rouser," said Tim with a grin. "On the Fourth of July in the year 1860, a group of Occoquan Republicans raised a liberty pole in front of Rockledge Mansion. You've seen the mansion, haven't you?"

"No, I just arrived. I've only seen the church."

"Well, you'll see it soon enough," said Tim. He pointed and said, "It's just over there, across from the ruins of the mill. Anyway, the liberty pole had Abraham Lincoln's campaign banner on it, as well as the American flag."

"That must have been quite a statement, being in the South and all."

"You're telling me," Tim said. "Later that month, the Prince William militia rode into Occoquan. They were coming from Brentsville, the county seat. They chopped down the liberty pole and took the flags and pole pieces to Brentsville. The story even made *The New York Times*!"

"Interesting," replied Harley, although he couldn't help but think that the pole-chopping was probably Occoquan's first—and only—fifteen minutes of fame.

"Lots of interesting things happened around here throughout the war," Tim continued, "including an encampment by Confederate colonel Wade Hampton. And there were several assaults by a United States ship called *Stepping Stones*. In 1862, Wade Hampton raided Occoquan and arrested my ancestor John for treason!"

"Sorry to hear it," said Harley. "I hope he survived."

"He was released in 1863 in a prisoner trade. Abraham Lincoln himself wrote a personal note to the secretary of war, asking him to find a position for John. He became a United States marshal."

"So, a happy ending," Harley said. "Is the Republican Party still active here in Occoquan?"

"Well, yes," said Tim with a smirk. "But I wouldn't say it is Mr. Lincoln's party any more. We Underwoods were registered Republicans through the 1960s, but Nixon's Southern strategy took our party away from us."

Harley had just a vague recollection of Nixon gaining votes by using race as an issue with white conservatives in the South. "Didn't mean to get political," Harley said.

"Oh, that's okay," said Tim. "I love the history of this place, and politics is a big part of it. Want to see the town?"

Harley wondered what was going on with this guy. It was a brutally hot Tuesday afternoon, and he was walking the streets of Occoquan seemingly waiting for random people to show up so that he could give them a history lesson. The guy was sixty, at most. *Doesn't he have anything better to do?*

"Over here you have the Yarn Shop," announced Tim, pointing across Washington Street. "It's run by some old ladies who have been here forever. Names are Doris King and Eleanor Buttress. Occoquan used to be full of places like this, but now it is getting much more trendy, with little bistros and whatnot. You'll see."

They walked north on Washington, toward the river. "Here you've got the Gold Emporium," said Tim, gesturing to his left. "Run by a family of Egyptians, the Ayads. Coptic Christians, I hear. You know about the Copts, right?"

"Oh yes," Harley replied. "I preached about Copts being killed by ISIS. That's why I'm here." Tim looked at him quizzically. "I gave a sermon that was a little too graphic, and people complained to the bishop. She thought Occoquan would be a better fit for my particular . . . shall I say . . . gifts?"

"Your gifts!" Tim laughed. "If you got kicked out of a church for exercising your gifts, I'd like to hear you, Pastor. Means you've got something to say. When do you start preaching?"

"This Sunday. I'll be here for the worship service, and then I move down here next week."

"Where will you be living?"

"Right there," said Harley, pointing to a Victorian townhouse on Mill Street, on the western edge of the housing development.

"Pretty fancy, Rev. Those are super luxurious for the Town of Occoquan."

"Yeah, I guess so," Harley admitted. "Seems that the developer was a Methodist, and when he finished the final townhouse, he had to dispose of the model home. He could have sold it, but his tax adviser suggested he donate it to the church. Some big write-off, I guess. So now it is the parsonage for Riverside Methodist Church, and I'll live there for as long as I serve as pastor. The current guy finished on Sunday and is moving out now; it will get cleaned up this weekend and ready for me. Even comes with a dock!"

"Sweet!" said Tim. "I assume you'll get a boat."

"Why not? Get a dock, get a boat."

"Here is where you will get your mail," said Tim, pointing left to the small post office on Mill Street. "No one gets residential delivery here. You'll be assigned a PO box, and you pick up your mail. The postmistress, Mary, knows everybody—and everybody's business."

"So, this really is a small town, isn't it?"

"One thousand and sixty-two residents," said Tim. "Part-time mayor, full-time sheriff, part-time deputy. We've got it all."

Harley was surprised that a town this size could still exist in the ever-expanding sprawl of the Northern Virginia suburbs. He would have thought that the county would annex it and suck it into Woodbridge or Lake Ridge. But somehow scrappy little Occoquan held on to its integrity.

Harley was suddenly reminded of a dream from two nights before, in which he was sitting in his first church meeting in Occoquan, listening to two older women engage in a lengthy debate about which color of beige should be used to paint the social hall. "Crumb cookie," said one. "No, cocoa butter," countered the other. "How about sand trap?" said the first. "I prefer chocolate turtle," replied the second. Harley felt his frustration growing and growing until he stood up and unleashed a string of expletives. As he thundered at the women, his body grew tall and his muscles burst through the fabric of his shirt and his pants, until he ended up towering over them in the small meeting room. The women cowered, silent and stunned, until he ended the meeting with the words, "The walls will be green." And then it was over. *That was not a nightmare*, thought Harley as he recollected the details. *Not at all. That was a sweet dream.*

"And here is the American Legion," said Tim, pointing to the building next to the post office. "I can't say I agree with their politics, but the grill in the basement has the best breakfast in town. If you can find a member to take you, you'll enjoy a full plate of eggs, bacon, and home fries for about five bucks, coffee included. And you can have a beer to go along with it—the bar is always open."

Harley smiled, wondering how it would look for the new preacher to be sucking down beers at breakfast.

Tim continued to narrate his tour of Occoquan as they walked west on Mill Street: A dive bar, a dress shop, another jewelry store, a Christmas shop, an art gallery, and even an apartment building with a ghost. "You'll have to take the ghost tour here at Halloween," he said, "since you are a spiritual guy."

"Tell me about the Riverview Bakery," asked Harley as he pointed to a shop on the south side of the street.

"Run by an Iraqi family, the Bayatis. The father is Muhammad, the mother is Fatima, and they have two daughters in their twenties, Norah and Sarah, and a son named Omar, who I think is a year out of high school. They set up shop about twenty years ago, after the Gulf War."

"Muslims?" asked Harley.

"Sure," said Tim. "They're accepted around here. I'm guessing they do most of our birthday and wedding cakes. And anytime you need a box of cookies, Muhammad is your man."

"We'll see," Harley replied. "Where do they stand on the invasion of Iraq and what has happened since then?"

"No idea," said Tim. "Muhammad never talks politics. I don't think they were fans of Saddam Hussein, but they can't be happy about the instability of the country now. I don't think that they are super religious, but who knows?"

The two walked past a brewpub, a bridal boutique, and a puzzle store. Tim pointed out the town hall, which had been an Episcopal church until the congregation shrunk to sixteen and closed. The two looked up the hill at Rockledge Mansion, an impressive stone structure that was the site of the short-lived liberty pole of 1860. Finally, they reached River Mill Park, a beautifully landscaped strip of grass along the river with a bandstand and public bathrooms and a walking trail. At the eastern edge of the park was a tiny town museum and a pedestrian bridge over the Occoquan River. The town had good walkability, as well as some natural beauty along the river.

"I've bent your ear enough," said Tim, "but I'm happy to talk with you about Occoquan any time."

"Thanks," said Harley. "You've been helpful. How can I reach you?"

"That's easy. I work part-time in the town maintenance department. Picking up trash, watering flowers, maintaining the gas streetlamps. You can leave a message for me at town hall. I'm not a social media or cell phone guy."

Harley stuck out his hand and said, "Good to meet you, Tim. I'm going to spend some time in the park, but I'll see you again soon."

"Maybe in church," said Tim as he shook Harley's and turned to leave.

"That would be great," said Harley.

Tim headed back into town while Harley continued west toward the end of the park. He sat on a bench overlooking the Occoquan River. Water poured over a dam and then danced down over rocks. Harley thought of his wife, Karen, and how much she would have loved the intimate feel of the town and the charm of the Victorian townhouse that would be his home. Although she thrived in the swirl of activities in the booming Sterling church, Harley guessed that that she would have appreciated Occoquan as a retirement spot. He felt unfaithful, being there without her.

Five large black vultures were eating the corpses of a couple of fish. One pulled the guts out of a fish as the others watched. *Will they be pecking on me next?* Harley looked at the bridge and thought of his daughter. When Jessica was a child, they would have walked across a bridge like that together, and maybe fed the ducks in the water below. He had such tender memories of her childhood— pushing her in a swing, buying her an ice cream cone, watching her talk to an imaginary friend—and over the last few years he began to dream of doing similar things with grandchildren, after Jessica got married and started a family.

Harley walked back to his car in the church parking lot. The shops and restaurants along Mill Street, which had been enticing an hour earlier, now looked shabby and uninviting. In another life, he would have been curious about the people who lived and worked there and interested in their lives. At that moment he only wanted to go home, back to Sterling. On Sunday at Riverside Methodist, he would have to fake some enthusiasm for his new congregation. The charm of the place was clearly no match for the force of his grief.

But Harley was not the only one suffering in Occoquan. That night, Norah Bayati, the daughter of the baker, was smothered in her bed.

CHAPTER 3

For his first Sunday at Riverside Methodist, Harley used an old preacher's trick. He offered the same sermon that he had given on his last Sunday in Sterling. He talked about Jesus being in a boat with his disciples on the Sea of Galilee when a great windstorm arose. Waves crashed into the boat, and the disciples called out in a panic, "Teacher, do you not care that we are perishing?" Jesus berated the wind and told the sea to be still—all of a sudden, the wind stopped and the sea became like glass. He turned to the disciples and asked, "Why are you afraid? Have you still no faith?"

In Sterling, Harley encouraged the congregation to continue to trust Jesus through the time of transition that lay ahead for them, and in Occoquan he promised that Jesus would be with them through any storms that threatened to swamp their little congregation. In both churches, he reflected on the tumult of his own life, and how storms were not always conquered. He wished his own sea would become calm, but it was still tossing him around. Still, he said that he had discovered that Jesus did care that they were perishing, and he gave everyone the help they needed to survive. "Even a little faith," he concluded, "can help us to face the future without being crippled by fear."

At Riverside, Harley's sermon was backed up by the mighty black Jesus in the stained-glass window, calming the storm and his frightened disciples. But nothing could ease the upset in the people of the congregation, because they couldn't stop thinking about Norah Bayati, the first murder in Occoquan in more than a century.

Police tape surrounded the Riverview Bakery, and gawkers hovered. Members of the family had been taken to the police station for questioning, but they were not making public appearances, slipping secretly in and out through a rear entrance. The bakery remained dark. Two days after the murder, word spread that Muhammad had been arrested for the death of his daughter, who had dishonored her family.

Harley heard all this at coffee hour in the church basement. Parishioners were welcoming to him, of course, since he was the new pastor and many were meeting him for the first time. But after introducing themselves, almost everyone commented about the Bayati family—how they seemed to be such a caring family, hard-working immigrants, lovely people, good Muslims.

"It is just such a shock," said one parishioner. *Of course it is*, thought Harley. Most went through life with a shadowy and cartoonish picture of death, but when death jumped out of the shadows, showing its true face, and violently snatched away loved ones—well, that was a high-voltage shock. It left people stunned and angry for far longer than they expected it would.

One familiar face in the congregation was Tim Underwood, Harley's tour guide from earlier in the week. At coffee hour, he hung back. "You preached a good sermon, Rev."

"Thanks, Tim," said Harley, finally able to take a sip of coffee. "I'm kinda surprised to see you. A lot of folks say they will come to church, and never do."

"Well, I liked talking to you on Tuesday. I wanted to see what you were made of."

"Nothing special, I can assure you."

"You know, I had no idea that you were the guy who lost his wife and daughter to the terrorist attack. You were all over the news last year, and I didn't make the connection until you talked about it this morning. I am so sorry."

"I appreciate it," said Harley. "And now you've got your own trauma here in Occoquan."

"Indeed we do. I wouldn't say I knew the Bayatis well, but I saw a lot of them. Watched their kids grow up here, go to high school at Lake Ridge and then commute to George Mason for college. Typical immigrant family, with kids living at home until they get married."

"What do you think of this talk of an honor killing?" asked Harley.

"Hard to say," said Tim, putting a hand through his beard. "They don't seem like super religious people, but maybe it is more of an Iraqi cultural thing. Even so, Muhammad always seemed so nice and gentle."

"But isn't that the typical description of a killer? You know, the neighbors saying, 'He seemed like such a mild-mannered guy.'"

"Pastor, you've got a dark streak."

"Let's keep that between us, okay?" Harley noticed a straggler from the congregation waiting for a chance to talk with him. "Tim, let's continue this conversation, maybe this week, after I get moved in."

"No problem, Rev. Welcome to Occoquan."

Harley waved to the guy in the corner of the social hall and motioned him over. The man was short and bald, in his mid-sixties and powerfully built from working out.

"Pastor, I'm Dirk Carter, and I've been a Methodist all my life. Been a member here at Riverside since they opened the doors."

"Good to meet you, Dirk," said Harley, shaking his hand. "What brought you to Occoquan?"

"The military," Dirk replied. "I was a Marine—or, to be precise, I am a Marine, since there are no ex-Marines. I got my start down the road at Quantico. Did a tour in Nam. Got moved around a lot, and kept cycling back to the DC area, sometimes assigned to Quantico, sometimes the Pentagon. When I got divorced in the 1980s, I bought a condo in Lake Ridge. It seemed central, and I like the water."

"Makes sense," said Harley.

"I liked your sermon," Dirk offered. "It seemed real to me. Not nice and neat, with a happy ending."

"There aren't many of those," Harley said. "At least not in real life."

"That's for sure," agreed Dirk. "So, I was wondering. Since you're a single guy—sorry about that, by the way—and I'm a single guy, would you like to get some lunch?"

Church volunteers were cleaning up the coffee, punch and cookies that had been put out for his welcome reception. The room was almost deserted, and it didn't look like anything else would be happening at the church that day. Sometimes, a group of church members would take a new pastor out to lunch on their first Sunday to help them to feel at home and answer any questions they might have. But no one had said anything about a meal. It was also Father's Day, so many people probably had plans with their families.

"Sure," said Harley. "Lunch sounds great."

They walked around the corner to the American Legion Hall. They were serving lunch in the grill, and sure enough there were guys sucking down beers at the bar.

"Hey, Jessica," said Dirk to the woman behind the bar.

"Hi, Dirk," she replied. "Your table is all ready for you."

She grabbed a couple of menus and led them to their table. She was an attractive woman in her thirties with green highlights in her jet-black hair, arms covered with tattoos, and a cigarette tucked behind her ear. There were a lot of smokers and huge flowerpots full of butts right outside the front door.

"Let this be my treat," said Dirk as they studied the menu. "None of this stuff is healthy, but it's all pretty good." After they ordered a couple of burgers, Dirk continued to tell his story.

"Like I told you at the church, I'm a lifelong Methodist. There are times when I think that the denomination is getting too liberal for me, but then I remember all the great people that I've known in the church. Mrs. Peterson, my Sunday School teacher, she was so nice to me. Reverend Smith got me through some tough times with my parents when I was a teenager. Chaplain Gerde, who kept me from losing my mind in Nam. All Methodists. So I'll never leave."

"Glad to hear it," said Harley. "The church has been good to me as well. I was an Army brat, and we were always moving around. But just about everywhere we went, there was a Methodist church. It gave me a sense of stability."

Jessica brought Dirk a beer and an iced tea for Harley. Looking at her nametag, Harley felt an unexpected pang of grief. Although his own Jessica had looked nothing like the tattooed waitress, seeing her name caused him pain.

Dirk said that he had been a fighter as a kid. "Always getting into scraps over stupid stuff," he admitted. "Always had a chip on my shoulder. I was probably on my way to reform school, but then one Sunday I was sitting in church. Didn't want to be there, but my parents made me. Reverend Smith read a verse I had never heard before: 'I have not come to bring peace, but a sword.' That got my attention. Words of Jesus, no less."

"What did that mean to you?"

"It let me know that Jesus was not a wimp. Willing to fight for what mattered to him."

"Of course, Jesus did not literally use a sword."

"Sure. But it got me thinking more about what it would mean to be a Christian and a fighter. I came to see that the two were not mutually exclusive, and when I turned eighteen I joined the Marines. Eventually, I heard another verse that really became a key one for me. I think the chaplain said it in Nam. Again, some words of Jesus, 'No one has greater love than this, to lay down one's life for one's friends.' I really saw that verse come to life on the battlefield. I swore to myself that I would show that kind of love."

Harley was impressed. "Dirk, I like the way you bring your work and your faith together."

"Well, I'm no saint," he admitted. "Far from it. I need forgiveness, and I ask for it every Sunday. I know I screw up. My son says I do the right things for the wrong reasons and the wrong things for the right reasons."

As he paused to take a swig of beer. Harley saw a strange look in Dirk's eyes—a flash of anxiety, or maybe even fear. But then Dirk changed the subject.

"You've been listening to me. Now I've got a question for you. Even though I like the Methodist church, I don't understand why it isn't taking a stronger stand against radical Islam. Why do you think that is? I mean, these terrorists are the biggest threat to our democracy and our Christian faith in the entire world. I don't have to tell you this—you've suffered personally. All I hear Methodist bigwigs talking about is Israel and Palestine, and our leaders are pretty damn critical of the way that the Israelis treat the Palestinians."

"True," said Harley, "but don't assume that Methodists are making a knee-jerk response. The denomination has refused to go so far as divesting from Israel."

"I should hope so!" Dirk replied. "Israel is the only true democracy in the Middle East, and we had better support them."

"I'm with you, in terms of supporting Israel. Their security is our security. But we cannot give them a blank check. I've been there, and I believe that the way they are treating the Palestinians is making the Middle East less stable, not more. Islamic terrorists feed off that stuff."

Dirk looked at his new pastor with grudging respect. Previous pastors had always tried to change the subject when he pressed them on denominational policies. He sensed that Harley was a straight shooter.

"Yeah, I guess you are right," Dirk shrugged. "In Nam, we always talked about winning hearts and minds. We've got to do the same today in the Middle East." He looked up and saw a young man across the room and called to him, "Hey, Will, come here." Then he turned to Harley. "Here's a guy who did a tour in Iraq and tried to win some hearts and minds."

A man with short brown hair, sad eyes and sunken cheeks walked over to their table. He looked as though he had just lost his best friend. Dirk introduced him. "Will is one of the few young vets who is a member of this American Legion. Most guys his age don't want to join. But Will has really gotten involved."

Will nodded and took a swig of beer. "There are some good men here."

"Pastor Harley and I were just talking about hearts and minds," said Dirk. "What was the name of your Iraqi translator, and what happened to him?"

"Nasim," said Will. "Really understood our mission. Did everything he could to help us."

"And where is he now?" Dirk prodded.

"Iraq. He wants to move to the US but hasn't been able to get a visa."

"That's not good," Harley said. "Is he in danger?"

"He's in a tough spot," said Will. "I don't like it."

"Want to sit down?" Dirk asked.

"No thanks," replied Will. Harley saw pain in his eyes, real suffering. "I was just about to head out." He took his last drink and left.

"Good kid," said Dirk, "but so serious. He's really struggled since coming back from Iraq. He has bounced from job to job, and doesn't have much of a social life that I know of."

"Speaking of Iraq," said Harley, "what do you think of the killing of this Iraqi girl here in Occoquan?"

"I can't say I'm really surprised. You can take an Iraqi out of Iraq, but you can't take the Iraq out of an Iraqi."

"So you think that it was an honor killing?"

"Looks like it. Rumors are, the girl was seeing an American guy, and that couldn't have gone over well with the old man. Maybe she was pregnant. Who knows?"

Harley chewed his burger and thought about what Dirk was saying.

"You may be right," he said, "but is there any hard evidence? No one around here seems to think that they were radicals."

"Yeah, it's surprising, for sure. I've never been in Muhammad's shop, and don't know much about his family. I did run into him once when I was doing some shopping on Mill Street. He seemed like a pretty assimilated guy to me. I asked him about the Gulf War, and he just shook his head and said how happy he was to get out of Iraq.

But, you know, Islam aside, cops are always going to look at family members first in a murder like this."

"Makes sense," agreed Harley. "I can't imagine the girl was killed in the course of a robbery. No one would break into a bakery looking for a lot of cash."

"Yes, it seems like a crime of passion. Could be a family member or a lover."

Harley remembered a retiree from the Sterling church who had come to him, requesting counseling for a personal issue. Harley hardly knew the guy but had heard a disturbing rumor about him. Apparently, his first wife had died under mysterious circumstances in the 1950s, when the two of them lived in Washington. The case had been all over *The Washington Post*, and although the man was investigated, he was never charged. He went on to have a successful career as a car dealer, and eventually retired and moved to Sterling. Then tragedy struck when his second wife fell down a flight of stairs in their retirement home and died of a broken neck.

"Pastor, I'm in so much pain. I've lost so much. Can you help me? I heard about your wife and daughter. You know what loss is like," the man had said. "I really need to talk with you, and only you. You will keep this between us, right? As a pastor, you are sworn to confidentiality, right?"

Harley nodded. "Tell me what's troubling you."

"My first wife was poison, so I poisoned her. My second wife was bringing me down, so I brought her down. There, I've confessed to God and to you. But you can tell no one, Pastor."

Harley was stunned by the revelation and wondered how he could possibly keep such a secret. But then a knock came on his door, and he opened it to see the middle-aged daughter of the man.

"Is he telling you about killing his wives? I'm afraid he's losing it," she said as she escorted her father out of the room. But Harley was left shaken by the experience.

Dirk was still eating and looking at his lunch companion, wondering why Harley had become so silent. Maybe he didn't want to talk about the death of the Bayati girl. Changing the subject, he said, "That's a nice place you've been given across the street. And what a great thing to have a dock of your own. Want to get a boat?"

"Yes, I would. I've never been a boater, but I would be crazy not to take advantage of this."

Dirk told him about the boat that he kept down the river at the Halliburton Marina, and how he'd be happy to take Harley there and introduce him to the owner. "They get lots of people who trade in smaller boats for larger ones, so I'm sure they can find you something," Dirk said.

Harley was really beginning to like this guy, a much warmer version of his own military father, who had died decades earlier. Their conversation was interrupted by Dirk's cell phone. "I've got to take this." After listening for a few seconds, he apologized. "I'm sorry, Pastor, but I need to go. I've got to talk to my son, Matt. He's FBI. I shouldn't tell you this, but you're clergy. Confidential, right? He's been investigating the Bayatis."

CHAPTER 4

The movers and their truck arrived in Occoquan on Wednesday afternoon, and Harley was waiting on the porch to meet them. They swarmed over the Victorian house for several hours, carrying furniture and boxes up the wrought-iron staircase on the side of the house, through the front door, and then into the various rooms of the three living levels.

The first floor was an open-air carport held up by sturdy concrete pillars covered with brick. The second level contained a kitchen on the street side, a dining room in the middle, and a living room with a porch facing the river. The third floor had two bedrooms with full baths, and a laundry room between them. The fourth floor was narrower than the other two because of the steeply pitched roof, but it contained a storage room and a large guest suite with a porch overlooking the river. The townhouse was much smaller than his parsonage in Sterling, but it had more than enough room for a single man.

After playing the role of traffic cop for several hours, Harley tipped the movers when they were finished. He surveyed the stacks of boxes throughout his house and realized that he would be unpacking for months. Although he had worked hard to downsize since hearing about his transfer to Occoquan, he knew that he had moved a ton of things that would still need to be sorted and discarded. The surplus furniture in Sterling had been no problem— several truckloads had been sent to Goodwill, and a number of items had been sold on Craigslist. All of Karen and Jessica's clothing had been donated to the church clothing closet and made available to low-income neighbors. Since he couldn't bear to sort through it himself, he asked for the assistance of several retired women from the church. They kindly boxed up all of the clothing and spirited it away. Even after the closets and chests had been emptied, a stray sock or scarf occasionally appeared, and Harley would well up with tears. He never dreamed that clothing could carry so much emotion.

As Harley stood motionless inside the front door, not sure where to begin, the doorbell rang. There stood Leah Silverman, an old friend from Duke, holding two containers of Thai food. "Harley," she said. "Welcome to the County of Prince William."

"Leah, come in." She entered and placed the food on the kitchen counter, then gave Harley a hug. "I'm so sorry about Karen and your daughter. I really should have called or sent a card."

Leah was a couple of years younger than Harley and had been an undergraduate religion major when he was a student at Duke Divinity School. The two of them had gone on an archaeological dig in Israel in the mid-1980s, part of a team that discovered a beautiful mosaic in the town of Sepphoris. Harley wrote in his travel journal about her in May 1985:

> *Arrived in Galilee. Visited city of Nazareth, hometown of Jesus, close to Sepphoris. Modern city is 70 percent Muslim and 30 percent Christian. Two groups cooperate. Tourism is booming, with visitors wanting to walk in the footsteps of Jesus. Our group visited Basilica of the Annunciation, a new church built over earlier Byzantine and Crusader-era churches. Thought to be site of childhood home of*

*Mary, where angel announced that Jesus would be
born. Question in the Gospel of John: "Can anything
good come out of Nazareth?" My team is beginning to
bond—five undergrads will be working in my square.
So glad I'll be digging with a cute girl named Leah.*

Leah was like a kid sister to Harley that summer, and they spent
many weekends together, hitch-hiking to Haifa for the gardens or to
Tel Aviv for the beach. She was a beautiful young woman with dark-
brown hair and an olive complexion, very fit from playing tennis and
racquetball, and always quick with a smile. Harley developed quite
a crush on her during the dig and always assumed that the feelings
were not returned because he was a Christian and she was a Jew.
They drifted apart after their summer in Israel, but then reconnected
after thirty years when all of the participants in the Duke digs got
together for a reunion. Harley had brought his wife with him.

"You live around here, don't you?" he asked. "I remember you
telling me that when I saw you at the Duke reunion."

"Yes, I've been in Occoquan ten years," she said. "I'm the CEO
of the Woodbridge Health Clinic, a nonprofit serving low-income
residents. God, it was so good to see you down in Durham. I just
cannot believe Karen was killed. I am so sorry, Harley. She was such
a lovely person."

Harley just nodded. "I'm sorry, too."

"One of my volunteers at the clinic is a member of your church,
and she told me about your arrival. She said you were moving in here
on Wednesday, and I guessed that you wouldn't want to cook on your
first night. So, I figured I would pick up some Thai and surprise you."

"Well, you succeeded," said Harley. "Thank you."

"I can just leave the food here and go. Or, if you want some
company, I can stick around."

"Company would be great."

Mealtimes were the loneliest part of his day since losing Jessica
and Karen. Pointing to the dining room, he said, "I think there is
a table under the boxes." He moved a few to the floor while Leah

dished the food onto paper plates. Harley tried not to stare. Leah was still fit and quite attractive. Her hair had turned silver and she had wrinkles around her eyes, but she was still the girl he had fallen for in the dirt of Israel.

"Harley," she said, as she put a plate of steaming noodles in front of him, "I am really sorry we lost touch. I would have liked to spend time with you and Karen and your daughter, especially since we were all in the DC area."

"Yeah, that would have been great, but work and family were so consuming." He offered her a glass of wine, and when she said yes he pulled a bottle out of the bag he had packed for his first night in the new house. Pouring two glasses, he asked her, "Tell me what brought you here and what you've been up to."

"Mainly work. After Duke I went to Carolina for a master's in public health."

"Traitor!" Harley blurted with a smile.

"Yeah, I know," she confessed. "But UNC was great for public health, especially health administration, and from there I worked my way up through a series of clinics in Greensboro, Richmond, and now Woodbridge."

"As long as you didn't become a Tarheel," Harley chided. "Coach K would never forgive you."

"Never. Blue Devils, forever." After taking a sip of wine, she asked, "So how about you? What brought you from Durham to Occoquan?"

"The bishop," Harley explained. "I met Karen on a blind date during my final year at Duke Divinity, and we got so serious that I wanted to be near her after graduation. She was living in Alexandria, so I sought out the Methodist bishop responsible for the DC area and pledged my allegiance to him. I moved to Virginia, we got married, and I started out as an associate pastor in Arlington. Next, I got a solo position in Annandale, then moved to Fairfax and finally Sterling. That was the peak."

Harley sipped his wine and sat quietly for a few moments. Leah just listened; she had always been a good listener.

"After losing Karen and Jessica, I slid downhill to Occoquan.

Now I'm just an unhappy old white guy with no future, no chance for advancement, nothing to look forward to. In other words, just like most other guys my age."

"This really isn't the pits, Harley. Sure, Prince William is an ugly stepsister compared to rich counties like Fairfax and Loudoun, but there are some great people here. And Occoquan? Harley, this town is a gem!"

He shrugged. "Yeah, except for the honor killing."

She flinched, and Harley could tell that the incident hit close to home.

"No one knows what really happened there," Leah said stiffly. "And even if it was a murder, one in a hundred years ain't bad. In other neighborhoods around here, gang members are killing each other every month."

Harley knew she was right about Occoquan but still couldn't help but feel that he had been demoted. On top of that, he looked around the region and saw progress for everyone around him—women, African-Americans, LGBTs, Asians, Latinos, immigrants from the Middle East. Everyone who was working hard was on the move, advancing, getting noticed. Not Harley. He was a middle-aged widower, a recently demoted white guy living alone. *Enough self-pity*. He changed the subject.

"So, have you been single all these years?"

"The past nine, yes," she answered. "I met Pat in the early nineties, soon after I moved to Richmond. I was playing a lot of tennis, and we met at the racquet club. Things progressed quickly, so we moved in together and then bought a house. In 2006 Pat got leukemia. A clinical trial became available at NIH, and I found this job in Woodbridge so that we could be closer to the treatments. Pat fought hard . . ." Leah paused and took another drink of wine. "The love of my life. Gone so quickly."

Harley reached across the table and put his hand on hers. "I'm sorry."

"Well, you know what it's like," she said, with tears welling. "Death is a monster."

"Indeed it is."

Harley liked the feeling of her hand but didn't want to send the wrong message. "More wine?" he asked as he lifted his hand and stood.

"You were alone at the Duke reunion, with Pat gone, right? I'm sorry we didn't get more caught up at that point."

"Well, the reunion was all about reliving our days on the dig, wasn't it? Feeling young and alive, skinny and tan?"

Harley smiled. "I have never been thinner than I was that summer."

"True that," said Leah. "Getting up at four in the morning, having a first breakfast in the dining hall, digging for four hours, having a second breakfast on the dig site, digging for another three hours, and being done by noon. Not the typical schedule for a college student!"

"But I'll tell you," Harley said, "I never felt healthier. I wouldn't mind getting up every day at four if I could be in bed by eight."

"Our world today just doesn't allow it," Leah lamented. "We bring our work home with us, get caught up on emails, and then unwind in front of the television. I'm lucky if I am asleep before eleven thirty."

"You and me both. When I get back from a church meeting at ten, I am usually so wound up that I cannot close my eyes before eleven. Junk TV and a glass of wine—or several glasses—are my bedtime rituals."

"Wild times in suburbia," said Leah, lifting her glass. "I'll never forget when we started to clear the dirt off of that mosaic. The artistry was exquisite. A piece of Roman art in the very heart of a Jewish community, with that beautiful woman, 'The Mona Lisa of the Galilee.' Changed what everyone thought of life in that ancient city."

"We did have a great time, didn't we?" Harley opened another bottle of wine. "Remember when we went to the swimming pool in Nazareth? At the end of the day, we put our thumbs out to hitch a ride back to the dormitories." Leah smiled as Harley refilled her glass. "A little pickup pulled over and the driver opened the door for you. He motioned for me to hop in the back. But then he sped off before I could climb in! I was terrified! I thought you were going to be raped and murdered!"

Leah was touched by how raw his emotions still were, three decades later. "I was just chatting with the guy, oblivious to the fact that you weren't in the truck."

"Well, I hope you had a good time," said Harley. "I was a wreck."

"What did you do?" she asked, sipping her wine. "I kind of forget."

"I kept my thumb out, and fortunately caught another ride a few minutes later. When I got back to the dorms, I ran to see if you were okay."

"Which I was," she said. "So sweet of you."

"I guess I shouldn't have panicked. Galilee was pretty safe in those days. Everybody hitched rides, and no one got in trouble."

"Yeah, it's different now. I was just reading a story online about Nazareth. Five Muslims arrested for declaring their allegiance to ISIS. The Christians of the city now worry that they are going to end up on the ISIS hit list."

"That's not good," said Harley.

"No, it's not. But it is not just ISIS that worries Christians. They are also concerned about extremism on the Jewish side. And that really makes me ashamed, as a Jew."

"I'm amazed you keep up with this stuff," said Harley.

"Well, I'm Jewish. What happens in Israel is important to me."

Harley stood. "If we are going to get serious, let's at least get comfortable." He pulled a couple of packing boxes off of a recliner and a couch in the living room and invited her to join him. Sitting comfortably in the living room, they continued to drink and talk.

"So, what's been happening from the Jewish side?" Harley asked.

"A couple of summers ago, Jewish extremists firebombed the Church of the Multiplication, near the Sea of Galilee. Remember seeing that church, with the mosaic of the loaves and fish?"

"Yes, I do. You say it was attacked by Jews?"

"Extremists, yes," said Leah. "The vandals wrote on the church walls, 'False idols will be destroyed!'"

"False idols? They think Christians have false idols? I never thought of myself as worshiping an idol."

"I guess you do, from their perspective."

Leah continued to talk about politics in Israel, and about her discouragement with the failure of the peace process. She was a bit intense, which Harley found simultaneously off-putting and intriguing, at least at first. Here she was, thousands of miles from Israel, feeling the tensions as personally as a Jew on the streets of Old Jerusalem. But gradually he became annoyed by her analysis, which seemed awfully detached from the pain of people like himself. She was beginning to sound like the Duke undergrad know-it-alls who had been so aggravating to him when he was in divinity school.

"Mutual concessions are essential," she insisted, blah, blah, blah. "But there is absolutely no trust between Israelis and Palestinians." *Sure, you are right*, thought Harley, *but what does all that have to do with me and what I have been through? Don't you read about the acts of terrorism constantly being committed around the world?*

Harley poured the last of the wine. "Open another one?"

"No, better not," she said. "Tomorrow's a work day."

As he sipped the last of his glass, Harley asked, "Leah, you seemed to react when I mentioned the killing of the Bayati girl a while back. Are you close to that situation?"

She thought for a moment. "Well, I don't normally talk about this kind of stuff, but you are clergy—confidential, right? And the girl is dead, so I cannot hurt her. She was a patient at my clinic, and after her death the medical examiner asked for her records. I reviewed them before turning them over to him and saw that she had come to us for birth control."

"Sounds controversial," said Harley, "especially in a traditional Muslim family."

"I would think so," Leah replied. "I never heard any more from the ME, but I assume that the records could become evidence in the trial."

"So maybe her father found out and became angry," Harley guessed. "That might support an honor killing."

"Or a lover's quarrel," Leah suggested. "Personal lives are messy. You know that as well as anyone."

They finished the wine, and when they got up they discovered that they were both a bit tipsy. "I don't think I can drive," Leah confessed.

"I better call an Uber."

"No, just stay here," insisted Harley. "It's a mess, but I can make up a bed for you."

"Won't the neighbors talk?" teased Leah.

"Not if you take the walk of shame at sunrise," he grinned.

"It's a deal," she said, and followed him up to the small bedroom on the next floor. They pulled some bedding out of a box and quickly made up the bed. "I'll be out before morning," she promised and then pecked him on the cheek. "Thanks, Harley."

He went to his larger bedroom down the hall, plopped down on his unmade bed, and as he drifted off to sleep he thought about how good it was to have a woman in the house. Just like old times.

CHAPTER 5

After two long days of unpacking and setting up his tiny office, Harley was ready for a break. He had carried a dozen boxes from his townhouse to Riverside Methodist Church, and spent hours arranging books on shelves and putting papers in his desk drawers and filing cabinets. He had even carved out time to prepare a worship bulletin for the Sunday service, and to write a sermon titled, "Can anything good come out of Occoquan?"

Harley sat in the kitchen of his townhouse, looking out the window onto Mill Street and waiting for visitors. He sipped black coffee and ate a danish from Auntie's Pie Shop. Dirk and Matt Carter had promised to introduce him to the pleasures of boating the Occoquan.

Harley had been worried that they would have to cancel their boat ride. A tropical storm made landfall in Louisiana and then moved northeast, dropping heavy rain and causing flooding throughout the South. Storms swept through Occoquan throughout the night, and Harley assumed that he would wake up to cloudy skies and a swollen river. But the opposite was true. The sky was bright blue and the river looked normal, with a slight breeze being the only vestige of the tropical storm. *Thank goodness for inaccurate weather predictions*, Harley thought as he drained the last of his coffee.

As he put his cup down, he saw the two men walking toward his house. Dirk was looking up at his son, who stood a head taller, and it appeared that he was trying to make him laugh. Matt didn't crack a smile. Although the younger Carter shared his father's powerful build, he had a head of thick brown hair. If Matt hadn't worked for the FBI, he had the movie-star looks to play an agent in the movies. Both men wore sunglasses, shorts and T-shirts. Dirk's shirt said *Margaritaville* and Matt's said *Marine Corps Marathon*. Dirk also wore an NRA-inscribed ball cap to cover his bald head.

After introductions, they went to the public dock near the restaurant called Maxine's. Harley asked Matt how long he had worked for the FBI.

"Thirteen years, sir."

"And do you like it?" Harley asked.

"Most of the time, yes," Matt said. Harley waited for him to elaborate, but Matt looked ahead and kept walking, without saying any more.

"Matt's always been a quiet one," said his more gregarious father. "Still waters run deep."

The roar of motorcycles quaked the town as a line of riders passed. Most of them appeared to be of retirement age, some dark skinned and others light and all with salt-and-pepper mustaches and beards.

"Occoquan is a biker town," said Dirk after they passed. "You'll see a lot of motorcycles outside of Maxine's at night. I suspect that this group is just out for a Saturday ride, and they are making a pit stop. Lots of Harleys—right, Harley?"

Harley smiled. "Wish my name gave me some stock in that company." Then, looking toward the water, he said, "Dirk, tell me about your boat."

"She's about nineteen feet long; a Sea-Ray. She's what is called a bowrider, which means that you have seating in the bow as well as in the stern. Inboard-outboard gasoline engine. Good for fishing, water-skiing, or just cruising around."

"Inboard-outboard?" Harley asked.

"You know what an outboard motor looks like, right?" Dirk asked. Harley nodded. "Well, an inboard-outboard has the engine in the back, like the outboard, except that it is enclosed in a compartment with a seat over it. Makes for a quieter ride."

Matt walked ahead of them onto the public dock and stopped at the boat matching Dirk's description. He climbed down a wooden ladder and got on board, put a key in the ignition, and pushed a button. Harley expected the engine to come to life, but nothing happened.

Dirk looked at Harley and said, "Matt is running a blower to get gas fumes out of the engine compartment before he starts it up. Otherwise, you could start the engine and have a nasty fire."

Harley took a seat in the stern over the engine compartment and looked around. Matt sat in a swiveling captain's chair behind the steering wheel on the right, and Dirk plopped down in a similar chair to the left.

"Ready to get underway?" Dirk asked.

Harley was surprised by how good it felt to be on the river. The sunlight shimmered on the water, and the deep green leaves of the trees along the banks made the river itself look green. A family of ducks swam beside them for a minute, and a fish jumped out of the water just a few feet from the bow. They moved slowly at first, passing under the Route 123 bridge as they headed east. Harley soaked up everything around him, letting the river work its calming magic on him.

"This part of the river is 'no-wake,'" said Dirk, "meaning you have to move slowly, running the engine about 1000 RPM. There are a number of houses with docks, and a couple of marinas up ahead. If we revved her up, our wake would cause all kinds of damage to the boats that are tied up. In about twenty minutes, we'll be able to let 'er rip."

"No problem at all," Harley replied. "I'm enjoying the sights." They passed a channel marker with a nest on top, and he asked the driver, "Matt, what kind of bird is that?"

"Osprey," Matt replied without turning around.

Okay, thought Harley. *I'm not going to get a lot out of this guy.* Shifting his attention to Dirk, he asked, "What other kind of birds do you see around here?"

"Ducks, of course. Seagulls. Hawks. Herons. There are even some bald eagles, with a nest near the river."

Harley's eyebrows went up.

"Spectacular birds," said the old Marine. "Keep your eyes open."

Motoring eastward, they passed the Occoquan Regional Park on the northern shore and saw several people putting red-and-orange fiberglass kayaks into the river. A man and a woman in their twenties were close to shore on stand-up paddleboards, trying to keep their balance. Dirk seemed to enjoy the fact that the woman was shapely in a bikini. In a minute, they passed the Lake Ridge Marina on the right.

"That's where I bought this boat," Dirk said. "Good place, but they concentrate on selling new boats. I'll take you down the river to Halliburton's. It's a mom-and-pop operation that has some good used boats. That's probably where you want to start off, right?"

Harley nodded. "Guess so."

Dirk pointed to a good fishing spot near the I-95 bridge and laughed about how he liked to wave to the commuters stuck in traffic in the lanes above, making them jealous. He asked Matt to tell Harley about the johnboat they used for their first fishing outings in the 1990s, but he didn't get a bite.

"I understand that Occoquan means 'at the end of the water,' but that's not really true, is it?" Harley asked

"No, there's a good bit of water between the town and the Potomac River," Dirk said. "A lot to see and a lot to do. The Occoquan River just keeps flowing, washing all the crap away." Dirk's words struck Harley as odd. The water all around him appeared to be clean and full of life, with no sign of human waste. *Crap?*

They passed a marina filled with yachts and a riverside restaurant, and Harley was surprised to see the restaurant next to an industrial site with huge piles of sand and gravel.

"That's a materials plant," explained Dirk. "Construction aggregate: Crushed stone, sand, gravel. The Occoquan is still a working river, you see, not just for bowriders and party boats. You'll see tugs pushing large barges up to the plant, and then leaving with loads of materials to take to construction sites up and down the Potomac River. Maybe even farther."

Next to the materials plant was the Route 1 bridge, parallel to I-95, and then came a railroad bridge carrying commuter trains and Amtrak trains along a north-south route. A long freight train roared overhead as they passed beneath the bridge, and the loud clacking of wheels on rails drowned out conversation for several minutes. Harley had never seen highways and train bridges from the perspective of a river, and he was struck by how the birds and fish seemed to be flourishing under and around these manmade structures. *Nature always finds a way*, he thought. An osprey screeched from the top of a nearby channel marker, warning them to stay away.

After gaining sufficient distance from the noise of the train bridge, Harley asked, "What are you hearing about Muhammad Bayati?"

Matt glanced at his father but said nothing. Dirk paused for a second. "Not much. Only what I read online. Muhammad is still in Prince William jail. He's got a lawyer, but all he has said is that Bayati is innocent and he looks forward to having his day in court."

"That's pretty typical," asked Harley. "Right?"

"I guess so," Dirk agreed. "I've never heard a lawyer say that his client is guilty. Not at this point, anyway."

"But what do you think?" Harley pressed.

Dirk spun his swivel chair and opened what looked like a glove compartment but was really a cooler. He asked his son what time it was, and the young man said eleven. "Close enough," Dirk said. "Want one?" he asked Harley. When the pastor said no, Dirk popped the can open and took a sip.

"What do I think?" he mused. "I think that most Muslims see us Christians as infidels. Many want to kill us. They don't have the tolerance for other religions that we talk about in church. Sure, some are peaceful and law-abiding people, but they see themselves as right and us as wrong."

"That's certainly true of the ones who killed my family," said Harley. Matt stayed silent, keeping his eyes fixed on the river.

"You know what I'm talking about, Rev," Dirk said. "You've suffered worse than the rest of us. These Muslims see everything as good and evil, and they want to wipe out people they see as evil. So yes, I can see Muhammad Bayati killing his daughter if she did something that he thought was evil. These people have no sense of forgiveness, no sense of compassion. They don't believe what Jesus says about turning the other cheek. If a family member does something bad and brings shame to the family, they take the sinner out!"

Matt turned again. He seemed to be searching for the right words. "Dad," he said, in a calm and measured way, "you know the investigation is still open. Don't jump to conclusions."

"Look, son, you and I both know, whether Muslim or not, these killings are usually crimes of passion. I don't think you have to look very far to find a suspect."

"Yeah, maybe," Matt replied, turning back toward the river, "but don't assume that this is a religious thing. I've got a Muslim friend at the Bureau. A stand-up guy. He hates what terrorists are doing to his religion."

"How long has he been here?" asked Dirk.

"He was born here."

"Well, there you go. He's an American Muslim, not a Muslim American. He's not like these immigrants who are bringing their jihad to America."

"Whatever," said Matt, keeping his eyes on the river.

"Personally, I think most Muslims in the US are good people," Harley offered. "But some get frustrated and are easily radicalized. Think of the Boston Marathon bombers. Or the guy who shot up the nightclub in Orlando. Or the young man who set off bombs in New Jersey and New York last year. Or this week's bombing in Brussels. That hit close to home."

"I bet it did," Dirk nodded. "I hate what those bombers did to your wife and daughter."

"That New Jersey kid worked in the family chicken joint," recalled Harley. "Played basketball with his buddies. Tangled with other kids in rap battles. Talk about all-American! Next thing you know, he is traveling to Afghanistan and Pakistan, and coming back as a changed person."

"That's what radical Islam can do," Dirk said.

"We have got to defeat ISIS," Harley said, "just like we defeated the Nazis in the Second World War. There is no way to make peace with them. Most of the time, I try to follow the example of Jesus, but Islamic terrorists make me want to take a page from the Old Testament."

"What page?" Dirk grinned.

"Something from Deuteronomy," said Harley. "Something like God's instructions to the Israelites: 'You must utterly destroy them. Make no covenant with them and show them no mercy.'"

"Preach it, brother!" whooped Dirk. "Utterly destroy them! Show them no mercy!"

Harley cracked a smile, feeling a sense of relief. Out on the water, he felt free to express himself, releasing some of the rage he had felt since the deaths of Karen and Jessica. Everyone wanted him to forgive, but in his heart he wanted justice. And now he had said it.

"Yes, that is a word from God for sure!" said Dirk, raising his beer in a toast.

"Guys, I need you to suspend your Bible study," said Matt, turning his head. "We are about to leave the no-wake zone, so I'll be revving our engine and planing."

Matt pushed the throttle forward, and in a minute they were moving at thirty miles per hour, shooting across Occoquan Bay and out into the Potomac. A strong breeze whipped across the water, creating little whitecaps, but the boat handled the waves well.

"Should have warned you that there was a small craft advisory today," shouted Dirk, smiling. "But don't worry. Weather Service guys are always cautious."

Conversation was difficult with the noise of the engine and waves against the hull, so Harley sat back and enjoyed the ride. He felt unburdened, and without a tinge of guilt for his hatred.

He thought about a recent therapy session where the grief counselor asked Harley if he were mad at God for what happened to his family.

"I understand why some people would feel that way," he said, "but I don't. I'm mad at a lot of people, but not at God." When the counselor pressed him, he explained that he had never understood God to be a divine puppet master, pulling strings to make people act in good or evil ways. He said that he believed in free will and in the freedom people had to choose good or evil, so his anger was directed at the terrorists who killed Karen and Jessica, the incompetent security forces that allowed it to happen, and the people around him who had no idea what to say or do. His rage was directed at people—not God. As far as he was concerned, God was off the hook.

But at the same time, Harley felt a distance from God that he had never felt before. His daily prayers felt dry and lifeless, and leading worship services gave him no experience of God's presence or power. He had always been lifted up by a service of worship, inspired each Sunday to march into the week with energy and confidence. But no more. Sundays were just another workday, and they left him feeling drained. His counselor suggested that Harley's rage was pushing God away, making it hard for him to feel any inspiration, and Harley had to admit that he was probably right. He always felt the presence of God most clearly through the people around him and their acts of communal kindness and prayer and generosity and vulnerability. His anger was a fire that was driving people away, and he felt like a firefighter trying to keep small brush fires from exploding into an inferno.

As they skipped across the water, Harley began to feel a strong connection with his boating companions. Dirk pointed to Mason Neck, the large peninsula that formed the western bank of the Potomac River, and shouted that it was the location of Gunston Hall, the home of one of the founding fathers, George Mason. He said that Harley could pull some enormous catfish out of the deep sections of the river around there. Stretching his hands out to four feet, he signaled the size of the biggest one he had ever caught. As the boat sped northwest, Dirk said that they were entering Gunston Cove, which bordered Mason Neck on the north and spilled into the Potomac. Straight ahead was Fort Belvoir, a large Army post that was the center of intelligence operations.

"Take us close to Belvoir," Dirk said to Matt, "so that Harley can see the landing boats."

Matt powered the boat toward the fort and then eased back on the throttle so that it slowed and settled down into the water. He steered close to shore so Harley could see the boats anchored at the Belvoir dock. They looked like the landing craft used at D-Day, with large, flat doors on the front that could be dropped to discharge soldiers.

"What are they used for today?" asked Harley.

"Hard to say," answered Dirk. "Modern battles don't tend to involve storming beaches, thank God. But I wanted you to see them, to remind you of the bravery of our fighting forces."

"Amen to that," said Harley, imagining soldiers facing withering enemy fire as soon as the doors opened and crashed down on the beach. He realized that violent conflict was sometimes necessary when facing an enemy such as the Nazis. Or the Islamic State.

"Let's drop anchor here and have some lunch," suggested Dirk. "Enough about terrorism and warfare. I'd rather talk fishing."

Dirk pulled sandwiches and cold drinks out of the cooler, and the three of them ate and talked about the fish that could be caught in the Potomac. Dirk described the bony fish called shad that could be caught easily, sometimes several on a single line, when the fish were running in large numbers. Matt told the story of an enormous catfish that he had once caught near Mason Neck, so heavy that it almost broke his line. Of particular interest to Harley was the snakehead, an invasive species with sharp teeth and a voracious appetite that had been dubbed "the Frankenfish." A strange fish with an organ that enabled it to take oxygen from the air, it could survive out of water for short periods. Dirk said that when this Asian fish first entered the Potomac, people were worried that it would eat up all the local wildlife and take over the river, but fortunately state officials and fishermen had started working together to keep the population in check. Dirk himself had been part of a snakehead derby, catching one and eating it. After finishing his second beer, he said that he wanted to help to fish this particular species into extinction—just like the American military should do to the Islamic State.

When they pulled anchor and started the engine, Matt asked Harley if he wanted to drive the boat. Harley took the wheel and was careful at first, but in just a few minutes he was pushing hard on the throttle and enjoying the thrill of piloting the boat at planing speed. He felt so free on the water, disconnected from the endless conflicts and concerns of life on land. As the wind whipped around him, Harley suddenly realized, *Yes, this is why the Holy Spirit is described as a mighty wind.* Feeling the spray of the water he thought, *This is the cleansing water of baptism washing away my sins.*

When they returned to the Occoquan River, they docked at Halliburton's and Dirk took Harley to meet the owner. By the end of the day Harley was the proud owner of a 2003 Chaparral, a twenty-three-foot bowrider.

CHAPTER 6

A week after Norah Bayati's death, the smell of baking filled the air outside the shop, and then several loaves of bread appeared in the window. The hanging sign on the door was turned from *Closed* to *Open*, and the glass shelves inside went from empty to full with cookies, cakes, cinnamon buns, and scones. A steady stream of people walked by the shop, and some peered in the window. But not a single person entered. Nobody wanted to be the first to patronize a bakery owned by a killer. At the end of the day, all of the baked goods were removed from the window and thrown away. Not a single item had been sold. It was the same nearly every day for two weeks.

Doris King of the Yarn Shop said to her partner, Eleanor Buttress, "This is ridiculous. I've known Fatima Bayati for years. Regardless of what her husband did or didn't do, she deserves to make some money for herself and her children."

Doris was heavyset, with bright-red, curly hair and the tenacity of a pit bull, while Eleanor—rail-thin with short-cropped white hair—was as stubborn as Doris but much less aggressive.

"I don't want a single dollar from my pocket going to help pay for the defense of a man who would kill his own daughter," Eleanor snorted while sorting out skeins of yarn. "Honor killing! Can you believe it? It's barbaric. I won't support any family that could do such a thing."

"But you don't know Muhammad did it," protested Doris. "What about innocent until proven guilty? Is there anything about the Bayatis that makes you think they would do such a thing?"

"Well, they are Iraqis," said Eleanor, not taking her eyes off the yarn. "And Muslim. And I know that Iraqi Muslims do such things."

"Yeah, well, remember Timothy McVeigh? He was an American Christian, and he blew up a federal building and killed hundreds of people. I don't stop buying from American Christians because they do such things."

"Suit yourself," said Eleanor, turning to arrange a display of knitting needles. And so Doris did. She marched down Mill Street, pulled open the door of the bakery, and bought a loaf of whole wheat bread. Word spread about her purchase, and a trickle of others began to patronize the Riverview Bakery once again. But business did not return to normal. The otherwise cohesive community of Occoquan was divided.

Jessica Simpson, who was taking a break from her job at the American Legion, stood smoking on the Mill Street sidewalk. Since Harley's townhouse was across from the Legion, they ran into each other frequently and usually stopped for a chat. The air that morning was crisp and cool, uncommonly so for the last day of June, and the sky was Carolina blue.

"So, will you go into the bakery?" Harley asked. She took a drag on her cigarette and squinted at him, then exhaled slowly as she thought about her answer.

"Sure, why not?" she replied, flicking an ash off of her tattooed arm. "They never did anything bad to me. And Omar used to work here at the Legion."

"Oh, really?" said Harley. He hadn't heard that about the Bayatis' son. "When was that?"

"For about a year, when he was in high school. He bussed tables, washed dishes, took out the trash. I always liked him; thought he was cute."

"So why did he quit?" Harley asked.

"He didn't," said Jessica. "He got fired. Some of the Legion guys gave him a hard time, talking to him in a funny accent and making jokes about Muslims."

"Like what?"

"Stupid stuff. Bad jokes about camels and harems and suicide bombers and Osama bin Laden. One I remember is, 'Did you hear about the Muslim party? It was a blast.'"

"Pretty lame," Harley said.

"Actually, there was one that I liked," Jessica recalled. "It wasn't anti-Muslim, exactly. It dealt with the 9/11 terrorists. Remember how they expected to go to heaven and be given seventy-two virgins? Well, they got to heaven and ran into George Washington, who was really pissed off. Then they met Thomas Jefferson and James Madison and James Monroe, equally furious, and the line went on and on. Turns out their reward was seventy-two Virginians!"

Harley smiled as Jessica continued. "On top of the joking, some customers would finish their meals and make real messes for Omar to clean up—chewing food and spitting it on their plates, squirting ketchup on the tabletop, nasty stuff."

"I can understand that they were angry, being vets and all."

"Yeah, but he was just an innocent kid," Jessica responded, snuffing out her cigarette in the flower pot outside the Legion. "Anyway, Omar started showing up late to work, and when he was on duty he dragged his feet and gave the customers dirty looks. The boss gave him some warnings about shaping up, but he didn't change his ways, so the boss cut him loose."

"What did he do?" asked Harley. "Go back to the bakery?"

"Guess so," said Jessica, knotting her black-and-green hair into a ponytail. "I think we kind of soured him on working with Americans. And that's too bad, because I think this place was an oasis for him, especially at the beginning. One slow evening, I remember him telling me about the abuse he got in high school, being called names way worse than anything these Legion guys said. And once he got jumped by a bunch of thugs after school who accused him of being a terrorist. Beat him up pretty bad."

"High school can be rough," Harley said.

"At least here at the Legion he got some respect from the folks in the kitchen, and a regular paycheck. I was sorry he got fired. I see him once in a while from a distance, as he walks to his boat, but we never talk."

"Omar has a boat?"

"Oh yes, he loves to fish. Talk about an oasis for him, out on the river. His family has a Sea Ray about the same size as the one owned by your buddy Dirk. Keeps it just a few hundred yards up the river from you, at a private dock just big enough for a couple boats."

"Interesting," said Harley. "Wouldn't peg the Bayatis as boaters."

"Hey, this is Occoquan. We have a river. Why would they not have a boat?" She playfully punched him on the arm. "Even you have a boat, preacher-man!" Harley shrugged and agreed with her.

Harley walked west on Mill Street toward the River Mill Park. Passing the Riverview Bakery, Harley saw that the windows were full of baked goods and no customers in the store. Shadowy figures moved around behind the counter, probably Fatima and one of her kids. He looked at the upper stories of the frame building covered in green shingles, where the Bayatis lived. He guessed that the second story was their kitchen and living room, and that the third floor contained their bedrooms. Someone had told him that they also had renters, and he was curious about where they could live, so he walked around to see the back of the building.

Turning the corner, he saw that the building was L-shaped, with a wing extending off the rear of the west side of the building. Wooden staircases connected balconies on each of the levels, giving access to a number of apartment doors on the back of the building. Harley guessed that the renters lived in apartments in the three levels of the wing, and then he tried to figure out which of the rooms had been the one where Norah died. Judging from the windows, there were numerous rooms on each level, so he was left without a clue.

Returning to Mill Street, Harley saw a midnight-blue Mercedes Benz pull up in front of the bakery. Two men got out. One was a gray-haired man in his sixties in a finely tailored summer suit. The other was a man in his thirties with a shaved head and muscles straining against the fabric of his open-collared silk shirt. He appeared to be a weight lifter. The two of them walked into the Riverview Bakery, and Harley felt overcome by curiosity. He plopped down on a park bench and pulled out his cell phone, ostensibly to check his email. But although his head was down, he kept his eyes on the bakery.

The older man spoke to a middle-aged woman in a head-scarf while the younger one stood by the door with his massive arms crossed in front of his chest. A young woman was behind the counter with the middle-aged woman, but she kept her distance. The older man seemed to be doing most of the talking, and as time went by the middle-aged woman moved back and forth as if agitated, pointing toward the door for them to exit. The older man gave her a little bow, and then motioned for the younger man to exit. They quickly returned to their car and pulled away.

Harley had no idea what he had just witnessed. The men were clearly not bakery customers. But at the same time, they did not seem to be law enforcement. Harley looked back at the bakery and saw the two women talking for a moment before they disappeared into a back room.

Harley walked toward the river and saw a Sea Ray bowrider that looked very similar to Dirk's. It was moored to a short dock big enough for just two boats. The dock appeared to be a remnant of Occoquan's industrial days, because it didn't have fancy lights, water hookups, or power connections.

Returning to the street and continuing toward the park, he passed the old brick bank that now housed a beauty parlor, and the wooden theater that had been transformed into a brewpub. Birds called out from the trees lining the street, and Harley enjoyed the peacefulness until a pack of motorcycles roared up Mill Street. One of the riders pointed to the bakery as the pack passed.

❋

Harley was weary but also excited to get out on the river with his boat. He sat at home, making a list of what he needed for his trip and thinking about what he had witnessed at the bakery. His eyes grew heavy as his third glass of wine settled his restless mind.

That night, Harley found himself sitting in the stern of his boat, going through his safety kit to make sure everything was there: flares, whistle, first aid kit. The sun was setting and turning the river red and gold. *Red sky at night, sailor's delight,* Harley remembered. His slip was on the western end of the community dock, so he had an unobstructed view of the sunset. He stopped his safety check to look west and enjoy nature's pyrotechnics. At that point he realized that he was trapped in his boat, with his feet somehow attached to the deck. Very strange!

Suddenly, a group of men carrying duffle bags walked across the parking lot toward the Bayatis' boat. The men appeared Middle Eastern, with brown skin and black hair. The first one on the boat was a young man, whom Harley presumed to be Omar Bayati, based on the description of the boy he had been given earlier. The others handed their bags to Omar, and then climbed on board, five in all. After a few minutes of preparation, Omar fired up the engine, untied the lines, and they began to move slowly down the river.

As they passed Harley's dock, heading east toward the Potomac, all five stared straight at Harley. Because he was trapped on the boat, he was terrified that they would see him and come after him. But something was strange: The men looked right through him, focusing their gazes on the shoreline. *What a relief,* thought Harley. *So good to be invisible.*

Harley made mental notes of their body shapes, facial hair and other features. He was sure he would have to testify against them, so he tried to remember everything clearly. He was a little surprised by the fact that Jessica was right—Omar was, in fact, cute. A really fine-looking young man with a slender face and soulful eyes.

Harley wanted to rush home and alert the authorities, but he remained trapped. He wanted to call the police, send up a flare or do something, but he couldn't move. He was sure that people were going to die at the hands of these terrorists, just as Jessica and Karen had been killed in Brussels. And then, the sky to the northeast erupted in a red-and-yellow fireball—not the sun, not a set of fireworks, but an explosion. The light was followed by a roaring shock wave that overturned Harley's boat, threw him in the water, and then he awoke.

❀

The room was full of sunlight that Saturday morning, and Harley's sheets were soaked. He awoke feeling both unnerved and relieved. Rolling out of bed, he rubbed his face and thanked God that it had only been a dream. But he couldn't shake the sense of dread that he might be living near a terrorist cell, right in the heart of historic Occoquan. Needing to clear his head, he threw on some clothes and left his house in search of a cup of coffee and some breakfast. As soon as he hit the street, he saw that the farmers' market near the park was open.

He strolled past the bakery and the hair salon and the brewpub. In the cul-de-sac that bordered the park, he saw a dozen white canopies and a crowd of people milling around. The day was unseasonably cool and the mood in the street was festive. Fathers pushed babies in strollers, mothers chased toddlers, elementary-aged children chased each other on the sidewalk, and mixed-race couples walked hand in hand. Little by little, Harley's dark mood brightened.

Harley saw that the Riverview Bakery was the first tent at the open market. Fatima and her daughter were standing behind a table covered with baked goods. He looked at the younger woman and tried to think of her name. *Norah is dead, so this is who? Sarah?* The two weren't doing much business, although the crowd in the cul-de-sac was large. Harley didn't want to buy from them, so he wandered to the right and began to inspect the fresh fruits in the first booth on the right side. Then he made his way around the semicircle, buying a cup of coffee at one booth, and a scone at another.

Numerous conversations filled the area, but the chatter was suddenly smothered by the roar of six motorcycles pulling up to the farmers' market. The bikers parked near the tent for the Riverview Bakery but stayed on their motorcycles and kept their engines running. These were not the harmless retirees who had rode through town last Saturday morning when he went out on Dirk's boat. This gang wore black leather with studs and chains and helmets with black visors obscuring their faces. The motorcycles had no license plates, either.

Most of the crowd ignored the bikers once their engines quieted to an idle. Children played and parents continued to shop. But Harley couldn't take his eyes off them. His breathing quickened and his heart pounded. Three of the bikers stayed on their motorcycles and scanned the area around them, acting like lookouts. The other three got off their bikes and pulled tire irons out of their saddlebags and stormed toward the Riverview Bakery tent, screaming at the Bayati women.

Harley felt as paralyzed as he did in the dream. Pandemonium erupted as members of the crowd closest to the bakery tent shouted and ran away, crashing into each other and knocking parcels to the ground. Fatima and Sarah Bayati ran into the park, covering their heads and crying for help. The motorcycle thugs smashed the bakery table with their tire irons, breaking the table in half and destroying the baked goods.

The attack seemed to go on for an eternity, but it was over in a minute. A siren could be heard as the thugs roared off in a matter of seconds and were out of Occoquan, scattering in different directions before the first police cruiser arrived.

Parents held tightly to their children, many people were crying, and some seemed to be in shock. A few ran up to the first police officer to arrive on the scene and tried to give a description of what had happened. The people who had fled into the park slowly returned, and Harley saw the Bayati women being helped by a large woman with bright-red hair. She had her arms around them and was trying to lead them to the police cruiser while offering them words of comfort. They were crying and trembling.

Harley remained frozen in place. Looking down at his feet, he felt a burning sense of shame.

CHAPTER 7

O ccoquan's rocks were old. On both sides of the river, ancient formations rose above the water and gave silent testimony to the region's history. They formed about 300 million years ago when the North American and African landmasses plowed into each other and created a supercontinent called Pangaea. The seam between these continental plates ran along the east coast of North America, with Virginia at the center, and the supercontinent remained stitched together for about 100 million years. Pangaea began to separate about 175 million years ago, creating the continents we know today, but it left behind formations such as the shelves of rock that stood on either side of the Occoquan River. These outcroppings had seen divisions between settlers and Native Americans, colonists and the King of England, the North and the South, blacks and whites, and now Christians and Muslims.

Harley saw evidence of this particular division when he was taking a short run on the Fourth of July along a one-mile loop from his townhouse to the River Mill Park, across the pedestrian bridge at the western end of town, through the woods on the other side of the river, and then back to town across the Route 123 bridge on the eastern edge of Occoquan. Directly across the river from his townhouse was an outcropping of rock, hidden by trees along the river but visible from the road that cut through the woods. These rocks stood as tall and strong as Easter Island heads, as they had for millions of years, but they were covered with graffiti, the work of numerous spray-painting vandals. The markings made Harley feel discouraged when he first saw them, but on his morning run he spotted a new one that stopped him in his tracks and made him shiver—the mark of the Islamic State.

Heat and humidity had returned to Occoquan after a few days of cool, dry weather, so Harley was panting and dripping with sweat as he inspected the graffiti. His shame after the attack at the farmers' market was now replaced by fear for his own safety. His mind raced with questions. *Who are they and how close are they—right here in Occoquan? What are they planning, and when will they strike—will it be today, a national holiday?* He realized that the symbol on the rock didn't necessarily prove that terrorists were at work. It could have been painted by the same sort of punks that put anarchy symbols on public buildings. Still, the discovery unsettled him, especially on the Fourth of July, the day he always felt the most patriotic.

After crossing the bridge back into Occoquan, Harley jogged down Commerce Street and took a right onto Washington. He glanced over at Riverside Methodist Church and noticed that the wood trim at the front of the church was in desperate need of paint, and also that the front door was slightly ajar. *What is going on?* The building should have been locked for the holiday, but the door was open. Since the graffiti on the rocks had put him on edge, Harley imagined robbers or vandals or terrorists breaking in and doing damage to the church. He stopped his run and walked carefully toward the building, pulling out his cell phone and punching in the numbers *9-1-1*, just in case. His heart pounding, he gently pushed open the front door, fully expecting to see a gang of thugs at work, or a badly trashed and desecrated sanctuary. What he saw was a gorgeous woman.

She was sitting in a pew and turned toward him when his opening of the door allowed a ray of light to shine down the center aisle. Her face was framed by carefully braided hair, her eyes sparkled in the sunlight, and her skin was copper and smooth. As Harley entered the sanctuary, she stood and smiled.

"Good morning. I was in here praying." She was tall and slender, in her early thirties, wearing tights and a running shirt. Harley was speechless.

"This used to be my church," she said. "I hope you don't mind me being here."

Walking down the center aisle, Harley found his voice. "Not at all . . . I'm Harley Camden. The new pastor."

They shook hands. "Nice to meet you. I'm Tawnya Jones. As I said, this was my church when it was Emanuel Baptist. I live in Lake Ridge now and was out for a run. We never used to lock the church, so I tried the door and found it open, just like the old days."

"Well, times have changed, and we do try to lock it," said Harley, "but I guess someone forgot."

"I just wanted to come see Jesus," said Tawnya, pointing to the stained glass at the front.

"Yes," Harley replied. "That's a beautiful piece of art."

"Black Jesus," Tawnya said. "I miss him. The new Emanuel is all high-tech sights and sounds, with no stained glass in sight. As a little girl, I loved black Jesus."

"I understand," Harley said to her. "Please sit. I'm glad you came back."

Harley sat in a pew across the aisle from her. Sunlight continued to pour in through the open door, illuminating bits of dust in the air. Tawnya seemed to feel very comfortable in the room, and she looked longingly toward the stained-glass window at the front.

"I sat right here with my family, all through my childhood," she recalled. "Whenever something bad happened, I would bring it to church and lay it before Jesus—the deaths of my grandfathers, my mother's cancer, even the ways that I was teased at school for being so tall. I brought it all to Jesus, and he helped me through my storms. I was fifteen when Emanuel moved to its new building, but until then I was in this pew every Sunday."

"I'm glad this place means so much to you," said Harley. "Even though it's now a Methodist Church, you are always welcome."

"Thanks for that," Tawnya smiled. "Glad I didn't have to break in."

"So, where do you live, and what do you do?"

"I live in Lake Ridge, in a subdivision off of Old Bridge Road. My husband and I bought a home there three years ago, and we have a two-year-old daughter. My husband's last name is Quander, and we use that name as a family, but I am Tawnya Jones professionally. I'm an attorney in the Department of Justice, Civil Rights Division, so I make the long slog into DC every day."

"What led you to go in that direction?"

"This church," she said. "Emanuel was really active in the Civil Rights movement, so justice is in this church's DNA. The marches and protests were before my time, but I learned at the feet of some warriors. Has anyone told you about Reverend Jones?"

"Jones?" Harley asked. "Yes, I think so. Tim Underwood said—"

"Tie-dye Tim!" she laughed. "You met Tie-dye!"

"Sure did. He was a big fan of Reverend Jones."

"Well, he's my great-uncle. Pastor of this church for many years. Retired now, but still active in community issues."

"So you know Tim Underwood?"

"Of course. I grew up here in Occoquan, just a block from here. My parents ran a small store that was in the family for generations. A black-owned business in the heart of Occoquan."

"Where is it now?"

"It closed in the early '90s when big grocery stores took all the business away. My parents sold the building and bought a couple of 7-Elevens on Route 1 in Woodbridge. My father also does commercial real estate development. They've done very well."

"What do you mean by 'very well'?"

"They're millionaires," Tawnya smiled. "My dad has always been very entrepreneurial. And he's about the only Republican left in our family. Most everyone became Democrats in the 1960s, but he said he was going to stay with his father and grandfather and great-grandfather in the Party of Lincoln. There aren't many black faces in the Prince William GOP, but he is one of them."

"I've heard that Occoquan is a Republican town."

"It certainly was. Proudly so, during the Civil War. And I think that history is part of what my dad holds onto. As for my mother, she has always gone her own way, politically. She usually votes for Democrats and cancels out my dad's vote."

Harley appreciated Tawnya's intellect and spunk, qualities that magnified her beauty. Since she was so plugged into the town, he asked her about the Bayatis.

"Don't really know them," she said. "We moved out of Occoquan just before they arrived. They seem to be good businesspeople, but I'm not sure that they'll ever fit in."

"Why's that?"

"You know, they're Muslims. Like it or not, this is a Christian town. Now don't get me wrong, they have a right to be here. I'm a defender of their civil rights, personally and professionally. But look around; there is one church in town, and we are sitting in it. There is no mosque here. No synagogue. We follow Jesus here."

Harley knew what she was getting at, although he wasn't sure that Occoquan was really a Christian town. After all, Leah Silverman lived there, and a lot of people throughout Northern Virginia weren't practicing any religion.

"I certainly want people to follow Jesus. I try to preach it every week."

"The world would be a better place if more people did," Tawnya said, crossing one slender leg over the other. "There is no way that Jesus could get behind the kind of killing that is done in the world today, whether it is gangbangers shooting up their rivals or terrorists killing innocent people."

"You are right. Defeating Islamic extremists has got to be a top priority."

"Wait a second," Tawnya interrupted. "You are the guy—the pastor—who lost his wife and daughter. Oh God, I am so sorry."

Harley nodded and thanked her.

"My husband works in Army intelligence at Fort Belvoir, and he was talking about you the other night. Reminded me about the Brussels bombing, and told me that he heard you were moving here. Reverend, you have my deepest sympathy."

"Please, call me Harley."

She stood, stepped across the aisle, took his hand. "Harley, I cannot imagine your pain. You seem like such a good man, and Occoquan is lucky to have you. May Jesus give you strength and help."

Harley loved the feeling of his hand in hers. Her beautiful face was just inches away, close enough that he could smell her perfume. He wished she would return to Occoquan and become a member of his church so that he could look at her every Sunday. Harley thanked her again, and then got the sense that the moment was becoming awkward. She did as well.

Tawnya gently let go of his hand, saying she was glad they had met and looked forward to seeing him again. Harley ushered her to the door. As they walked out into the sunshine together, she said that she was going to continue her run. Taking note of his running clothes, she said, "Look, we're both runners. We should go for a jog together." Then she gave him a quick hug and ran up Washington Street toward Lake Ridge.

✵

Harley locked the church and walked the short block home. He showered and dressed for the day, and then headed to the dock to prep his boat for the evening. He had invited Leah to join him for the Fourth of July fireworks, which were being launched from the Lake Ridge Marina east of Occoquan. Harley figured that they would have the best possible view from the water, so he asked her to join him on the boat for an evening picnic on the river beyond the Route 123 bridge. But when Harley took the cover off of his boat that day, he discovered the mysterious black marks and started scrubbing, working himself into a lathered sweat.

An hour into this job, the Pakistanis called to him from the dock and asked him for a ride—a request he couldn't honor. Finally, he hit the showers a second time and put on a fresh set of clothes for the evening.

Leah arrived at seven, dressed in tennis shoes, shorts, and an Indigo Girls T-shirt. "Happy Fourth, Captain Harley," she said as she handed him a bottle of white wine for the picnic. "Here's a little something for your cooler."

Harley thanked her and invited her in. "I'm still unpacking," he explained as he waved a hand toward the boxes stacked in the dining room and living room. "But who cares, since we are going on the boat."

"You're right," she said. "I'm excited about seeing your yacht. Let's go!"

Harley put the wine on top of a six-pack of beer in the cooler, gave Leah a picnic basket to carry, and the two of them walked down the wrought-iron stairs and across the parking area to the dock. The temperature was cooling a bit, but the air remained uncomfortably humid.

"It should be nicer on the water."

Once on the boat, Harley turned on the blower and showed Leah its various features, including its small bathroom. "That could come in handy," she said, "especially if we drink all the wine I brought, plus that six-pack."

"Right about that," said Harley. "I remember the time we went to the beach in Tel Aviv, and we had such a hard time finding a bathroom. I've never been in such pain."

Harley fired up the engine, asked Leah to untie the lines, and in a minute they were off. Reconnecting with Leah was one of the happiest surprises of his move to Occoquan, and he hoped that they could get into a habit of regular meals together. Since the deaths of Jessica and Karen, Harley had struggled with the loneliness of dinnertime, and realized how much he had failed to appreciate the simple joy of eating and talking with loved ones around a table.

Karen had been a creative cook, which he had taken for granted. Jessica had been an enthusiastic storyteller, which he had failed to appreciate. His eyes misted up, but then he spotted a log in the water brought downriver by a recent thunderstorm. Wiping his eyes, he steered around it, pointed it out to Leah, and said that they would have to watch out for it when they returned in the dark. They motored slowly east on the Occoquan River, past the osprey nests on the channel markers, and found a place to anchor on the far side of the Route 123 bridge. "Not a long cruise, but you get a sense of the boat. Some other time, we'll go out on the Potomac and drive her fast."

The boat had a table in the stern, where they set up cheese and crackers alongside a plate of fruit and a couple of sandwiches. Harley poured Leah a glass of wine and popped the cap off a beer for himself. He lifted his beer in a toast. "From the Mediterranean Sea to the Occoquan River."

"L'chaim," she responded, winking at him. "To life."

"Speaking of the Mediterranean," said Harley, "do you remember the boat that was broadcasting Top 40 music when we were in Israel?"

"Oh yeah," recalled Leah. "The Voice of Peace. I haven't thought about that for years. But I remember their slogan, 'From somewhere in the Mediterranean, we are the Voice of Peace.'"

"That's right. I can remember listening on my transistor radio, lying in my bunk in the A-frame dorm. Rumor was that the station was started with money from John Lennon."

"Peace through pop music. Arabs and Israelis, rocking out together. What a concept."

They began to eat, and Leah asked him how things were going at the church. He described the congregation and its issues, and then told her about running into Tawnya Jones in front of the black Jesus. She said that she had heard of the Jones family but didn't know Tawnya personally.

"And black Jesus? What's that?" she asked. She had never been inside the church, so he told her the story of Emanuel Baptist, founded by a former slave, and how it became Riverside Methodist.

After pouring Leah some more wine and opening himself another beer, Harley asked if she had heard about the incident at the farmers' market. She nodded. "They haven't caught the attackers, as far as I know. They scattered quickly, and who knows where they came from. At least the Bayatis escaped physical injury."

"I'm guessing the attackers were just trying to send a message," Harley said.

"A pretty violent one," replied Leah. "Their tent and table was completely trashed, and they lost all of their goods. I'd call it a hate crime."

Harley put a piece of cheese in his mouth and chewed instead of responding. He was still ruminating on the appearance of the Islamic State symbol on the rocks. He wondered if it would be so bad if the Bayatis packed up and moved out of town. Swallowing, he asked, "Has anyone ever linked the Bayatis to terrorism?"

Leah's expression made Harley want to take his question back.

"No!" she said, sharply. "Are you kidding? They have been here for twenty years and are bakers. How does that fit a profile for terrorism?"

Harley shrugged. He hated to look stupid. "There is just so much lone-wolf stuff going on," he suggested, trying to redeem himself.

"Well, not the Bayatis," Leah snapped. "Harley, you have got to understand. We Jews have suffered so much from guilt by association. You know the history. Centuries of being called Christ-killers. Hitler blaming us for Germany's loss in the First World War. Any time I see Muslims being associated with terrorism just because they are Muslim, I just have to defend them. Holocausts come out of that kind of suspicion."

Harley knew she was right, but he couldn't shake the fear that had grabbed him when he saw the graffiti on the rocks. *And*, he wondered, *how can she know for a fact that they are innocent people?*

"Harley, you remember what our prof taught us about Sepphoris, right? You've got a role to play in making Occoquan such a place. If we can't figure out how to live and work together like the people of Sepphoris, we've got no hope for the future. Any peace on earth has got to start in places like this."

Harley sipped his beer and looked at the deep-green leaves of the trees on the shoreline. Where was the sweet companionship that they had enjoyed when she spent the night at his house? His rage was returning; Leah was really getting under his skin. *Peace on earth! Who is she kidding? How can she be so naïve? Karen and Jessica believed in peace, and look what happened to them.*

"Harley, you need to be a bridge," she said. "Just like that bridge over the river. As a pastor, you have the challenge of making connections, bringing people together."

He looked up at the bridge and then at Leah, hoping that she did not see his rage. Such self-righteousness and condescension. *Who is she to tell me about my job? Who is she to challenge me to build bridges to Muslims, after my family was killed by those gutless terrorists?* He turned back to the trees, hoping that their deep summer green would calm him. *Come on, cool down, boy. Green is a calming color, right?* That's what he had heard. It was why people sat in "green rooms" before going on television. Hospitals painted rooms green to relax patients.

Harley felt unnerved by a mix of love and anger as he looked at Leah, a confusing blend of emotion reserved for the people closest to him. He had not felt this way since he was married. Karen was a smart and attractive wife, loving and devoted, but she had driven him crazy at times. She always pushed him to take bigger and bigger churches so that he could make more money, but she herself had never been willing to take a full-time job. Sure, there was a lot asked of her as a pastor's wife, and she did it well—helping to lead the Methodist Women, chaperoning youth mission trips, showing concern for senior citizens. She worked hard in the church and certainly made him look good. They talked about it and even fought about it, but she always said that she was too busy with church and parenting to take on a full-time job. Love and anger—he felt it toward Karen, and now, with tears welling, he was feeling it toward Leah.

Fortunately, a boat pulled up alongside them, and Harley recognized the owners as his next-door neighbors. He wiped his eyes, cleared his throat, and called out, "Hey, Bill and Jean. You here for the fireworks?" They nodded. Harley introduced Leah and the four of them chatted for a few minutes. Harley was grateful for the distraction. After the other couple got settled and focused on their own picnic, he said to Leah, "Let's not talk about work. It's a holiday.

Tell me what you're going to do for vacation this summer.''

Leah could tell that Harley was irritated, but she wasn't exactly sure why. He was a different person from the divinity school student she met thirty years ago. She lightened the conversation, telling Harley about her plans to go with a group of friends to the Jersey Shore. Harley pretended to listen as he looked into the water, which darkened as the sun went down. He had never been on the river at night before, and he didn't realize how inky black it would become. He imagined himself slipping into the water and disappearing into its depths, into a place of darkness and silence and endless sleep. But then the sun dropped below the horizon and fireworks erupted over the river, pulling Harley out of his morose funk.

Leah craned her slender neck up to watch the show, suddenly filling Harley with longing. He loved her smile and her bright eyes, and he needed her in ways he couldn't express. The fireworks turned out to be a soothing balm for Harley, except for the grand finale, which gave him a momentary flashback to his dream of the terrorist explosion.

After motoring through the black water to Harley's dock, with both of them keeping an eye open for logs in the river, Leah thanked him and said goodnight. She stood there for a moment, creating an opportunity for some additional conversation. Harley didn't respond. Their rekindled friendship still felt fragile to him, like a baby osprey in a nest, and he didn't want to cause additional damage. He wanted them to continue to get together, so he kept it light, gave her a peck on the cheek, and promised that they would connect again soon. She slid into her car and drove off, while he headed into the house and continued his drinking. After falling asleep in his chair, he got up at four in the morning, staggered to the bathroom and then to bed, and ended up oversleeping his alarm.

When he arrived at his office, it was ten in the morning, about an hour later than usual. He had a bad hangover and a message on his church answering machine. It was from a corrections officer at the Prince William County Adult Detention Center, asking him to visit Muhammad Bayati.

CHAPTER 8

Muhammad Bayati was on a hunger strike and the jailers wanted Harley to meet with him. *But why?* The baker was a Muslim and Harley didn't even know him or his family. What he did know was that he wasn't going to figure things out by sitting at his desk, so he picked up the phone and called the Prince William County Adult Detention Center.

"Officer Reddick, please," Harley said to the receptionist, rubbing his temples to try to ease the pain. "Reverend Harley Camden, returning his call."

"Thank you, Pastor, for returning my call," said the young cop. "We have a situation here that we think you might be able to help us with. One of our inmates, Muhammad Bayati, has been on a hunger strike for several days. He is protesting his incarceration, and objecting to the time it will take to get him to trial."

"You do know that he is a Muslim, don't you?" asked Harley. "I'm Methodist."

"Yes, sir."

"So why are you not calling an imam?"

"We did, sir," said the officer. "An imam was here the day before yesterday, but he was not successful in getting Mr. Bayati to eat."

Great, thought Harley. "So why me?"

"We went online and found that your church was the only congregation in Occoquan," explained the officer. "We thought that you might have some influence as a neighbor and a clergyman."

Harley wondered if there was going to be any way out of this. "I need to tell you that I do not know Mr. Bayati. I have only lived in Occoquan for a few weeks."

"Yes, sir," the officer replied. "We would still like you to come in. We do not want to have to arrange for a doctor to force-feed him. That is a tough process, and it always leads to a lot of publicity."

Harley leaned back in his chair, thinking. In the Washington area, most people wanted publicity. But not the jail, of course. "Okay," he said. "I'll come in. I've never been to your jail, so give me the procedure."

After hanging up, Harley thought about the many bizarre situations that he had been forced into as a pastor. Once, he spent an hour counseling a distressed stranger on the phone, and after hearing several grunting sounds realized that it was an obscene call. Another time, a homeless guy came into his office and said that he had seen Harley's wife at a local diner with another man. Turns out the woman was a heavyset blonde, quite the opposite of his thin, brunette wife. And then there was the time that Harley was asked to visit a man who had grown up in his church but then moved to another town to become a police officer. The guy was in a tough spot, Harley was told, and really needed support. When he asked for the man's address, he was given the address of the Fairfax County Jail. The police officer had been arrested for robbing a store. Now Harley was going back to jail, to visit a Muslim accused of murder.

Harley got up, straightened his tie, and headed for the door. He knew he needed a cup of fresh coffee, so he walked across the street to Auntie's and bought a large. Sipping the steaming, black coffee, he looked around the pie shop, smelled the fragrance of the cooling baked goods, and wished that he could hang out there all day and write a sermon. But he knew that pastors were both called and sent, and right now he was being called to the Prince William County Adult Detention Center. There was no way around it. It felt like the irresistible call of God. And as someone who had been feeling distant from God, he knew he had to respond.

Most days since the deaths of Karen and Jessica, Harley felt impotent and powerless. But not when he was driving, oddly enough. Getting behind the wheel of his new Volkswagen Passat, he punched the gas, leaving Occoquan through the woods along Tanyard Hill Road, getting a rush from the acceleration. Harley's gray sedan didn't attract much attention from police officers, nor from anyone for that matter, but he loved its power as he darted into traffic or blasted along an interstate.

Harley had purchased the car the previous summer, needing to replace his ten-year-old Honda Accord but also wanting to drive something that didn't remind him of Karen whenever he looked at the passenger seat.

The GPS took him along a route he had never driven before, with most of the mileage being on the heavily wooded Prince William County Parkway. Harley sensed that he was running parallel to the Occoquan Reservoir, although the water was completely out of sight. He entered the city of Manassas and found the adult detention center in the center of town, an imposing brick building that was far larger than he expected. After parking, he passed through a metal detector, identified himself to an officer behind a bulletproof window, and was buzzed through a series of heavy metal doors, each of which locked with a decisive clank. Harley's heart beat faster as he moved deeper into the jail. After reaching a sparsely furnished reception area, he took a seat, closed his eyes, and calmed himself with deep breaths while two officers fetched Muhammad Bayati.

Harley had reached a visitation area with ten rooms for private conferences, each with a heavy door with a window. He realized that he was dressed casually for a jail visit, wearing khaki pants, a short-sleeve, button-down blue shirt, and a blue-and-brown patterned tie. In the cooler months, he might have worn a sport coat. On a visit like this he should have worn a clergy collar.

Finally, a short, slender man entered the room with his hands behind his back. He was followed by two guards, one of whom stopped him and unlocked his handcuffs before ushering him into a visitation room. The man glanced at Harley before entering, then turned his eyes forward and walked to a chair on the far side of a table in the middle of the room. He sat and rubbed his wrists to soothe them after being released from the cuffs. The guard turned to Harley.

"Pastor Camden, this is Muhammad Bayati. You have twenty minutes. Good luck."

Harley walked cautiously into the room, jumping slightly when the guard closed the heavy steel door behind him.

"Mr. Bayati?" he asked, putting out his hand for a shake. "I'm Harley Camden, the pastor of Riverside Methodist Church in Occoquan." The inmate looked him in the eye and offered his hand but didn't say anything. "May I sit down?" Harley asked. Muhammad nodded.

"You probably wonder why I am here," Harley continued. "I was called by a corrections officer since I am the only clergyman in Occoquan."

"I've heard about you," said Muhammad. The man had a brown face with deep lines, bushy eyebrows and large brown eyes that were as dark and deep as the inky water of the Occoquan River at night. Muhammad was balding, with a fringe of gray hair around the back of his head. His orange jail jumpsuit hung on his slender frame, and his long fingers continued to massage his wrists.

"I understand that an imam visited you a couple of days ago," Harley offered. Muhammad nodded. "Was that helpful?" the pastor asked.

"We prayed together," Muhammad said. "Prayer is always helpful." He looked Harley in the eye and said nothing more. He seemed comfortable with awkward silences.

"So, you pray five times a day?"

"Of course. I am Muslim."

"And how does it help you?"

Muhammad squinted. "You should know how. Prayer reminds me of who God is, and where I stand in relation to God. Allahu Akbar."

"Which means what?" asked Harley.

"God is the greatest."

"Indeed," said Harley. "God is the greatest. Have you been able to keep up with your prayers here in jail?"

"Of course," Muhammad answered, with just the hint of a smile. "There is not much else to do."

Harley realized that he had asked a stupid question, so he changed the subject.

"Let me tell you a little about myself." He described how he had served churches in the Washington area for thirty years before being assigned to Occoquan, always trying to help people to live their faith and to serve the needy. Realizing that Muhammad might not know anything about the Methodist Church, he talked about the denomination's openness to interfaith relations with Jews and Muslims. He concluded by becoming more personal and telling him that he had recently lost his wife and daughter. Looking Muhammad in the eyes to gauge his reaction, he said, "They were killed by terrorists at the Brussels airport."

Muhammad's eyes welled up, which was not the reaction Harley expected. "I was informed of your loss when you arrived in Occoquan," he said. "You have my sympathy."

Harley thanked him but felt a little off balance. *Why would this guy feel any emotion about the killings of two people that he didn't know, by terrorists he didn't know, in a country that he has probably never visited?*

"You may know that the Qur'an says that whoever kills a person unjustly, it is as though he has killed all mankind. I condemn the killers of your wife and daughter."

"The killers deserve condemnation," Harley said. "They are not men of God."

"Nor is the person who killed my daughter," Muhammad said. Harley wondered, *How do I know that you did not kill your daughter?* He looked long and hard at Muhammad, trying to pick up on any expression or body language that might signal guilt. Muhammad simply sat there silent and grief-stricken.

Harley refrained from judgment. "I think we have much in common," he said. "We serve the same God, a just God."

Nodding, Muhammad said, "God has judged the killers of your family. May he do the same to the one who murdered my daughter."

"Do you have any idea who he is?" asked Harley.

"A suspicion, yes. I learned that my daughter was seeing a man, an American, a non-Muslim."

"And why do you suspect him?"

Muhammad leaned back. "Women are not killed in their beds by strangers. The one who murdered her knew her. Perhaps they quarreled. I do not know." His words were calm and measured, and Harley guessed that he was either innocent or in complete denial.

"So why are you here?" Harley probed.

"Some neighbors heard me arguing with Norah. The day of her death, we had a fight about her relationship with this American. It was a bad fight, a loud one. I lost my temper, I admit it. I grabbed her by the shoulders, and she took hold of my arms, scratching me deeply with her fingernails. We struggled until I pushed her away. After her death, the police heard about the argument, saw my wounds, and made me the suspect. It didn't take them long to find my DNA under her fingernails."

"People are calling it an honor killing," said Harley.

Muhammad's eyes flashed with anger. "Absurd. Such killings are barbaric. I am an American. I left Iraq to escape such brutality. I came to America because it is a land of justice, and now I am getting no justice."

"I'm not being accusatory; it's what people are saying."

Muhammad's expression changed from anger to sadness. "I know."

"So why have you started a hunger strike?" Harley asked.

Muhammad ran a hand across his bald head. "To bring attention to my case, and move it more quickly to trial. My lawyer says they have to begin a speedy trial within seventy days, but that does not sound speedy to me! I think Norah's death was a priority for the police until I was arrested. Now, no one cares. The prosecutor is going to take his time and build a case around the idea of an honor killing. But nothing could be further from the truth. I need to get to trial, prove my innocence, and return to my work at the bakery."

"But you are going to destroy your health by starving yourself."

"God will take care of me," Muhammad said. "My incarceration is unjust, and God is a God of justice. He will help me get through this."

Harley thought for a moment about what his next move should be. "What do you think Jesus would want me to do? After all, we both honor Jesus, right?"

"In my faith, he is a great prophet," said Muhammad. "And as an Iraqi, I cannot forget that the Wise Men came from the east, maybe even from my homeland, to visit the baby Jesus."

"Exactly," Harley said, a little surprised that Muhammad knew that Bible story. "Jesus is a prophet for you and the messiah for me. He teaches that we should help the hungry and the thirsty, and visit people in prison."

"Indeed he does," Muhammad agreed.

"So perhaps you are the hungry one in prison that I am supposed to help."

"Maybe," said Muhammad, "but I don't know what you intend to do."

"The Bible says that when I help a person like you, I am really helping Jesus."

Muhammad looked at him quizzically. "So I am Jesus for you? I do not see how that can be. I am not a prophet."

"We don't have to get too spiritual about it," said Harley, backing off a bit. "But I think I should help. What can I do for you?"

"Anything to get my case some attention," suggested Muhammad, "and move it more quickly to trial. I am angry that I am locked up and forgotten, falsely accused of a crime that I did not commit. I came to this country because of its rule of law, and now look at what is happening to me."

Harley pondered for a moment, and then thought of Henry Kim, the husband of his colleague Emily in Sterling. He wrote for the Metro section of *The Washington Post*. Maybe Henry could do a story on Muhammad.

"If I could get a journalist to write a story on your case, would you be willing to stop your hunger strike? It won't get you out of jail, but a big story might get the wheels turning a little faster."

"A big story?" asked Muhammad. "Not just in the county paper, but in a big paper like *The Post*?"

"Yes, absolutely."

Muhammad thought for a moment and nodded. "I would agree to that."

"I'm sure your family would appreciate it," said Harley. "They must be worried."

"They trust God, as I do. God is merciful and just."

"God is also love," added Harley. "Our Bible says that God is love."

Muhammad cocked his head slightly. "That is different from our understanding. We have many names for God, but love is not among them."

"For Christians, love is at the core of who God is," explained Harley, offering an insight that had been at the center of many of his sermons. "God reveals his love by sending Jesus to bring us forgiveness and new life. And the response we are supposed to make is to love one another—a love that should be extended to friends, enemies, blacks, whites, Muslims, Jews, fellow Christians. It is all supposed to come down to love. In fact, the Bible insists that those who say, 'I love God' but hate their brothers and sisters, are liars."

"I would agree with that," said Muhammad. "Loving God does require that we love the people around us."

"Of course, it's easier said than done," observed Harley. At that moment, the heavy metal door opened behind him, and the guard said, "Time's up."

❃

That night, Harley slept soundly and had the most vivid dream. He was walking along a dusty road in the Middle East, with the sun burning brightly in a cloudless sky. Ahead of him were two women with headscarves and flowing clothing, carrying baskets and walking toward a town perched on a hilltop. He tried to catch up with them, but he couldn't do it—they stayed ahead of him and never turned around to reveal their covered faces. They passed a field where sheep were grazing, then an orchard filled with olive trees, and finally reached the outskirts of the town. It looked to be a town out of the Bible, with people in robes walking the streets and doing their business in sunbaked shops and residences. As they entered the town, a group of eight Roman soldiers marched past them, looking powerful and dangerous with their swords and shields. But Harley and the women kept their heads down and avoided any trouble.

The soldiers exited by a paved road that passed through the main gate of the town, and the women led Harley along this street, which was lined with colonnaded buildings. After a few blocks, the street crossed the city's main road, which was paved with limestone blocks and full of people with animals pulling wagons. The buildings along this road had grand columns and entrances covered in finely crafted mosaics, and people were doing business in shops all along the route, gesturing wildly and making a lot of noise in their negotiations. There were many people in tunics, which was typical Roman dress, but there were people in robes as well, which Harley associated with Judaism. He saw a stone on the street with a carving of a seven-branched candelabrum, a clear sign that this was a Jewish town—or at least a town with a Jewish community.

The two women led Harley to a large building with a huge mosaic floor, one that contained scenes from the Nile, colorful depictions of plants and animals and people. He wanted to linger and look at it closely but sensed that he needed to stay with the women, so he kept walking. The two guided him to a large public building that was the city's market, and there they stopped at a shop and talked with a merchant in a tunic. Harley moved closer and saw that one of the women was entering into an intense negotiation. The other became distracted by two Roman soldiers standing nearby. Although Harley could not see the women's faces, he had a clear view of the expressions of the shopkeeper and the soldiers. The shopkeeper shook his head and scowled as he bargained with the first woman, while the soldiers broke out in smiles. It seemed that the second woman was teasing them, maybe even flirting. Harley realized what an unusual place this was, with Romans and Jews coming together for business and pleasure. *Weren't they sworn enemies? Didn't the Jews mount revolt after revolt against the despised Roman Empire?* He recalled that when the Romans put down the first Jewish revolt, they destroyed much of Herod's temple in Jerusalem, leaving only the large foundation stones that remain standing to this day as the cherished Western Wall. During the Bar Kokhba revolt, the Romans destroyed almost 1,000 villages and wiped out most of the Jews of the land by killing them, selling them into slavery, or forcing them to flee.

The first woman finished her negotiations, paid the shopkeeper, and put several yards of cloth in her basket. The second woman flipped the end of her scarf in a flirtatious wave to the soldiers. Then they turned around and revealed their faces. Harley couldn't believe who he was seeing. The two were Karen and Jessica, living in Eirenopolis.

CHAPTER 9

The summer slump hit Riverview Methodist on the Sunday after the Fourth of July. Interest in the new pastor was waning, vacation trips took people away, and the twenty-year-old air conditioner struggled to cool the sanctuary in the middle of a brutal heat wave.

When Harley stepped into the pulpit to start the service, there were only a few dozen people in the pews. A few more trickled in during the first hymn, but it soon became clear that he would be preaching to a small crowd. He apologized for the warmth of the room, encouraged everyone to make themselves as comfortable as they could, and promised to keep his sermon short. He was especially concerned about an elderly woman in the third row. She was dressed in her Sunday best, not the lightweight casual clothes favored by younger church members. Harley worried that she would be overcome by heat and pass out in the middle of the service, which he had seen several times in his previous churches. Once, he watched from the pulpit as a woman fell over in the row right behind his wife, Karen. He was preaching on the healings of Jesus and had to move straight from "Jesus wants to heal us" to "Karen, please turn around and help Louise." Most of the people in the church were confused but assumed that his request was somehow a part of his sermon.

Fortunately, everyone made it through the service and then headed out quickly to find relief in places with better air conditioning. Harley greeted members at the door of the church, thanking them for coming and wishing them well as they stepped out into the summer sun and the hot, humid air. Dirk Carter was one of the last to leave, dabbing his forehead with a handkerchief.

"Harley, we have got to do something about that AC. This is no way to worship, unless you are going to do a sermon on the fires of hell!"

Harley smiled and agreed that it needed to be fixed.

"Of course, it will be expensive," said Dirk. "New HVAC systems are going through the roof. I don't know if the church members can afford it."

"Here's an idea," suggested Harley. "We announce a fund drive and say that it will start the next Sunday. On that day, we shut the system off entirely. People will be so miserable that they will pay anything to get some relief."

"Not bad," Dirk said, smiling. "Then, next winter, we'll shut off the heat and make an appeal for a new furnace. Gotta hit 'em where it hurts."

Dirk invited Harley to lunch at the American Legion. As the two walked toward the river on Washington Street, Dirk asked Harley if there was any debris accumulating around his dock. Harley said that he wasn't sure, so they went to check. Harley was surprised by the quantity and size of the logs and debris that had floated downriver after a heavy rain the night before.

"Those are like underwater mines," said Dirk. "Nasty hazards. They lurk just beneath the surface, ready to damage your hull or break your propeller. You think you're going to have a nice day on the river, and then bam—they come out of nowhere and hit you when you least expect it."

"Like most of life's problems," said Harley.

"Amen to that," agreed the old Marine. The two men pushed the logs and branches out into the current so that the river would take the debris away. After that, they headed to the Legion for food.

The dining room felt like a walk-in refrigerator compared to the church, and the cool air was a welcome relief. Dirk and Harley were given menus by Jessica, who recommended the tacos.

"They are not the best I have ever had, but not the worst."

They talked for a few minutes about the church as they sipped their drinks. Harley felt a growing affection for the old Marine and sensed that he was going to be the rare church member who turned into a real friend. Shifting the conversation, Harley asked, "So, how are the guys at the Legion?"

"Same old, same old," Dirk responded. "Had a funeral last week for one of the last of the Second World War vets."

"That group is getting so old. Hard to believe that the generation is almost gone." Harley drew a figure on the condensation of his iced tea glass, and then asked, "How about that young man I met on my first visit—Will?"

"Will Beckley," said Dirk. "I don't know. He's always been serious, but he seemed particularly intense on the day you met him. He might be struggling with something, but I can't say since I haven't seen him. In fact, I don't think I've run into him since the day you met."

"Any idea?" Harley remembered the pain in his eyes. "Could it be something from combat? Post-traumatic stress?"

"Could be. Guys come back from combat with so many demons." Dirk paused as though he was about to say more, then thought better of it. Harley sat back and waited, playing Muhammad's game of being comfortable with awkward silences. Dirk spun his beer bottle a couple of times and took a drink.

"Can I tell you something in confidence?"

Harley nodded.

"Remember I said that Norah Bayati was involved with an American? Well, I just heard a rumor that the guy was Will. He lives in an apartment building behind the Bayati bakery. People are saying that they saw him—or a guy like him—sneaking over to her room late at night."

"But how could he get to her room?" asked Harley. "Doesn't the family all live together?"

"Not Norah," said Dirk. "She was the oldest, and a few years ago she moved from the family apartment to a separate apartment in the back. The top one."

Harley was struck by the fact that Dirk knew so much about the Bayati living arrangements but then realized that there had been a lot of talk about the details of their lives in recent weeks. Harley had learned that it was unusual for the daughter of an Iraqi immigrant to move out of her father's house before she was married but surmised that the apartment was a cultural compromise. She had her own place, which was what young Americans wanted, but she was still under her father's roof, which was what Iraqi parents would require.

"So, has Will been questioned by the police?" asked Harley in a hushed tone.

"Not that I know of," said Dirk. "There's no evidence, really. It's just a rumor."

"That would be terrible if he was involved with her and killed her."

"You're right," said the Marine. "Personally, I don't believe it. Don't want to believe it. But if it turns out to be the case, it's another good reason not to get involved with these people."

"What do you mean?"

"We shouldn't get entangled with people like them—Iraqis, immigrants, Muslims. Bad things happen." He took another swig of beer. "Speaking of entanglements, I heard you made a jail visit to Muhammad Bayati."

"Uh-huh," said Harley, after taking his first bite of taco. "An officer from the jail called and asked me to come talk with him. They are concerned he's been on a hunger strike."

Dirk arched an eyebrow, drained the rest of his beer, and then held up the bottle so that Jessica would bring him another one. "Who cares?" he said to Harley. "Let him starve himself."

"You know that won't happen," said the pastor, surprised at Dirk's attitude. "They'll get a doctor to force-feed him. But they would rather have him start eating on his own."

"We'll all pay for it either way," said Dirk, finally beginning to eat. "I just resent that you had to spend your time talking to him—time that I am paying for as a member of your church!"

"Hold on, Dirk," Harley protested, putting down his taco. "I can appreciate that you put money in the offering plate, but I am not your private chaplain. I've got to pursue my ministry as I feel called by God. Visiting prisoners is part of what I do."

Dirk might have been able to intimidate previous pastors, but not Harley. "I'm not trying to tell you what to do. But I don't like the idea of you—or anyone—giving aid and comfort to the enemy."

"You don't know that Muhammad is an enemy. He is an American citizen and has worked in this town for what—twenty years? If anyone should have a beef with Muslims, it's me. But I'm willing to consider him innocent until proven guilty."

"You've got a right to have a beef, Harley. More of a right than I do. If you can have a civil conversation with a Muslim, you are a bigger man than I am. But Muslim or not, I still don't like the idea of you spending time with a guy in jail who has no connection to our church. For God's sake, take care of your congregation!"

"We're going to have to disagree on that one, Dirk," said Harley, returning to his tacos. "I'm going to take care of you and the other members of Riverside, sure. But I've got to do what I feel called to do."

Jessica put Dirk's second beer on the table, and he immediately took a swallow. "Suit yourself," he said. "But think about the message you are sending. Some of the guys here at the Legion might benefit from the church, but they are going to steer clear if they hear you are spending time with Muhammad. And how about the Ayads? You know who they are—the Coptic Christians who own the Gold Emporium? What kind of relationship are you going to have with them if you sympathize with a killer who is a Muslim?"

Harley was about to respond when Jessica passed by the table and interrupted.

"Cut it out, Dirk," she said. "Harley is doing his job and you know it." Dirk gave her a sideways glance. "He doesn't lecture you, so don't lecture him."

"Sure he lectures me!" said Dirk. "He is my preacher!" She moved on to another table, and he continued. "This stuff is just personal for me. You know that I was in Vietnam, and all the protests back home really got to me. And when Jane Fonda visited Hanoi and sided with the Viet Cong, that made me go nuts."

"Yeah, I hear you," said Harley. "But I'm not siding with the enemy. I'm doing my ministry. And please don't accuse me of not sympathizing with the Copts." With the hint of a smile, he said, "Part of the reason I am your pastor is that I preached a sermon about the murder of Copts. You know, by the Islamic State."

Dirk took another swallow of beer and nodded. "I get it. The thing is, we are at war. It's a different kind of war than we have fought before, but it is still a war. The Islamic extremists are trying to destroy us, both overseas and here at home. We have got to fight back, or we are going to lose our homes, our families, our way of life."

"I think we are doing that," said Harley, sipping his iced tea. "I really do. The military has made good progress against the Islamic State."

"But how about here in the United States?" interrupted Dirk. "There could be a sleeper cell right here in Prince William County."

"As a matter of fact," said Harley, "I saw the symbol of the Islamic State painted on the rocks across the river."

"There you go. You don't have to turn on the TV to see that symbol. It's right here. We don't know where they are hiding, but we have to send the message that we will show no mercy to terrorists on our soil. Look, I don't know if Muhammad is a killer or not. Don't know if he is part of a terrorist plot or not. The truth will come out. But we have to communicate determination and strength, or we are lost."

"But don't we have to be careful about not painting every Muslim with the terrorist brush?"

"Well, yes," admitted Dirk. "We are a country of law and order. But in a time of war, we have to err on the side of national security. In war, there is always collateral damage."

"Meaning what?" asked Harley.

"Innocent people are going to die," said Dirk. "It's a fact of life, Harley. War is a dirty business, and noncombatants die. It is part of the price of winning."

Harley pondered that for a minute, trying to figure out how the deaths of Muslim bakers could be considered a legitimate part of a war on terrorism. Maybe if Muhammad turned out to be guilty of murder. Maybe if he or his family was part of a sleeper cell. Still, at this point, it seemed like a stretch.

"Winning is important to me," Dirk explained. "That's why I voted for Trump. He knows how to win. Who did you vote for?"

"That's kind of personal, don't you think? I thought we had secret ballots in this country."

"Sure, but what's the big deal? The election is over and Trump is in the White House. It doesn't make any difference at this point. I'm just curious."

"I voted for Hillary. Not enthusiastically, but I thought she had the right qualifications."

"But what about the email thing?" interrupted Dirk.

"Yeah, that bothered me. But it was not a deal-breaker. What really impressed me was the way she spoke so clearly about her faith. You know that she is a Methodist, don't you?" Dirk nodded. "I do believe that she has sincere Christian faith. She has spoken about the importance of taking care of the poor, visiting prisoners, and welcoming strangers. Now, I know that we were electing a president, not a pastor, but still it matters to me."

Harley spoke the truth, but at the same time he had to admit that the presidential election had been a small matter to him, coming so soon after the deaths of Karen and Jessica. Trump and Clinton dominated the news cycle for months, but Harley saw very little through the fog of his grief.

"In any case, Trump won and I'm glad," said Dirk. "But let's move on. You know that Matt has been watching the Bayatis, right? Well, he used to be watching them. He's now on to something else— that's a different story. Anyway, I've been keeping an eye on them, especially the son, Omar. Maybe you've seen him around town."

"No, I don't think I have," said Harley. He wasn't going to admit that he saw him, or someone like him, in a dream. "The mother and daughter, yes. But not Omar."

"Well, the family has a boat, and Omar has been going out in it. He works mornings at the bakery, then goes to school at George Mason during the day. Late in the day, I've seen him going out in the boat. Maybe he's fishing, but I don't know. He could be up to no good."

Harley was intrigued, knowing that Omar had been bullied in high school and hassled at the Legion. On the surface, he seemed ripe for terrorist recruitment. But he sensed that Dirk was being paranoid, and he didn't want to fuel the fire. Plus, he had promised to help Muhammad by trying to get Henry Kim to write a story. Nothing good could come from encouraging Dirk to investigate a nineteen-year-old college student who had a dead sister and a father in jail.

Dirk was a little surprised that Harley didn't want to talk about Omar, so he leaned back, put a toothpick in his mouth, and said, "I'll let you know if I see anything. Nothing is more important than keeping our community safe. You know what they say, 'See something, say something.' Got to be on the lookout for hidden threats—logs in the river, terrorists in the town."

"Yes, please do," said Harley. "Keep your eyes open. But my guess is that the FBI has got this."

Dirk thanked Harley for the lunch and then invited him to come hear him play guitar at Maxine's.

"What?" said Harley, surprised. "You play guitar?"

"Sure," Dirk nodded. "And sing. Mostly country music. Old time stuff, Hank Williams and whatnot. Been playing for years."

"Well, I never would have guessed it," said Harley. "You are a man of many talents. When do you play next? I'll put it on my calendar." He reached for his smartphone and realized that it was not in his pocket. "I must have left it at the church."

Dirk told him that he would be playing at seven o'clock on Saturday night, at the outside River Bar, and encouraged him to stop by. Harley promised to plug it into his online calendar, and the two of them headed out the door and parted company on Mill Street. As Harley turned the corner and walked toward the church, he ran into a couple unlocking the front door of the Gold Emporium. *Must be the Ayads.* He decided to introduce himself.

"Good afternoon," Harley said, offering his hand. "I'm Harley Camden, the new pastor of Riverside Methodist Church. I don't think we've met."

The Ayads shook his hand and said they were very happy to meet him.

"I'm Youssef," said the husband, "and this is my wife, Sofia." The two were short and heavy, with dark hair, light-brown faces and big smiles. They looked similar to one another, as people often did after years of married life.

"We are just getting home from church," said Sofia. "Would you like to come in for tea?"

"No, but thank you."

"A least get out of the heat," insisted Youssef, opening the door of the shop. "Let's talk inside where it is air-conditioned."

Harley stepped into the Gold Emporium. It was an old-fashioned jewelry store, with framed pictures on the walls and glass-topped showcases across the back and the sides. Behind the back showcase was a worktable with a gooseneck lamp and large, mounted magnifying glass, where jewelry could be cleaned or repaired. A staircase ran behind the work area. Harley assumed the couple lived in an apartment upstairs. A few padded chairs were lined up across the front wall of the store, and Youssef quickly pulled three of them into a conversation circle.

"Sit, sit," he said to Harley, motioning to a chair.

"So where do you go to church?" Harley asked when they were all seated.

"St. Mark Coptic Orthodox Church," Sofia answered, "up in Fairfax. We feel very much at home there."

"The Coptic Church is one of the oldest Christian groups in the world, isn't it?" asked Harley.

"Indeed it is," said Youssef, "and the largest Christian community in the Middle East. We are proud to trace ourselves back to St. Mark, who introduced Christianity to Egypt just a few years after the ministry of Jesus."

"That explains our church name," added Sofia with a smile.

"I'm so sad about what ISIS is doing to your brothers and sisters throughout the Middle East," said Harley. "The executions. The beheadings. Absolutely horrible."

"Yes," agreed Youssef, "but persecution is not new to the church. We grieve those who have died, but give thanks for their faithfulness."

Harley wondered how the Ayads could stand to live so close to the Bayatis, given the violence being inflicted on Copts by Muslims. "And now we have experienced a murder right here in Occoquan— not a Copt, but a Muslim."

"Isn't it terrible?" said Sofia. "We are still in shock. Fatima is one of my closest friends."

Harley was stunned, but he tried not to show it.

"We moved to Occoquan at the same time," explained Youssef, "completely coincidentally. At first I was not sure what to make of Muhammad, since relations are strained between our religions back in Egypt. But here in the United States, we both had a hard time getting started in our businesses. The old-timers in Occoquan were not helpful."

"One day," Sofia added, continuing her husband's story, "Youssef and Muhammad found themselves in the permit office together, trying to get permission to modify these old buildings for their businesses. They were both getting the runaround from county officials, so they complained to each other and then decided to help each other. Ever since, it has been a beautiful friendship."

"We never had any children," continued Youssef, "so Norah, Sarah and Omar became like our children. We are not as close to them now as we were when they were young, but even so, Norah's death has been devastating."

Harley paused. "I had a chance to visit Muhammad in jail."

"I'm glad you did," said Youssef. "I saw him before we took a trip to see relatives overseas, and I need to visit again. I regret that our travels took us away at such a difficult time."

"He understands about that," said Sofia in a soothing voice. "He knows how important it is to be with family."

"Everyone is wondering about Muhammad's guilt," said Youssef, "but let me tell you what kind of a man he is. Do you remember when the terrorists killed those twenty-one Coptic Christians on the beach in Libya?"

"Of course," said Harley. That incident had been the subject of his controversial sermon.

"Muhammad came to my shop after that horrible day. He had tears in his eyes, and he told me how moved he was by the faith of those Christians, how they bravely professed their trust in Jesus in the face of a certain death. He thought the murders of those innocent men was an abomination. He said that he wished he could have been there, so that he could say to his fellow Muslims, 'Their God is my God.' Can you believe that? Muhammad, a devout Muslim, wanted to point to the faith of those Christians and say, 'Their God is my God.'"

Harley made his living by speaking, but he couldn't find the words to respond to what he was hearing.

"They are such a good family," added Sofia. "Always devoted to their children, trying to support them when they had troubles at the public schools."

"Fatima invited us to a fast-breaking dinner soon after I met Muhammad," said Youssef. "During Ramadan, the first year we were in the United States. We were so impressed by their hospitality. That deepened our friendship, and our meals together have continued to this day."

The conversation bounced back and forth between the two like a ping-pong ball, and Harley could do nothing but watch.

"In the year 2000, Fatima was in a terrible car accident," said Sofia. "She lost a lot of blood. I rushed to the hospital and made a donation. It turns out that we have the same rare blood type. That made us feel like sisters."

"They certainly are like sisters," Youssef said. "Sofia has been with Fatima every day since Norah's death, except when we had to be away."

The door opened and a woman with bright-red hair stuck her head in.

"Hello, Ayads," she called out. "Welcome home. We missed you." Then she looked at Harley and said, "I think I know you: the new pastor of the Methodist church. I'm Doris King. I saw you at the park, the day that the hoodlums attacked the Bayatis."

Once again, Harley felt a deep sense of shame.

CHAPTER 10

Cotton-ball clouds in a brilliant blue sky, dry air and temperatures in the eighties made for a perfect day. Harley desperately wanted to escape Occoquan and enjoy the day alone on his boat on the Potomac River. His week had been filled with numerous hospital visits and counseling sessions, plus a couple of contentious church committee meetings filled with people anxious about the ailing air conditioner and the anemic church budget. He was confused by his conversation with the Ayads and unnerved by his encounter with Doris King. Striding along Mill Street, Harley was hoping that he would not get sucked into a conversation with anyone—just as he ran into Tim Underwood.

"Pastor, how's it going?" chirped Tie-dye Tim. "Long time no see."

Tim was sitting in a Town of Occoquan golf cart, with a toolbox in the seat next to him. Harley had no choice but to stop and chat. "I hear you visited Muhammad Bayati."

"Yes, I did," said Harley, gathering that small talk was out of the question. "Word gets around, doesn't it?"

"Well, this is Occoquan," said Tim with a smile. "No secrets here. I think you did the right thing."

"Thanks. Not everyone would agree."

"Since when does that matter? Remember the liberty pole?"

"Yeah," Harley nodded. "That was not a smashing success. Well, it was smashed, but it was not a success. So, what's the word on the street?"

Tim sat back and stretched, settling in for a long talk. "The Prince William police caught one of the thugs who attacked the Bayatis."

"Really?"

"Yeah. And get this, he's not anti-Muslim."

"What?"

"No, the guy *is* a Muslim. No kidding. He is an Iraqi immigrant, just like the Bayatis. The police are holding him and questioning him right now."

"Why in the world would he attack them?"

"Who knows?" said Tim. "A personal beef? Something tribal? Sunnis versus Shiites?" He shrugged.

"Well, that does surprise me," Harley said.

"I guess we'll see if he has any connection to Norah's death," Tim continued. "It would be nice for Muhammad if the guy confessed."

"You're right," agreed Harley. "But at least Muhammad has ended his hunger strike. Did you see the article in Thursday's *Post*?"

"Yes, I did."

"It was written by a journalist named Henry Kim. He is married to one of my colleagues in Sterling. I called him right after I met with Muhammad, and he got interested in the case. He wrote the article, which I hope will speed up the process for Muhammad. But most importantly, he agreed to start eating again."

"Good work, Pastor."

Harley leaned against the golf cart. "Hey, Tim, I've been wondering. Do you know Will Beckley?"

"Sure. The young vet."

"I've heard a rumor that he was involved with Norah Bayati."

"Yeah, I've heard that, too. He lives right behind the Bayatis. But I don't know. They don't seem like a match to me."

"What do you mean?"

"Well, Norah was a real pistol—exuberant, energetic, surprising. In high school, her parents wanted her to dress modestly, covered up, so she would wear skirts with multicolored leggings underneath. She wore headscarves, but always with the wildest patterns. I loved to watch her leave her house and run for the school bus. I never knew what crazy outfit she would be wearing."

Harley realized that he had composed an inaccurate mental picture of Norah. She had not been a meek and submissive Muslim girl. "Did she have a problem with the local high school kids?" he asked.

"Surprisingly, no," said Tim. "Most of them loved her. Sure, the cool white kids snubbed her, same as they treated most of the blacks and the other immigrants. But Norah was a champion of the underdog, and she didn't care if kids were poor or awkward or new arrivals from Africa or Central America. She was elected homecoming queen! She had so many friends that she won in a landslide. She rode into the football stadium in a convertible, along with the rest of the homecoming court. When the car stopped she jumped off the side—wearing leggings under her dress. She ran to the center of the field and the crowd went wild!"

Harley smiled and shook his head. "So, you are saying that Norah was a bit much for Will Beckley?"

"Yeah, probably. I know that opposites attract, but Will seems to be so reserved. So quiet. But what do I know? I've never been married."

"Some couples do surprise you."

"In addition, Norah was gorgeous," Tim added, blushing slightly. "I mean, she was beauty-pageant beautiful. The hair, the eyes, the perfect skin. I think she could have been Miss Iraq, or at least first runner-up."

"Really?" said Harley. "She must have had lots of guys interested in her."

"Oh, yeah. The Bayatis tried to set her up the old-fashioned way. I saw a steady stream of eligible young Iraqi men coming by to court her. But since no one ever came twice, I'm thinking she didn't care for her parents' matchmaking."

"I don't think I'd want to be an Iraqi kid in America," Harley admitted. "It's tough to be caught between two worlds."

"Norah always turned heads," Tim added. "Here in Occoquan, and wherever she went. I liked watching her, and I'm sure Will Beckley did as well. Heck, I'll bet those FBI guys liked taking her picture more than they liked taking pictures of Muhammad and Fatima."

"You know about them?" Harley asked, surprised.

"Sure! Everybody knows about them. They've been watching the Bayatis for a few months now. For a week, they even had a stakeout in an empty apartment in Will's building. One of the guys is the son of your buddy Dirk."

Harley knew this, of course, and had assumed that it was confidential. But he was beginning to see that it was hard for anything to remain confidential in Occoquan.

"Yes," he said. "I knew Matt was FBI."

"Maybe he was the one involved with Norah," suggested Tim. "He sure had his eye on her—officially, that is."

Matt had been given the job of watching the Bayatis, so of course he would be keeping an eye on the beautiful Norah. A young man and a young woman, in close proximity, day in and day out. Naturally, they weren't supposed to have any contact, but nothing was sweeter than forbidden fruit. *Could the two of them have been involved? Did Matt somehow contribute to her death? Or did he kill her?* Harley's thoughts were racing.

Matt had been awfully reserved when they had their day on the river, so maybe he was grieving her death or struggling with guilt. But Harley told himself not to jump to conclusions, especially based on a single day with the man. Perhaps Matt wasn't wrestling with anything at all, but was simply a no-nonsense, serious guy.

"I really can't say," Harley responded, finally. "I've only met him once."

"Don't get me wrong," said Tim, realizing that Harley might take offense at such an insinuation. "I'm not accusing the guy of anything. I'm just saying that he is one more guy in the orbit of Norah Bayati."

"Fair enough. It sounds like she was able to draw a crowd. Problem is, I've not heard any talk of a motive, except for those who want to accuse Muhammad of honor killing."

"That's right," agreed Tim. "And I'm not buying it."

"Neither am I, at least not now."

"So maybe this violent biker will prove to be the one. Who knows what has been motivating him. We can just be glad that Doris King gave a good enough description of his motorcycle that the police were able to pick him up."

Doris King? Why did she have to be the one with the eagle eye? Harley thought back on the destruction of the Riverview Bakery tent, and how he had felt strangely gratified by the bikers' attack. It felt like frontier justice to him, a rebalancing of the scale that had been tipped by the killings of Karen and Jessica. But if the thugs had been Muslims, what was the point of the attack? He shook his head and said, "I have absolutely no idea what his motive might be." Then, since they were talking about the bakery, the two men who visited Fatima Bayati popped into Harley's mind, and he asked Tim who he thought they might be.

"Well, I can't say for sure," Tim admitted, "but it sounds like they might have been Jefferson Jones and his partner, Abdul."

"Jones?" asked Harley. "Any relation to Tawnya?"

"Her father," said Tim. "He has gotten into real estate development and is pretty aggressive about going after distressed properties. I think he takes Abdul with him to intimidate people. The guy is ripped!"

"No kidding."

"Not that I've ever heard of Abdul hurting anyone," Tim clarified. "Jefferson is known for making cash offers and never paying a penny more than is absolutely necessary. Some people complain he is trying to rip them off, but the truth is that he knows what the market will bear. Abdul goes with him on his business meetings, and doesn't say much. Just looks tough. When a deal is completed, Abdul gathers a team of contractors and goes to work on tearing down or renovating a place."

"So why do you think they were visiting the Riverview Bakery?"

"Classic distressed property. One family member dead, another in jail, family trying to keep the business afloat. Plus, I've heard a rumor that Jefferson wants to buy up the whole block and redevelop it. Wine bars and gourmet restaurants instead of neighborhood bakeries and such."

"What's the deal with the Abdul guy? Name seems Muslim. He seemed African American to me, not Middle Eastern."

"He is African American. Converted to Islam while in jail. From what I've heard, Jefferson Jones took a chance on him, and he has stayed out of trouble for as long as they have worked together."

"Could he have had anything to do with Norah's death?"

"No idea," Tim shrugged. "At this point, everyone is a suspect."

Muhammad. Will. Matt. Abdul. The Muslim motorcycle guy. The list of suspects seemed to be growing every day. A month ago, Harley would have thought that such a case would be open and shut. Occoquan had more drama and mystery than a city ten times its size. Harley didn't know what to say, so he just stood there and stared toward the river.

"So where are you heading, Rev?" Tim asked, trying to lighten the mood.

"Over to Town Hall to get my car sticker. Then maybe a boat ride."

"Your sticker fee will help to pay my salary."

"Money well spent," Harley smiled.

"While you are there, check out the town photos by Omar Bayati. Really elegant black and whites. The kid has talent."

Harley thanked Tim, gave him a pat on the shoulder, and then continued his walk west on Mill Street. He looked up and down the street, hoping that he would not run into Doris King, the one person in Occoquan who had quickly developed the ability to make him feel awful about himself. Fortunately, there were enough people on the sidewalk that he figured he could duck unnoticed into an alley or a shop if he crossed her path.

He passed the Riverview Bakery, which had returned to its normal activity level on a Saturday morning. Somehow Fatima and her children were keeping up with demand, even without Muhammad.

He looked into the brewpub, where waitresses were sweeping the floor and moving chairs in anticipation of the lunch rush. Then he looked into the bridal boutique and puzzle store, tenants of a ramshackle old industrial building on the river, before crossing the street and entering Town Hall.

The building still looked like an Episcopal Church from the outside, and as Harley pushed through the red front doors he discovered that it resembled a church from the inside as well. The pews were gone, as were the pulpit and altar, but the nave in which the congregation gathered for worship had been largely untouched. Rows of chairs filled the space, facing the raised chancel in which the town council gathered for monthly public meetings. The right side of the room had been partitioned off for office space for the mayor and town clerk, but the walls were only six feet high, so the soaring ceiling of the nave remained in place. The room felt sacred to Harley—not in the sense of Christian holiness, but in terms of respect for local governance, practiced in Occoquan for almost 300 years.

He looked around the freshly painted white walls and saw a display of photographs carefully mounted in black frames between the clear church windows. Moving closer, he saw that the first photo was a black-and-white picture of Rockledge, the stone Georgian mansion that had been the site of the liberty pole. On the matte was the name Omar Bayati, with a small head shot. *So that's what he looks like*, thought Harley: A slender face like his father's, and the same large brown eyes. Cute, as Jessica Simpson said he was. Next was a picture of the pedestrian bridge shrouded in fog, again by Omar. Moving along the wall, he saw a shot of the town museum by another photographer, and then pictures of the various shops and residential buildings along Mill Street, ending with a photo of Riverside Methodist Church. About half of the photos had been taken by Omar, and in Harley's opinion they were the best— carefully composed and attentive to the distinctive atmosphere of the little town. If Omar learned his craft at Lake Ridge High School, he clearly had an excellent teacher.

Harley moved to the window of the town clerk's office, introduced himself and then purchased a sticker for his car. He asked the clerk about the photographs on the wall and learned that they were the winners in a contest tied to the town's annual arts and crafts festival.

"Omar Bayati took first place," she explained, "so he was invited to display a number of his photos. The other prize winners were allowed to contribute the single photo they considered to be their best. It's remarkable that Omar took the top prize, since he was competing against professionals. He's a talented young man." She sighed. "It's just too bad about his family." Harley agreed that his work was quite good, thanked the clerk, and exited quickly into the brilliant sunshine. He sensed that the clerk wanted to get into a conversation about Omar and his family, but Harley was done with chatting for the morning. He wanted to escape to the water as quickly as possible.

❋

Harley fired up his boat and pulled away from the dock, enjoying the slight breeze rippling the surface of the river. The boat cut effortlessly through the water, and Harley loved the feeling of moving forward with no friction, no resistance, no tension, no struggle. He headed for the channel under the Route 123 bridge, not wanting to run into the rocks lurking beneath the water near the Occoquan shoreline, and then watched as the boat's small wake sent ripples toward the shore and caused the sunlight to dance. He looked toward Maxine's and saw children running along the public dock, chased by parents who didn't want them to fall into the water. Ducks paddled out of his way, and a heron swooped down in front of him. As he passed under the bridge, Harley felt his blood pressure dropping.

Boating had become meditation for Harley, an activity that enabled him to practice what his contemplative friends called mindfulness— focusing awareness on the present moment. On the boat, he had to pay attention to where he was going, with eyes open for kayakers and floating logs, but none of this activity required much mental energy. He simply looked and listened and experienced the river, occasionally adjusting the throttle and turning the steering wheel.

After passing under the I-95 bridge, Harley looked to the shore and saw the huge rocks that had been put in place 300 million years ago. They were covered with large trees whose roots reached around the rocks, hugging them tightly and finally plunging into whatever soil they could find. He couldn't tell if the rocks were supporting the trees or the trees were supporting the rocks. Harley envied that. He thought that such rootedness was a virtue. He wondered what it would feel like to hold on to something so solid, and to be able to grow and thrive with such a firm foundation. An old hymn began to play in his head: "On Christ the solid rock I stand, all other ground is sinking sand."

Harley believed in Christ, but he had no roots. He had grown up an Army brat, moving around the country and then ending up in Germany for his high school years. He came back to the US for college and divinity school but didn't feel a connection to any one place until he became involved with Karen and moved to Alexandria. His dad was a no-nonsense Army officer, a veteran of Vietnam with a three-pack-a-day habit, and he died of lung cancer a month after Harley graduated from college. His mother was softer and more spiritual, but she retired to Florida and remarried. Harley enjoyed visiting her in her new home and liked her new husband, but she developed ovarian cancer and was dead by the time Harley turned forty. He had grown up as an only child and often longed for a larger family. That was one of the reasons that Karen and Jessica were so precious to him, and why he became so close to Karen's parents in Alexandria.

Throughout his ministry in the Washington area, the five of them gathered frequently for birthdays and holiday celebrations. Sometimes Karen's brother from Spokane would join them, along with his family, but usually it was just Jessica, Harley, Karen and her parents. They loved to eat and drink together, whether they were having a Fourth of July picnic or Christmas dinner. But after the Brussels bombing, Karen's parents moved to a retirement facility in Annapolis, and he rarely saw them. He came to realize that Karen and Jessica were his roots, and without them he had nothing holding him in place.

Harley found himself thinking of Karen's parents as he steered the boat into the Potomac River and headed north. They had lived in the Mount Vernon area of Alexandria, and on their many visits Harley and Karen enjoyed walking along the trail bordering the river, which offered stunning views of the river and the Maryland shoreline. Now Harley was able to see their neighborhood from the water, which gave him a new perspective. It struck him that travel in colonial Virginia had been largely water-based, but now it was primarily land-based, with people moving around by cars and trucks and busses and trains. He enjoyed seeing the area from the water and feeling a connection with years gone by. One of his favorite destinations had become George Washington's Mount Vernon home, which was hard to see from the land but spectacular from the water.

As he motored north, he heard another powerboat approaching from the rear. He turned and saw that the boat was gaining on him quickly and would overtake him on his port side. It was a bowrider, similar to his own, with one person aboard. As the boat passed, a little closer than Harley liked, he looked carefully at the driver and saw a familiar face—Omar Bayati. He wouldn't have recognized him if he had not just seen his picture at town hall, but he was sure that it was Omar. Speeding ahead of him was the Bayati boat that he had seen docked on the Occoquan River. *Finally*, he thought, *the mystery man has revealed himself.*

To escape Omar's wake, Harley steered right and headed toward the Maryland shoreline. Omar continued on a northward course, motoring toward Gunston Cove and Fort Belvoir. Harley wondered where Omar was heading, and as he adjusted his course he thought about what he should do. Harley felt strangely powerful at the helm of his 270-horsepower boat, and as he watched Omar's boat disappear into the distance, he figured that he could follow the young man without raising any suspicions.

Harley set a course for Fort Belvoir, following Omar, who motored slowly along the shoreline, keeping out of the restricted area marked by government buoys. Harley puttered around in the middle of Gunston Cove, trying to look like a pleasure boater and not attract

Omar's attention. Finally, Omar dropped anchor a few hundred yards from shore and simply sat in his captain's chair, looking at the dock and the scattered buildings along the shoreline. Then Omar pulled out a fishing rod, attached some bait, and began to fish.

After a few minutes, Harley figured that he would look suspicious if he continued to motor back and forth in the middle of the cove, so he took a last look at Omar and turned for home. He gunned his engine and returned to planing speed, heading south to the Potomac River and finally to the Occoquan. The mindfulness he had enjoyed on his way out was now replaced by speculation about what Omar had been doing on the river, so close to Fort Belvoir. *Is he part of a terrorist plot to attack the fort? If so, what's there that would make it a target? Did Omar paint the symbol of the Islamic State on the Occoquan rocks?* Harley's ruminations took him to a very dark place, and by the time he pulled into his dock, he was convinced that Omar was the mastermind of a local sleeper cell.

Harley had a late lunch on the porch of his top-floor balcony, which gave him a view of the river to the east and the west. About an hour after he returned home, he saw a bowrider moving slowly westward through the no-wake zone. He picked up a pair of binoculars that he kept on the porch for bird watching and saw that it was Omar. Harley watched him pass under the Route 123 bridge, motor in front of the Victorian townhouses, and then pull into the Bayati dock. Omar climbed out of the boat and left the dock with nothing but a fishing rod and tackle box. Harley didn't see any fish.

✳

The afternoon was filled with sermon revisions, but Harley couldn't keep the events of the day out of his mind. He wasn't sure what he had seen, or whether it mattered, but his gut told him that Omar was trouble. After making sure that the sanctuary was set for the Sunday service, he returned to the riverfront and asked for a table at the River Bar outside Maxine's. He wanted to have something to eat and catch the beginning of Dirk's set at seven o'clock.

As he was escorted to his table, he heard a voice from a table at the edge of the bar.

"Reverend Harley!" He looked around, not recognizing the voice. Then he spotted the beautiful Tawnya Jones, sitting at a table with a man.

"Tawnya? Good to see you."

Tawnya introduced him to her husband, Clyde. They shook hands and then Tawnya invited Harley to join them. He tried to beg off, but she took the bold step of asking him if he was meeting anyone for dinner. When he said no, she insisted that he eat with them.

Tawnya told Clyde about how she and Harley had met at the Riverside Church and that Harley was the pastor who had lost his wife and daughter in the terrorist attack. She reminded Harley that Clyde worked in Army intelligence at Belvoir and said that they were enjoying a night away from their two-year-old daughter. She looked even better at the bar than she had looked at the church, with makeup on her face and her braided hair now accented by large gold earrings. Harley couldn't tell if Clyde was annoyed that Tawnya changed the course of their date night by inviting Harley over, but it was pretty clear to him that Tawnya was in charge.

"So, what brings you here tonight?" Tawnya asked.

"My friend Dirk plays guitar here."

"Oh yes, I know who that is," Tawnya said. "We've seen him here before. Not exactly our favorite music, but he plays and sings pretty well."

The trio made small talk for a while and Harley steered the conversation toward Clyde. "What's it like to work at Belvoir? I know you can't talk about what you do, but what is the place like?"

"It's a beautiful place, really. Surrounded on three sides by water, and heavily wooded. I'm a big runner, and I love to hit the trails on my lunch hour."

"We both love to run," Tawnya interrupted. "But you know that, Harley. You caught me in the middle of a run."

"So, Army intelligence is there, where you work," probed Harley. "What else?"

"There is a hospital that serves a lot of service members and families," said Clyde. "The officers' club is fantastic, with a beautiful view of the Potomac. And there are a number of areas that are no longer used, but are mothballed and protected."

"Such as what?" asked Harley.

"Well, Fort Belvoir was the center of the US biological weapons program from the '40s through the '60s."

"Really?" said Harley. "What is going on now?"

"Nothing active," Clyde said. "But you cannot just put old biological weapons in a landfill. They are in a secure location."

"By Gunston Cove?" asked Harley.

Clyde smiled. "You know the old saying, Harley. 'If I told you, I'd have to kill you.'"

CHAPTER 11

On Sunday morning, Harley took his coffee up to the top level of his townhouse and looked westward up the river in the early morning light. He saw the Bayati boat tied to the dock and bobbing in the water. No sign of Omar.

In the morning service at Riverside Methodist, he found himself frequently distracted by thoughts of Omar and was anxious to get down to the docks. Once he returned home, Harley grabbed his binoculars and saw that Omar was untying the mooring lines, preparing to leave the dock. Minutes after Omar pulled away, Harley prepared to chase.

In his sermon that morning, he quoted the Danish philosopher Sören Kierkegaard, who had said that "purity of heart is to will one thing." As his boat engine throbbed at idle speed, Harley realized that he was feeling a purity of heart that he had not felt for many years, and it was based on his single-minded desire to stop a terrorist plot.

As soon as Omar's boat passed under the bridge, Harley pushed the throttle forward and pulled out of his slip, steering carefully to avoid banging into the dock supports on either side. He looked around and was relieved to see a number of kayaks, canoes and powerboats on the river—this meant that he wouldn't attract Omar's attention as he followed him through the no-wake zone. The day was hotter than the one before, creeping into the low nineties, and the humidity lay like a damp wool blanket on the river. Plenty of people would be on the water in an attempt to cool down, providing lots of cover for Harley.

A breeze blew across the river, and Harley remembered a similar breeze swirling around him on one of the greatest adventures of his teenage life. He was living on an Army base in Germany, where his father was stationed, and he had been hanging out with a group of classmates on a Friday night. They were bored, having spent the last few Fridays at the bowling alley, and were looking for something new and different. One of them suggested that they climb the base water tower, which stood about 130 feet tall. Harley was not a fan of heights, so he held back at first, but peer pressure quickly took over and he found himself alongside his buddies, sneaking through the woods surrounding the tower.

First challenge was to scale a fence, which fortunately was not topped with barbed wire. Second challenge was to reach the bottom of the ladder, which was suspended above their heads to prevent just this sort of an unauthorized adventure. One guy put another on his shoulders to reach the ladder and lower it for everyone else. The third challenge was to avoid being caught, so they waited in the trees until the military police did their patrol along the road by the tower. Once the Jeep passed, the guys figured that they had time to get up and down without detection.

Up they went, climbing the ladder single file, hand over hand. There was a cage around the ladder, so Harley was not afraid of falling off the tower, but he feared losing his grip and falling on the guy beneath him, creating a deadly chain reaction of bodies crashing into each other. He concentrated on the rungs of the ladder, one after another, making sure that his hands and feet always had a good grip. His breathing became labored as his heart pounded. About halfway up, a refreshing breeze caressed him. He had ascended beyond the tops of the trees around the tower and reached the point where the wind was not blocked.

"Feel the wind," Harley said to the guy below him.

"Kinda scary," said his buddy. "Just keep going." But Harley was not scared; the wind felt like the Holy Spirit.

From that point on, Harley lost his fear. In fact, the danger made him feel alive. He made it to the top, walked around the entire tower on the catwalk, and even left a message in permanent marker, *Harley was here.*

Just as the breeze had calmed Harley on the water tower, it gave him a sense of peace on the river. *Is this completely irrational? Perhaps.* Harley could have been killed on the tower, just as he could die on the river. But something about the wind told him not to worry.

"All will be well," it seemed to be saying. "You are doing the right thing. Trust my power."

Harley continued to follow the Bayati boat into Occoquan Bay and the Potomac River. He dropped back a bit on the open river because the traffic was lighter and he didn't want to spook Omar. He kept him just within eyesight as he traveled north on the familiar route toward Fort Belvoir. Then, when Omar slowed his boat near the Belvoir shoreline, Harley cut back on his throttle as well, and cruised slowly westward in the middle of Gunston Cove.

There were several jet-skiers darting around the cove, so Harley figured that their noise and wake would keep Omar from focusing on him. Harley pulled out his binoculars and trained them on Omar, who had killed his engine and was floating freely. The young man had a camera with a telephoto lens, and he stood in the center of his boat taking pictures of the shoreline.

He cannot be doing nature photography, thought Harley. *No way. There are no historical buildings along the shore, no subjects for pictures like the ones on display at Occoquan's Town Hall. He must be doing some kind of surveillance, some kind of spy photography.*

Just then, a police boat appeared, lights on and siren wailing. It was on a course for the Bayati boat, moving at high speed. "Got him!" said Harley out loud. Keeping his binoculars on Omar, he saw the young man drop his camera and leap into the captain's chair. He cranked the ignition, hoping to run away from the police boat. *Stupid plan*, thought Harley, *but hey, the kid is still a teenager. He is as good as caught.*

The police boat sped past the Bayati boat and headed farther east into Gunston Cove. Harley saw a look of relief on Omar's face, but it only lasted a second. Next, Harley saw raw terror, and when he shifted his binoculars he discovered the reason—Omar's engine was on fire!

In his haste to escape the police boat, Omar had forgotten to run the blower in his engine. He cranked the ignition and set fire to the fumes in the engine compartment. Within seconds, tongues of flame were visible and thick black smoke billowed out of the boat. Omar grabbed a small fire extinguisher and shot it at the engine, but the flames were already out of control. Harley saw him grab his camera and stumble toward the front of the boat, desperate to escape the flames. It would only be a matter of minutes before the gas tank exploded.

Harley felt a breeze across his face and knew that he had to do whatever he could to help the boy. He dropped his binoculars and pushed his throttle forward. His boat quickly accelerated to planing speed and arrived at the bow of the Bayati boat in seconds.

"Get off your boat!" he shouted to Omar. "Swim to me. She is going to blow!"

"I can't swim!" yelled Omar in a panic. He looked small and helpless in the bow.

Pushing the throttle again, Harley made an arc in front of the Bayati boat, and when their hulls were almost touching he yelled for Omar to jump. The young man leapt off the bow of his boat and landed in the stern of Harley's boat, immediately losing his balance and falling onto the rear bench seat. Harley forced the throttle all the way forward, causing the boat to leap almost out of the water. When they reached planing speed, they heard a loud explosion behind them. A ball of fire rose high into the air, followed by an enormous cloud of black smoke. The Bayati boat was engulfed in flames.

Omar held his camera to his chest and stared in shock at his ruined family boat. He looked like a stunned child, with eyes wide and mouth hanging open. Harley knew that they couldn't leave the area until the firefighters and police arrived, so he slowed his boat to a crawl once they reached a safe distance.

He swiveled in his captain's chair and said, "Young man, you almost met your maker."

Omar nodded, and then whispered hoarsely, "Thank you, sir."

"Just abiding by the law of the sea," Harley said. "If someone is in trouble, you must help them."

"But only if you do not endanger yourself," said Omar. The boy knew his rules of the nautical road. After a few seconds, he added, "You put yourself in danger. I appreciate it."

"So, what were you doing out there?" Harley asked.

"Taking pictures," the young man said.

"Of what?"

"The shoreline."

"That's a United States Army Fort," Harley said, gravely. "I suspect you are up to no good."

Omar looked almost as scared as he did when he was trapped on the boat. "No, sir. Photography is my hobby."

"You take good pictures, I know," said Harley. "I have seen your work in Occoquan. But you were not preparing for an art show today."

Omar looked around, desperately wanting to get off of Harley's boat. When he saw there was no escape, he asked, "Who are you?"

"Harley Camden."

"Do you live in Occoquan?"

"Yes."

"Wait a second. I know your name. You visited my father, didn't you? That was good of you."

The police boat appeared again with its siren and lights on, but this time it was heading east on Gunston Cove. It circled the burning boat, looking for people in the water. Harley pointed to the police boat and said to Omar, "I could turn you and your camera over to them."

The young man held his camera even tighter to his chest, and stared down at his feet, not wanting to look Harley in the eyes. "Go ahead. It's a free country. I can take pictures of whatever I want."

"All right," said Harley, "let's go over to them and I'll tell them my suspicions."

Omar realized that Harley had called his bluff, and he squirmed in his seat. At that point, a fire boat appeared around the eastern end of Fort Belvoir and motored up to the burning boat. A large water cannon was directed at the fire, and within seconds it was out.

Harley pushed his throttle forward to move toward the boats filled with police and firefighters. As he did, Omar said, "Wait. Let's talk. I don't think you need to tell them about the pictures."

"Why not?" asked Harley.

"Because I'm not going to do anything with them. If you want, I'll give them to you."

Harley thought for a moment "All right," he said, "I'll consider it. Let me hold on to the camera, and I won't turn you over to the police."

Omar handed him the camera and showed him where the memory chip was inserted. They pulled up alongside the police boat, and Omar explained to the officers that he had caused the fire by failing to run the blower before starting the engine. Harley vouched for him by saying that it was a rookie mistake and could have happened to anyone. Since the hull of the boat had remained intact, miraculously, the officers said that the fire boat would tow it to the Town of Occoquan. They explained that Omar would have to take responsibility for the boat being salvaged or transported to a dump, and the young man agreed that he would do that. They took down his personal information and said that they would be in touch with him as they filed their report on the incident.

※

The trip back to Occoquan looked like a funeral procession. The fire boat pulled a charred hull, and behind it was a bowrider containing two solemn men, the older one with a camera slung over his shoulder. As they entered the Occoquan River, Omar turned around and looked at Harley with anger in his eyes.

"What's the matter with you?" snapped Harley.

"You've got nothing," muttered Omar. "I should tell the cops you tried to molest me."

"Good luck with that," said Harley. He sounded confident, but he wasn't. Omar's threat was not only unexpected but deeply unnerving. "Your best bet is to say nothing at all," Harley scolded.

The two said nothing for the rest of the trip, both acutely aware of the damage that each could do to the other. The air remained hot and still, and Harley wondered where the wind of the Spirit had gone.

CHAPTER 12

Harley dreamed he was in his twenties, on his summer semester in Israel, digging in the Galilee. A warm breeze caused a grove of pine trees to sway gently, and a pair of birds flew in gentle circles above him in a cloudless sky. He had spent the day working in the same square as Leah Silverman, enjoying playful banter while sifting dirt in the search for ancient coins and sherds of pottery. Leah's legs were brown from weeks in the sun, slender and long beneath her cutoff jeans. She wore a yellow T-shirt from a Go-Go's concert with the sleeves rolled up, a red bandana on her head, and aviator sunglasses. Harley enjoyed looking at her across the sifter, and he loved to make her laugh.

When the workday was over, he returned to his A-frame dorm for a quick nap before their afternoon classes. Dozing off, he was visited by a wingless but clearly supernatural messenger who told him that Leah was pregnant. Harley was shocked, since the two of them had not slept together and he was not aware that she was seeing anyone else. *Pregnant? How could that be?* Then the angel said, "Harley, do not be afraid to take Leah as your wife."

What? That was more unexpected than an unplanned pregnancy. "She will bear a son, and you are to name him Jesus."

When Harley awoke from sleep in the A-frame, he wondered whether the angel was speaking the truth or not. *How would I know?* He had never received a message from God in a dream. *What would Leah say if I approached her and asked if she were pregnant? Would she marry me? Would she even consider raising a child with me?*

In the dream, Harley wrestled with these questions as he lay in bed and looked out of the dorm at the rays of afternoon sunlight coming through the pine trees of Galilee. Justice was important to him, as was personal responsibility, so he thought Leah should be held accountable for her unplanned pregnancy. He felt anger toward her for flirting with him on the dig site and then spending the night with someone else. But he also had compassion for her and didn't want to do anything to embarrass her or cause her public humiliation. Wrestling inside him were the virtues of justice and love, fighting for dominance inside Harley just as they had battled inside Joseph. He went back and forth and finally concluded that he should go ahead and marry her.

Harley awoke from his dream in Occoquan, feeling even more confused. He had experienced a dream within a dream. As the fog lifted, he realized that the promise of intimacy with Leah was a fantasy. He was hungry for closeness and camaraderie, attraction and affection, but the reality of his life was that he had ended their Fourth of July boat ride with a slow boil of anger and frustration. The dreams seemed to be challenging him to make a commitment to Leah, an offer of unconditional support as she brought a new life into the world. But what was that life, if it was not a baby? *Leah is surely not pregnant,* he thought, *not at age fifty-five.* Only in the dream was she a fertile young woman. But the dream inside the dream was so vivid. *What was God saying to me? Or, if it was not a message from God, what is my subconscious saying to me?*

Looking around his bedroom, he quickly took stock of his reality. In the dream within a dream, he felt love and connection. But in the real world, he faced overwhelming fear and judgment and rejection.

He was suddenly terrified by the thought of what might happen to him as a result of taking Omar's camera. Members of an ISIS cell might attack him and kill him in the carport beneath his house. The police could arrest him for possessing evidence of a terrorist plot. Maybe Omar would follow through on his threat to accuse him of sexual abuse. His congregation would fire him and his friends would desert him.

He sat up, rubbed his eyes, and tried to control his breathing. *Settle down. Don't panic. You are allowing yourself to be dragged to a very dark place. The fact is that you are holding on to the camera of a young man whose life you just saved. Nothing more, nothing less. There is no evidence of anything. Your suspicions are just your suspicions. Remember, when you get stressed, the best thing to do is focus on your daily routine. What was it that the angel said? "Harley, do not be afraid."*

Rolling out of bed, he headed downstairs to make coffee. As the coffeemaker gurgled, he glanced at the clock on the microwave. He had an hour before he needed to be in Woodbridge for a clergy breakfast. Routine would help him. He picked up *The Washington Post* on his front porch and read about another terrorist attack by a lone-wolf soldier of the Islamic State, this one a vehicular attack in a crowded Spanish beach town. Five people dead, seventeen injured. It was certainly good that the regular army of the Islamic State had been so badly degraded, but defeats on the battlefield did not reduce the frequency of these random attacks. If anything, they seemed to be increasing, as ISIS shifted its attention.

Harley thought more about his rescue of Omar. He was still fearful, but his panic was subsiding. Reflecting on the moment he pulled close to the Bayati boat, he wondered what had driven him to do what he did. *Did I really want to save Omar, or did I secretly hope that the fireball would kill us both?* While such a death would have been agonizing, he wouldn't be facing the tension he was experiencing now, the struggle between love and justice that Joseph had experienced in Nazareth. Looking from his kitchen to the dining room, he saw Omar's camera on the table, containing what he assumed were surveillance pictures of Fort Belvoir. Harley had looked at the digital photos on the camera screen the previous night, and he saw just a few buildings and roadways in very high resolution. He realized that the pictures alone were not proof of a terrorist plot, but they must have been taken with malicious intent. There was simply no other reason to be shooting such photos. And then his mind shifted to the dream of fertile Leah, which was a much happier focal point, a balm for his fearful heart. *What kind of new life am I supposed to be supporting in all this? What risk am I being challenged to take?*

Harley sipped his coffee while getting dressed, thinking about how the struggle between judgment and compassion had appeared first in Joseph's dream, and then continued throughout the ministry of Jesus. In fact, it was one of the dominant themes of the New Testament, hidden in plain sight. *Why didn't I see it before?* Checking the weather report on his smartphone, he saw that the day was going to be another hot one, so he skipped the tie and put on a lightweight sport jacket. Then he headed out the door for his clergy breakfast, grabbing Omar's camera as he passed the dining room table and throwing it into his trunk for safekeeping—and just in case he was called on by authorities.

✳

Walking into the Bob Evans in Woodbridge, it didn't take him long to find the clergy breakfast. Ten men were sitting around a long table, and about half were wearing clergy collars. Harley was surprised that there were no women but then figured that such gatherings were rather old-fashioned and might not appeal to younger female pastors. He saw an empty seat, asked if anyone was sitting there, and then introduced himself to the men on either side, one in a collar and one in a golf shirt.

"Hi, I'm Harley Camden, the new pastor of Riverside Methodist in Occoquan."

"Welcome. I'm Jim Black, the pastor of Sacred Heart Catholic Church in Woodbridge."

"And I'm Tony White, pastor of New Life Community Church in Lake Ridge."

"Black and White," said Harley, trying to remember their names. "Sounds like a joke."

"We've heard them all," said Father Black. "Please, have a seat."

"How long have you been here, Harley?" asked Pastor White.

"Arrived in June. The bishop moved me down from Sterling."

"I feel your pain," said Father Black. "You and I get moved around by our bishops, while White here can stay where he is as long as he keeps his customers satisfied."

"Church members," corrected White.

"Whatever," said Black. "You keep your flock happy, and you can stay for years and years."

"True enough," White agreed. "But if I make them unhappy, I can find myself on the street without a job. You guys have security as long as you stay loyal to the bishop."

"But sometimes that loyalty gets sorely tested," added Harley. "So, what's the news in Woodbridge?"

"We were just talking about one of our younger colleagues," said Black. "Nice guy, a regular at these breakfasts, a Lutheran. He seemed to be doing well at his church, but then he started disappearing for hours at a time. His church administrator would ask where he was going, and he would give evasive answers. She got concerned enough that she notified the bishop."

"The bishop sent a member of his staff to find out what was going on," White added. "The pastor was not in his office that day, but a church member had been to lunch at a local restaurant and reported that the pastor was there, sitting at a table in the corner. The bishop's assistant found the pastor and asked him what he was doing. The guy said that he was performing intelligence work, meeting with informants and assisting authorities with matters of national security."

The blood drained out of Harley's face. He could only croak out the words, "That's odd."

"Very much so," continued Black. "Long story short, he was having some kind of psychotic break. Total delusions. The bishop pulled him out of his church and put him on administrative leave. I sure hope he is getting the help he needs."

"Amen to that," White said. "He was a heck of a preacher. Very passionate and engaging. He preached so well at a community Thanksgiving service that he made me jealous."

"Well, it's often the passionate ones who go off the rails," said Harley. A wave of paranoia swept over him; he hoped that no one had observed him on the water with Omar.

"Yeah, we've lost some good ones from the Catholic Church," Black noted. "Although, when you calculate how much trouble they cause, the cost of cleaning up their messes always exceeds the benefit of whatever gifts they have."

"Better to be boring," said White.

"Fortunately, that's your gift," cracked Black, smiling.

A pastor at the end of the table asked the newcomers to introduce themselves and then said that they would order breakfast, share some announcements, and then have a prayer when their food arrived. Harley scanned the menu but could hardly focus on it since the story of the Lutheran pastor had spooked him so badly.

Fortunately, the time of announcements gave him a few minutes of welcome distraction. Father Black said that a pro-life demonstration was being planned for a local women's clinic, which struck Harley as a black-and-white response to the problem of unwanted pregnancies. But then Black added that he had found an immigration attorney who was charging his parishioners very reasonable rates as she helped them to navigate the citizenship process. A number of pastors around the table nodded and asked if they could get her number. Pastor White announced that a talk on sexual purity would be offered at his church and invited the group to publicize it among their youth leaders. Harley conjured a mental picture of the poster for the event, with the word *sexual* in black letters and *purity* in white letters. Then White encouraged his colleagues to join him in an effort to curb payday lending, which was drawing his low-income church members into a downward spiral of debt.

After the food was delivered and the pastor at the head of the table said grace, Harley continued his conversation with the clergy on either side of him.

"I know that your Lutheran colleague was dealing with some mental issues," he began, "but I am sure there are some serious national security issues all around us. What would you do if a member of your congregation told you about a terrorist plot?"

"I'd go right to one of my deacons who works for the CIA," said Pastor White, as he took a bite of toast.

"It depends," responded Father Black.

"Depends on what?" asked Harley.

"Depends on where I heard it. If it was in the confessional, I would have to keep it confidential."

"Really?" said White. "Even if the plot posed a real danger?"

"Yes. The seal of the confessional prohibits me from disclosing anything I hear. What is said is between the parishioner and God."

"Isn't there anything you can do?" asked Harley.

"Of course. I can encourage the parishioner to report what he has heard. Or to turn himself in, if he is part of the plot."

"That sounds righteous, in theory," White observed, after swallowing another bite. "But what if lives are lost because the plot is not revealed?"

"I cannot break the seal," said Black, "even under the threat of my own death. Some things are more important than life and death."

White shook his head in disagreement.

"What I hear you saying is that you cannot reveal what a person says, but you can try to persuade them to do the right thing," Harley said.

"Exactly," said Black. "Confession is all about getting right with God, and doing the right thing is always part of reconciliation."

"I have always found that people are more willing to speak honestly when they know that I will keep things secret," Harley said.

"That's the key to confession," said Black.

Pastor White wiped his mouth with a napkin and said that he would have to run. Harley looked at the time on his cell phone and realized he needed to leave, too.

✳

Back at Riverside Methodist, Harley pulled into the parking lot and checked his trunk to make sure that Omar's camera was safe and secure. Then he entered his office by the side door and punched the button on his answering machine. There was only one message, and it made his heart skip a beat.

"Harley, it's Leah. I won't leave a detailed message on your office machine, but I'd like to get together. Are you free for dinner tonight? Give me a call."

Harley felt a rush of relief. He had been afraid that he scared her off, and it felt good to hear that she wanted to see him. But his relief was immediately replaced by embarrassment as he thought about his dream from the night before. "Do not be afraid to take Leah as your wife!" He picked up the phone and Leah answered on the second ring; dinner at her place at six.

Leah's condominium was at the top of the hill on the western edge of Occoquan, on the rocks high above the Rockledge Mansion. Harley arrived on time with a bottle of red wine. She welcomed him with a tentative hug, not sure where they stood. Harley immediately apologized for the way he treated her on the boat, saying that he had been struggling with anger and had a tough time controlling it.

"Harley, you deserve to be angry," she said, taking the bottle of wine out of his hands. "If I had lost my family as you did, I'd be furious."

"Still, I shouldn't take it out on you."

"Yeah, you're right," she agreed, motioning him into her living room. "But I am sure I said things that set you off. I can be pretty assertive, and that leads to some strong reactions."

"Yeah, that thing about me being a bridge to Muslims, that was asking a bit much."

"Oh, I meant that," said Leah. "Still do. You are in a perfect position for that."

Harley felt a burning in his neck, the return of his anger. *Is she trying to provoke me? Or does she have some kind of fantasy about me? Why would she say such a thing?* He rubbed the back of his neck and tried to calm himself. He told himself that she had a right to her opinion, and he didn't have to agree with her.

"I'll try to do better," Harley promised, not wanting to get into a fight. "You are important to me. I don't want to ruin our friendship."

"Same here. That's why I invited you over. Let's drink this nice-looking bottle and have something to eat. This can be a reset for us."

They sat together on a couch and ate the cheese and crackers that Leah had put out. Harley poured them each a glass. In a few minutes they were relaxed and enjoying each other's company. Leah's legs were as slender and tan as they had been in Harley's dream. Harley thought of the Leah of his dream—young and beautiful and pregnant.

"Harley, you are blushing," said Leah.

"Must be the wine," he blurted nervously.

Moving into the dining room, they had a light dinner of chicken Caesar salad and continued to drink wine. Harley asked her about her work at the clinic, and she described how difficult it was to get people to change their behavior and make healthy choices. Harley said that the very same was true in the life of the church.

"The more I tell people what they should do, the more they push back," he admitted.

"That's natural," Leah said. "Throw people off balance and they will try to regain equilibrium."

"So, how can people be changed?"

"Persuasion. Appeal to their self-interest. Help them to see that a new course is going to help them."

"Give me an example," said Harley.

"I can't be too specific, with healthcare confidentiality and all that. But a physician at the clinic recently talked with a grandmother about the babysitting she was doing for her grandchildren. The doc found out how much they meant to her and asked if she wanted to continue to be involved in their lives as they became teenagers and young adults. The woman said yes, of course, and then the doc said that she could achieve that goal only if she quit smoking. The woman is a chain-smoker, three packs a day. She agreed to join a smoking cessation class, based on her desire to be with her grandchildren."

"Sounds like the key is to figure out the person's motivation."

"Exactly."

"Well, I've got someone I need to figure out," said Harley as he finished his wine. "I have no idea what is driving him. But once I do, maybe I can persuade him to change."

CHAPTER 13

The morning rush was over when Harley opened the door of the Riverview Bakery and stepped inside. Only Fatima was behind the counter, sweeping the crumbs generated by a stream of customers on a busy Tuesday morning. She wore a colorful hijab and a white baker's smock. The intoxicating aroma of fresh baked goods made Harley regret that he had never entered the shop. He paused for a moment, took a deep breath, and scanned the place. The display cases were picked over but still held a number of breads, pastries, and muffins, and behind the counter were shelves containing jars of jams and marmalades. To the left of the cash register was a carafe with a sign offering free coffee and to the right was a plate containing samples of the morning's blueberry muffins. Harley stepped to the counter and introduced himself.

"Pastor Camden, so good to finally meet you," said Fatima. Her round face glowed as she smiled, and the scar on her left cheek became more pronounced.

"Please call me Harley," he replied, wondering if her scar was from her car accident.

"You were so kind to visit my husband in jail. You helped him very much. The article in the newspaper seems to be working."

"He deserves a speedy trial."

"Would you care for some coffee?" asked Fatima, washing her hands in a sink behind the counter.

"No, thank you. I had some this morning."

"How about a piece of muffin?"

"Don't mind if I do."

Fatima handed him the sample plate, along with a napkin. He popped a small piece in his mouth. It was moist and delicious, filled with fresh berries.

"That's excellent," said Harley. Fatima smiled. "How is your son, Omar?"

"Embarrassed," she admitted, shaking her head. "He knows that his carelessness caused the fire. I suppose I owe you thanks for helping him as well."

"You are welcome. But boaters do help each other. It is the law."

"Still, you risked your life to rescue him. He might have died if he had stayed on the boat. You are earning much *hasanat*."

"Much what?"

"Hasanat: Credit for good deeds. After death, God weighs your bad deeds against your good deeds. If the balance tips toward good deeds, you enter heaven."

"Interesting," said Harley, realizing that she was identifying one of the major differences between Christianity and Islam.

As a Christian, Harley did not believe that he could ever do enough good to earn a spot in heaven. The line from the Book of Psalms—"I am a worm, and no man"—was the Biblical verse that he felt best captured the human condition. He believed that he was saved only by the grace of God. He grew up being taught that he gained access to this free gift through his faith in Jesus, not through any good works that he might do.

Harley changed the subject. "I did not see the boat this morning. Was Omar able to get it hauled away?"

"Yesterday," she said. "The insurance company came and

inspected it. A total loss. And then the hull was pulled out of the water and taken to the dump."

"I'm glad you had it insured."

"Yes, we'll probably replace it someday. But it is a low priority at this point in our lives."

Harley nodded. He understood that the replacement of a powerboat was a small matter for Fatima, with her husband in jail and her daughter freshly buried.

"You do have my sympathy for what you have suffered," he said. "Your daughter's death was a terrible loss."

"Thank you," said Fatima, her eyes welling up. "I still cannot believe she is gone."

On the wall behind the counter, Harley saw a framed photograph of the Bayati family, a formal portrait of all five of them.

"Is that Norah?" She was as gorgeous as everyone said, with a broad smile and eyes that seemed to see all and know all. Her vitality radiated from the frame, and Harley thought that she looked familiar. Then he remembered the face of the woman in the mosaic at Sepphoris.

"Yes, it is," said her mother, proudly. She started to say something else but got choked up.

A small bell tinkled as a customer came through the door. Harley stepped aside and let her pass. Fatima wiped her eyes and greeted the young woman, there to buy a dozen muffins to take to her workplace. When the transaction was complete and the customer gone, Harley asked, "Is Omar here today?"

"Yes, he is. He has summer school classes this afternoon but is working in the back this morning."

"May I speak with him?"

"Of course." Fatima disappeared through a swinging door and remained in the back room for several minutes. Harley heard voices, talking calmly at first and then rising in pitch and intensity, sounding argumentative. Then complete silence, followed by Omar coming through the door brushing flour off his hands. Right behind him was Fatima. Both of them looked stressed.

"Good morning," said Omar in a flat tone. "How can I help you?"

"I was hoping we could talk. Do you have a minute?"

"I don't know," the young man replied. "I'm pretty busy." He turned his head and looked at his mother.

"Go ahead," she said to him. "Talk to Pastor Camden. He helped you."

"Sort of," snapped Omar.

"Show some respect," said Fatima. "I can handle things here while you go out and talk."

Omar shook his head and gave Harley a dirty look. But he didn't want to get in deeper trouble with his mother, especially after his carelessness with the boat. He removed his apron and put it on the counter. "I don't have much time," he said. "I have class this afternoon."

"This will only take a few minutes," said Harley as he opened the door for them to exit.

Omar was silent as they walked westward on Mill Street, toward the park. Harley knew all about sullen teenagers, having worked with youth groups through most of his ministry.

"Omar, I am very sorry about your sister," Harley said as they walked side by side. "She did not deserve to die."

"I know that."

"Her death is a tragedy. It is causing you all to suffer."

Omar looked straight ahead, not turning to meet Harley's eyes and clenching his mouth.

"I lost my wife and my daughter a year ago," Harley said. "I have also suffered."

These words caused Omar to glance briefly at Harley, but then he turned forward again. After a few seconds, he asked, "How did they die?"

"That's not important now. What's important is that we talk, and come up with a plan together."

"A plan to do what?"

"To do the right thing."

"Whatever," said Omar flatly.

"Here's the deal. I have your camera and your pictures. I want to return your camera to you, but I want the pictures destroyed, and I want you to stop whatever you are doing."

"I'm not doing anything."

"I don't believe that," Harley stated firmly.

"Believe what you want."

The two of them continued to walk toward the park, passing the entrance to the pedestrian bridge across the river. They were close to the spot where the Riverview Bakery tent had been attacked by the bikers.

"What will the Muslim bikers do to you if you stop taking pictures?"

Omar's head jerked around. "What are you talking about?" The young man stopped and looked at his feet. "That was a misunderstanding. My mother is not going to press charges."

"Really?" said Harley. "That was quite a violent attack."

"That's our personal business," Omar explained. "No one else needs to be involved."

They continued walking along the perimeter of the park. Reaching the farthest bench, Harley asked if they could sit and look out at the river. Omar sneered and crossed his slender arms. "Is this where you try to molest me?"

Harley sat on the bench. "We can talk with you sitting next to me, or with you standing there. Your choice."

Omar began to feel awkward about standing with his arms crossed, so he sat at the opposite end of the six-foot wooden bench. The two of them looked out over the river.

"Omar, I want what is best for you," Harley began. "I want your sister's killer to be caught. I want your father to get out of jail. I want your family to be able to run its business. I want you to live without fear."

"I'm not afraid," Omar huffed, staring straight ahead.

"I think you are," Harley said quietly. "I think you are afraid because I feel afraid. And I trust that my emotions are similar to yours."

"That's messed up," said Omar.

"I believe that you and your family are in a bad place. You are frightened. I want to help you."

"How do I know that's true?"

"I helped your father," Harley said. "I risked my life to save yours."

Omar turned his face away from Harley and wiped tears from his eyes.

"If I'm going to help you, I need to know what is going on," Harley continued. "In the Christian Church, we have what is called the seal of the confessional. That means that whatever you say to me remains in complete confidence. It is the same as if you were speaking to God directly."

Harley was stretching the truth, since the seal only applied to an actual Roman Catholic confessional. But he had every intention of maintaining confidentiality with Omar. "I know you are not Christian, but I can promise to keep your secrets."

Omar looked at him with an expression of wariness. "You are promising that you will keep all my secrets? You will not tell anyone?"

"No one."

"Not my parents? Not the police?"

"Absolutely no one. What you say to me is between you and God."

Omar looked around to see if there was anyone within earshot. It was now mid-morning on a weekday, and the park was deserted. An osprey winged above the water, screeching.

Omar rubbed his chin and then put his hands at his sides, gripping the front planks of the park bench.

"I was three years old when 9/11 happened," Omar began. "By the time I started school, the United States had invaded Iraq. A lot of my classmates were military kids, and their fathers were deployed. I got called a lot of names. Hajji. Taliban. Al-Qaeda. Osama. Saddam." He closed his eyes tightly, suppressing a tear. "One day in fourth grade, a kid named Mike didn't come to school. The word spread that his dad had been killed in Iraq by an IED. Mike was out for a week, and I felt really bad for him. When he came back, I wanted to tell him that I was sorry, but he gave me a hateful look. After school that day, he and a couple of his friends beat me up, saying that Iraqis were scum.

I couldn't do anything except cover my face until a teacher pulled them off. I went home with torn and dirty clothes, feeling ashamed."

Harley remembered how confused he had been by the invasion of Iraq, a military action that seemed to have no connection to the terrorist attacks of 9/11. Sending soldiers into Afghanistan had made sense to him, since the attacks were linked to al-Qaeda and the Taliban in that country. But Iraq? The hijackers had been mostly from Saudi Arabia, with others from the United Arab Emirates, Lebanon and Egypt. There was not an Iraqi in the bunch. He tried to picture little Omar being beat up for having a family connection to Iraq.

"Sounds like you were the whipping boy."

"Yeah. The kids said they hated Osama bin Laden and Saddam Hussein, and wanted to kill them. But since I was convenient, they went after me."

"Did your parents do anything?"

"Sure. They talked to the principal. Had conferences with teachers. Brought stuff from the bakery to international days. But what could they do, really? They were powerless."

"How were things for your sisters?"

"Not as bad. They got teased, but no one beat them up. And Norah, she was amazing—able to take control of any situation. She was way ahead of me at school, and by the time I got to high school she was a legend." Omar smiled.

"You must miss her."

"God, yes. Her death is the worst thing that has ever happened to my family. Her killer deserves to die. And there is no way that my father should be in jail. His arrest was a complete injustice."

"I suspect you are right."

"What do you mean suspect?" said Omar with a flash of anger. "He is completely innocent. If you really want to help us, you need to believe that."

"I'm still learning," said Harley. "Figuring things out."

Omar returned his gaze to the river and continued his story.

"Anyway, I'm eight years younger than Norah, and five years younger than Sarah. When I arrived at Lake Ridge High School, the teachers and administrators had a high opinion of my sisters, especially Norah, which helped me as a student. But among my classmates, they were unknown. I had to find my own way."

"Must have been tough."

"Yeah, anti-Muslim feelings were running high, which made me want to keep my head down. I focused on art classes, especially photography. And I made some friends in the Muslim American Cultural Society. They rallied around me when I got jumped and beat up one day after school by a bunch of jocks who called me a fag and a terrorist."

"That's an odd combination."

"Not really. Have you heard the expression 'Man Love Thursday'?"

"No."

"US soldiers use it. The joke is that on Thursdays in Afghanistan, men have sex with each other so that they will not have lustful thoughts on Friday. That's the Muslim day of prayer. The jerks that beat me up had heard that from their fathers."

"Once again, you were the whipping boy."

"So, I started hanging around more and more with my fellow Muslims. And this is where I have to know that you are going to be completely confidential."

"Yes," said Harley. "I promise."

"Not that I have done anything wrong. But you cannot speak of any of this to anyone. People could get hurt, including my mother and sister."

"I am sworn to secrecy. Absolutely."

"A small group of guys offered me support after I was beat up during my junior year. They lived in Lake Ridge and would invite me to their houses on the weekend. We would play video games, surf the internet, do stuff like that. One guy was getting really serious about Islam, and was always talking about sharia law and how great it was. He called the US military 'crusaders,' and talked about how it was time for Muslims to fight back. Although he never used the term ISIS or Islamic State, I suspected that he was making contact online."

"What did the other guys think about this?"

"They were not as serious. We were just high school guys, hanging out together and acting tough. Occasionally, some older guys would join the group. Guys in their twenties who would arrive on motorcycles and bring us beer. They talked about their respect for ISIS, and that made me nervous."

"What would they say?"

"They would talk about ISIS fighters as being studs, battling the oppressors and going to heaven as servants of God. They said it was time for Muslims to take action in America. There were six of them, and they lived nearby in Woodbridge. One of them said after a night of drinking that he wanted to make Woodbridge the city of jihad."

"And what were their plans?"

"They didn't say much at first. I thought they were just acting tough. But at the same time, I was having a hard time at the American Legion, and ended up getting fired. I was angry at the way I was treated there, especially by the vets. I was sick of being looked down on. One of the guys from Woodbridge took me aside and said that they were going to send a signal to the crusaders. He told me that they accepted me and respected me, and that they wanted me to play a part. He said that I could earn hasanat."

"Credit for good deeds."

"Exactly. They knew that I was a good photographer, so they asked me to use my boat to get close to Fort Belvoir and take some pictures. They were planning to blow something up as a sign of their strength."

"And what did you say?"

"I said that I didn't want to be involved in anything that would kill. The Qur'an does not support the taking of innocent lives. He assured me that their target would not be occupied by people. It would send a message, but not kill."

"So that's why you were spending so much time on the water."

"Yes, I took a lot of pictures, all along the shoreline. I especially focused on the old landing craft that were docked there. I thought that the destruction of one of them would send the right message."

"Did you give the pictures to these guys from Woodbridge?"

"The first set, yes. That was last year, after I graduated from high school. My boat was out of the water all winter, but when I launched it this spring, I started to have second thoughts. I was about to back out of the plan when Norah was murdered. Her death and the arrest of my father made me furious, and I threw myself back into the photography. I wanted to punish the people that had killed my sister and jailed my father." Omar turned to look Harley in the eyes.

"But then everything changed. I heard one of the Woodbridge guys saying that Belvoir had a stockpile of biological weapons, and that this would be their target. He said that they were going to get revenge for God. I said no way—releasing biological weapons would be genocide. The guy said martyrdom was an automatic path to heaven. I went home immediately, swearing that I would never meet with those guys again."

"But what happened?" asked Harley. "Why were you on the river again on Sunday?"

"They put me in an impossible spot. You know the attack on our bakery stand, right here in the farmers' market? That was the Woodbridge guys. They told me that they were sending me a message, and that they would do even more damage if I backed out of the plan. They threatened to kill my mother and Sarah. So, I continued to take pictures, up until Sunday afternoon."

"Have you given any photographs to the Woodbridge guys?"

"Not since the first set. Nothing related to the stockpile. They are all still in the camera."

"Good," said Harley. "You've done nothing that cannot be undone."

Omar appeared relieved. "How can I get out of this, and keep my family safe? I don't want us all to die."

"Neither do I," said Harley. "Are you willing to talk to the police?"

Omar thought for a moment. "Not the ones who arrested my father. I don't trust them . . . and remember, this is all between me and God."

CHAPTER 14

"City of jihad." Harley let the phrase roll around in his mind as he prepped his boat for a trip to Nationals Park in Washington. On the one hand, the word *jihad* meant "striving," so it could include a struggle for peace and justice and enlightenment. He knew that many people used the word to describe their efforts to be good Muslims or to share the message of Islam with others. But the Woodbridge guys proclaimed a holy war—not peace. *Are they working on explosives or stockpiling weapons? Finding another powerboat to use in their attack on the cache of biological weapons?* Harley's mind spun as fast as the propeller on his boat engine.

He was cleaning up his boat for an afternoon trip to watch a ball game that started at four o'clock. It was a church activity, one that he had announced from the pulpit and opened up to anyone in the congregation. Dirk Carter had signed up, as had Tim Underwood, who was now a regular attender at the church. Mary Ranger, the postmistress of the Occoquan Post Office, was enjoying a day of vacation and joined the activity with her husband, Paul. They brought their three elementary-school-aged granddaughters, who were staying with them for part of their summer vacation. At the last minute, Harley had one cancellation, so he offered the ticket to Leah, who left the clinic early so that she could join the group.

At two, the passengers started arriving, and Harley welcomed them and helped them to climb onto the boat. He put children's life jackets on the three little girls and ushered them to the bow along with their grandfather, Paul. Taking seats in the main part of the cabin were Dirk, Tim, Mary, Leah and Harley, and Mary promised Paul that she would switch places with him as they made their way up the river.

With Dirk acting as first mate, they got underway quickly and motored toward the concrete Route 123 bridge. An osprey swooped near their boat—maybe the same one that Harley had seen from the park. From the swivel chair next to Harley, Dirk told the group that ospreys bred on the channel markers up and down the Occoquan River, and then migrated to Central and South America for the winter. "Scientists can track them," he said, "by putting satellite transmitters on their backs. The record for migration is twenty-seven hundred miles in less than two weeks."

"What do they eat?" asked Leah.

"Live fish," said Dirk. "They are excellent anglers, diving into the water and coming up with fish in their talons. They like these shallow waters where the fish swim close to the surface."

"I saw a bald eagle this morning," announced Harley. "A spectacular bird."

"Right about that," agreed Dirk. "There are a number of nests on Mason Neck. I'm glad you saw one."

Mary Ranger was heavyset and in her late fifties, with short, bleached-blond hair and a big smile. She knew everyone in town, given the fact that there was no residential delivery and everyone picked up their mail from a post office box. She asked Harley how he was settling into Occoquan, and then talked with Leah about the activity at her health clinic. After telling Tim about a dead bush at the edge of the post office parking lot that he really ought to replace, she teased Dirk about allowing his mailbox to overflow.

"That's because I never get any good mail," he complained. "Can't you do something about that?"

Harley was happy to have his boat full of people, especially on such a lovely summer day. He had realized that a large part of his anger over the past year was grounded in loneliness. Yes, he was rightly upset about the way that Karen and Jessica had died, and the injustice of their killings continued to anger him, but on a more fundamental level he simply missed them. Companionship was as life-giving to him as food and drink.

"Dirk, how is your music going?" asked Tie-dye Tim.

"Not bad. I feel like I'm not drawing the crowds I used to, but Maxine's still likes to have me."

"Well," said Tim. "Occoquan is changing. There are not as many white people as there used to be, natural fans of country music."

Dirk nodded. "Yes, that's true. A lot of changes going on. Not all of them good."

"But there are certainly some good ones," interjected Leah. "The new places to eat and drink are great, I think. They are turning Occoquan into a real foodie town."

"Yeah, but they are driving up rents and making it harder for regular people to live around here," complained Dirk. "I thought the area was fine as it was."

"What, you liked the Yarn Shop?" teased Tie-dye.

"No, not really. I'm not a yarn guy. New restaurants are fine, but I like slow change," said the Marine.

"You'll have to get used to things changing," said Leah. "Racially, culturally, economically. The people I'm seeing at my clinic are not the white folks of old Prince William County."

"You Republicans used to be change agents," Tie-dye said. "Now you are change resisters. Remember the liberty pole?"

"Sure I do," said Dirk. "I've got no problem with liberty. In fact, we Republicans are still all about liberty. We hold on to the Bill of Rights: freedom of religion, right to bear arms, right to privacy."

"You say you support freedom of religion, but all through Northern Virginia you have people objecting to the building of mosques," Tie-dye said. "Did you hear what happened in Culpeper? A Republican led a protest that resulted in a sewer permit for a mosque being denied. Now the project is on hold. Those kinds of permits are routinely approved for churches."

"I think that's dead wrong," insisted Dirk. "Anyone who wants to worship in peace should be allowed to do so. Freedom should be for everyone—that's what I fought for. I'll do anything to protect my family, my community, and the American way of life. Anything." He turned in his swivel chair and faced forward along with Harley. "They think I'm a dinosaur, but I'm not. I just value tradition."

"I hear you, Dirk," said Harley. "Where would the church be without tradition?"

"Amen, brother."

"At the same time, you know what God says, don't you? In Revelation? 'I am making all things new.'"

"Now you're just meddling, Pastor," Dirk smiled.

"Hey, look at that," one of the girls in the bow shouted, pointing to the port side.

"Snake," said Dirk, standing up to get a better look. "Northern watersnake. They can get pretty big, up to almost four feet, but they are harmless." The girls squealed as they watched it traverse the river.

Dirk settled back in his swivel chair and continued to face forward. Tie-dye Tim, Mary and Leah chatted on the stern bench seats. Harley looked around to make sure that everyone was safe and comfortable, and then checked his instrument panel. He sensed that Dirk wanted a little quiet time, so he let him be. The girls were having a good time up front with their grandfather, watching for birds and fish and maybe even another snake.

Tradition, Harley thought. So important to the church. And yet, congregations that remained trapped in the past were doomed, because God was always working for transformation, leading people into new understandings of themselves and the people around them.

For most of Christian history, slavery was accepted by the church. Women were long considered second-class citizens. Homosexuals had been routinely condemned. *Bad traditions!* Harley thought.

Harley's awakening on homosexuality had come through a friendship with a fellow seminarian, an Illinois farm boy from a very conservative family, who came out in the 1980s. Although members of the Methodist Church debated the morality of homosexuality for decades, using a variety of biblical and theological arguments, Harley was convinced that gays and lesbians could be good and moral people. For proof, he looked no farther than his friend, who had been a good and righteous man, faithful to the church, and never sexually exploitative.

Tradition. What about hatred toward Muslims? Is my intervention with Omar another awakening?

Harley sensed that God was leading him into a deeper relationship with Omar and the Bayati family. As he thought about the New Testament, he realized that Jesus always reached out and embraced people at the margins of society—the poor, the sick, women and children. Jesus got in trouble for eating with tax collectors and sinners, and for criticizing the religious leaders of his day. There was something edgy about Jesus, a willingness to enter into uncharted territory with nothing but love and acceptance. Maybe Jesus would reach out to Muslims today, people who were on the margins of American society. As radical as such an approach seemed, Harley had the feeling that it was absolutely central to the tradition that Jesus started.

"Ready to leave the no-wake zone?" asked Dirk, pulling Harley out of his meditation.

"Yeah, right," he responded, realizing that he had become oblivious to the channel markers. He warned his passengers that he was about to accelerate and told them to hold on to their hats. For forty-five minutes they raced up the Potomac River, bouncing over the waves and enjoying the breeze on the water. Everyone seemed to enjoy the speed, especially Leah, who had not been out of the no-wake zone on their previous trip.

Harley thought she looked fantastic, with the sun reflecting off her sunglasses and the wind in her hair. He was so glad that she had agreed to come on the trip. On the left they saw George Washington's

Mount Vernon, and on the right they got a look at Fort Washington, a stone structure designed to protect the city from a river attack. "The British attacked it during the War of 1812," shouted Dirk over the engine noise, "and the Americans chickened out. They retreated from the fort and blew it up. Not our finest moment."

Approaching Alexandria, Harley pulled the throttle back and slowed as they passed through another no-wake zone. Mary changed places with Paul, while Leah and Tie-dye continued to chat. Speaking over the windshield, Harley asked Mary if she had an impression of the Bayatis.

"Solid citizens," she said. "Always polite and careful."

"What did you think when Muhammad was arrested?"

"I was shocked," Mary admitted. "I had seen him in the post office with Norah over the years, and he was never anything but respectful. My impression was that he adored her."

"Yeah, but you don't know what goes on behind closed doors," Dirk interrupted. "I heard she could be pretty feisty."

"True," said Mary. "That was her reputation. And Lord knows that it is hard for immigrant kids to navigate the United States, caught between family traditions and American freedoms. But I still think that Muhammad was crazy about her."

"We'll see," Dirk responded. "The courts will sort things out."

Mary turned to give attention to her granddaughters, and Harley pondered her words. He figured that a postmistress knew more about the people of a town than anyone else. And if she believed that Muhammad was innocent, she was probably correct.

So, that left which prime suspects? Will? Matt? Abdul? The Muslim motorcycle guy, or one of his Woodbridge buddies? Harley didn't sense that Omar suspected the Woodbridge guys, but there was no question that they were violent. Maybe one of them was involved with Norah and not even her brother knew it.

"Did I tell you I went to the hospital?" said Dirk, out of nowhere.

"No," Harley responded. "Really?"

"Chest pains. Really excruciating. Spent a night in the hospital."

"I hope you are okay."

"Yeah, the docs aren't exactly sure what happened. The good news is that I didn't have a heart attack."

"Well, that's great," said Harley. "Thanks for informing your pastor, so he could visit."

"Look, I don't need any hand-holding."

"Still, I would have liked to visit. It's my job."

"You can save it for some little old lady. Speaking of hospitals, I heard you almost ended up in one when you pulled the Bayati boy off his burning boat."

"Actually, it went well. Got him well away before the explosion."

"You were lucky."

"No doubt about it. I had to make a split-second decision, and it worked out."

"What were you doing there, anyway?"

"Just enjoying my boat," Harley said, hoping that he wouldn't sound like he was lying.

"Really?" Dirk replied, less than convinced.

"You know the spot, Dirk. You took me there."

"Just be more careful in the future. That kind of recklessness can get you killed. I don't want to lose my pastor."

The boat pulled up to the dock outside Nationals Park in time for the first pitch, and the group had a great time watching the Washington Nationals beat the New York Mets, four to three. Harley enjoyed seeing the little girls enter the ballpark for the first time, eyes wide with amazement at the size of the park, the deep green of the field, and the bright lights of the digital scoreboard. As they munched on popcorn and hotdogs, he remembered taking Jessica to her first game at Camden Yards in Baltimore, since there was no Nats Park at the time—a magical moment for any parent and child.

Their trip home on the boat was uneventful, and they tied up in Occoquan just as the sun dipped below the horizon. Harley said goodbye to everyone, and Dirk stayed behind to help him put the cover on the boat.

As he left, Dirk said, "Harley, thanks for your concern about the hospital thing. I'll tell you when I really need you."

CHAPTER 15

"Harley, do you have time to talk this morning?" Mary Ranger asked from behind the counter of the Occoquan Post Office. "I'll have a break in about an hour. Can I stop by your office?"

Harley walked across Washington Street toward the church, wondering what in the world she needed to discuss. She and Paul had seemed very relaxed and happy the day before, so he didn't think that they were having marital problems. The fact that she had signed up for the baseball game and brought her grandchildren gave him the impression that she liked him personally. Mary was active on the Riverside Methodist worship committee, so if she didn't care for his preaching or the way he led the services, she certainly could have said something at a committee meeting. Harley was stumped.

Over the course of his ministry, he had a terrible record of guessing what problems people were facing. He once assumed that a couple was having money problems, only to discover that the husband was gay. Another time, he guessed that a conservative family was leaving the church because of his preaching, only to discover that their best friends had moved away and they had lost their anchor in the congregation. Then there was the unpleasant experience of meeting with a man who said he wanted to discuss the music program only to end up attacking Harley on his failures of leadership.

As he approached the church, he noticed that a sign on the corner of Commerce and Washington, which said *Historic Occoquan Welcomes You*, was on its side. It looked as though a motorist had clipped one of the large wooden posts supporting it. *Probably a drunk leaving the brewpub in the middle of the night*, thought Harley. He turned the key in the side door of the church and entered his office, walking first to his window air conditioner to crank it up and cool the room. He booted up his computer, knowing that he would have to spend a few hours on his Sunday sermon, and then checked his answering machine for messages.

"One new message, zero saved messages," said the electronic voice. The new message was a pleasant surprise—an invitation from the Ayads to come over for dinner that night. He immediately grabbed the phone and returned the call, telling Sofia that he would be very happy to join them.

Then he organized a stack of the church's mail, which he had picked up that morning at the post office. Flipping through the envelopes, he separated the items addressed to him from the bills that he would give to the church treasurer. Harley thought about the church secretaries and office administrators that had always done this kind of work at his previous churches, ensuring that his mail always appeared in a neat pile in his office cubbyhole. Now, sitting in his silent office, he realized that he didn't really mind sorting the mail at the start of each day. But he did miss having another human being in the office, a living person to keep the building from being so deathly quiet.

Knowing that he wouldn't have time to get into his sermon before Mary's arrival, he walked into the sanctuary to check the level of disorder from the Sunday service. Riverside employed a cleaning service, so Harley didn't have to act as church custodian as well as pastor. A team came in once a week to scrub the bathrooms and vacuum the sanctuary and office, and every month they did a complete dusting and polished the floors of the social hall downstairs. But the team did not straighten up the sanctuary after Sunday worship, so every week Harley put hymnals back in pew racks and picked up worship bulletins from the floor. It was menial work, but Harley considered it to be an act of pure service to the congregation, and he enjoyed the sanctuary as a place where his mind could wander in unexpected directions. Through it all, black Jesus gazed down at him from the stained-glass window, calming the waters and asking the questions, "Why are you afraid? Have you still no faith?"

Harley flipped through a set of brochures in an information rack near the entrance to the church. Many were outdated, advertising church programs that had died years before. He tossed entire stacks of brochures into a recycling bin. He marveled at how people were reluctant to dispose of anything associated with the church, assuming that it must have some kind of holiness attached to it. *Better to clear the deck and make space for brochures that actually look forward*, he thought. As he tossed away a final stack, he heard Mary Ranger calling out to him from the office.

"Harley, thanks for making time for me. I know you must be busy."

Everyone always says that, thought Harley. "No problem. Happy to meet with you."

"That was so much fun yesterday," Mary said as she settled into a wooden arm chair in front of Harley's desk. He sat down in a similar chair across from her. "Paul and the girls really enjoyed it. Paul is taking off the whole week to babysit, and I'm glad that I could take off Monday and Tuesday to have some fun together. When the grandkids come here, we call it 'Camp Occoquan.'"

"Sounds like fun," said Harley. A wave of grief passed over him as he realized that he would never be able to offer such a thing.

"Yes, we walk along the river with them, get ice cream, feed the ducks. There is so much here that kids love."

"I bet."

"And your boat is great," Mary continued. "Taking it to the ballpark was a real treat. We've talked about getting one, but have never moved seriously in that direction. You know what they say:

Better to have a friend with a boat than a boat of your own."

Harley nodded, hoping that she would get to her point. "So, Mary, how can I help you?"

"There's just something that I think you need to know," she said, getting serious. "It concerns Tim Underwood."

"Oh, really," said Harley. "Is he okay?"

"As far as I know, yes. But there is something from his past that I feel I must tell you. If you just bumped into him on the street, it wouldn't be a big deal. But since he has been coming to church here, I think you need to hear about it. If you are going to be his pastor, you need this background."

"Go on," he said.

"Tim is about my age," Mary said, running her fingers through her short blond hair, "not quite sixty. As long as I have known him, he has lived in his parents' house on Tanyard Hill. His dad was dead when I started work here in 1985, but his mother lived in the house with Tim until she died just two years ago. He always took care of her, and never married."

Harley felt a chill as he conjured an image of a decrepit Victorian mansion, one filled with sickening family secrets and supernatural horrors.

"Anyway," Mary continued, "Tim has always worked for the maintenance department, so he spends a lot of time in the community. You see him doing his work, I know. About twenty-five years ago, when Tim was in his mid-thirties, he starting paying a lot of attention to a young woman in Occoquan, a teenager named Holly. He would talk with her at her bus stop in the morning, and sometimes follow her home in his little cart in the afternoon. Her parents got concerned, and asked her what was going on. She said that he was just a funny guy, harmless. I think she enjoyed the attention. But they didn't like it one bit. They told him to stay away from her."

Harley started to feel a little sick to his stomach. "How did Tim react to this?" he asked.

"I think he brushed it off as a big misunderstanding. Tried to laugh it off, as Tim is wont to do. He kept his distance for a while, but this is a small town, and people are going to run into each other. When Holly's parents saw him talking to her on a street corner, they threatened to get a restraining order."

"That's serious," said Harley. "What happened?"

"Well, they weren't successful," Mary reported. "The standards are pretty high for a restraining order. Tim had never laid a hand on her, so the judge said that he couldn't issue an order. But he reminded Tim that he was a grown man, and he ought to stay away from her. The parents were so upset that they put their house on the market and moved out of town."

"Do you think they overreacted?"

"Probably. But Tim was being inappropriate, no doubt about it. Maybe even obsessed. He was given the label of 'creepy guy,' which has stuck with him to this day."

"That's kind of odd," said Harley, "since I've never heard anyone say that about him."

"You're just not talking to the right people," said Mary. "Any parents of children or teenagers will tell you that they keep their kids away from him. The reputation has stuck, and it just gets passed from generation to generation."

"Kind of sad to have to carry that burden."

"Maybe," said Mary. "Maybe not. You are in a better position to judge than I. I just thought that you needed to know."

"Yes, thank you. That is good information to have."

"I better get back to the post office. My break is over. I feel better for having gotten it off my chest."

Harley walked her to the door and stepped into the bright sunshine alongside her. Enjoying a breath of fresh air, he walked with her across the parking lot and said goodbye as she walked north on Washington Street. Then he saw Tie-dye Tim in his golf cart next to the broken Occoquan sign. A midnight-blue Mercedes pulled away from the curb, and Tim gave it a wave. *The world is just a little too small in the Town of Occoquan*, thought Harley.

"Was that who I think it was?" asked Harley, as he stepped across Commerce Street.

"Jefferson and Abdul," said Tim, nodding. "Jefferson was very concerned about the sign. Abdul, of course, said nothing. Just sat there looking pumped."

"Nice of Jefferson to be concerned."

"Yeah, he loves the town. Told me that he would make a special donation to get it fixed."

"Well, that's being a good citizen," said Harley.

"Good citizen," agreed Tim, "and good businessman. He's got his eye on redeveloping Mill Street, and he'll need the approval of the town council."

"So, what do you think happened here?" asked Harley.

"Definitely a vehicle that jumped the curb. You can see the tire tracks in the flower bed. But it was a hit-and-run, sometime last night."

"One too many at the pub?"

"Probably," Tim agreed. "I've seen similar accidents before. Would be nice if someone took responsibility, but I doubt anyone will."

"Can you get it back up?"

"Sure thing. The sign itself was not damaged, just the posts. Remount the sign on some new posts and we'll be good to go."

"I guess you're the guy to do it, Tim."

"That's why they pay me."

Harley gave Tim a careful look, trying to picture him as the creepy guy who followed a teenager home from the bus stop. He had a hard time seeing it. But then he remembered Tim's description of Norah Bayati, and how he had become a bit more emotional than seemed appropriate. Maybe he still struggled with being obsessive.

"Thanks for the boat ride yesterday," Tim continued. "That was a lot of fun. Hope I didn't make Dirk too mad. You know, with my busting on Republicans and their anti-Muslim bias."

"He's a big boy," said Harley. "He can handle it."

"Speaking of Muslims, I talked with your buddy Omar this morning."

"Why do you call him my buddy?" asked Harley, surprised.

"Well, you saved his life. And then you spent yesterday morning with him in the park." It was impossible to keep a secret in Occoquan.

"Okay, so what did Omar say?"

Tim leaned back in the seat of his golf cart and stroked his gray beard. "I ran into him on Mill Street when I was picking up some trash. Asked him how his father was doing in jail, and whether there had been any developments in the case. He told me that his father was doing okay, and he was glad that he was eating again. But he said that the police had suspended their investigation since they seem convinced that his dad is the killer."

"Yes, that fits with what I've heard," Harley said.

"So then I asked him if anyone had questioned Norah's boyfriend. He said that he had heard about an American boyfriend, but no one knew who he was. Norah was very secretive about seeing Americans, because she knew her parents would object. Omar said that his family had told the police about a boyfriend, but they had no evidence to go on. Her apartment was small, just a one-room efficiency with a bed and kitchenette. They went over it completely and found no fingerprints except from Norah, her sister, her mother, and her father. There was nothing in her room to implicate anyone else, not even anything in her cell phone. Nothing to link her to a boyfriend. It was a total dead end."

"Strange that the police would give up so easily."

"Well, they felt that Mohammed was their man. They knew that Norah was trying to break away from her family, working for the county after college. They knew that she had fought with her father about seeing an American. It was natural that they would focus on Muhammad. Anyway, I told Omar that I had seen a white man with dark hair, probably in his thirties, entering Norah's apartment on several occasions. He went to the back wing late at night, up the outside staircase to her room. I never saw him leave, but of course I didn't just hang around watching."

"Why didn't you report this to the police?" asked Harley.

"I didn't see him on the night she died. And hey, it's not a crime to visit someone in their apartment. If Norah wanted to have an American boyfriend, good for her. I'm not going to stick my nose where it doesn't belong."

"Really, Tim? It seems to me like you do a pretty good job of nosing around."

Harley's comment seemed to annoy Tim a bit, so he pushed back. "Do you want to hear what Omar said or not?"

"Okay, go on."

"So anyway, I told Omar about the dark-haired man, but made clear that I had not seen him on the night of her death. He asked me who it could have been, and I said I never saw him up close or in the light. He asked if he came in a car, and I said no—he was always walking. He would come between the buildings behind her apartment and go straight to her room. Omar asked me if I knew anyone in town who would fit that description, and I said I had thought about that question quite a bit. The only two I could come up with were Will Beckley and Dirk Carter's son, Matt. Omar said that he knew Will and didn't think that Norah would be interested in him, but he wanted to hear more about Matt. At first, he wasn't sure he had ever seen Matt."

"Wait a second, Tim. Are you serious? Matt could have been Norah's boyfriend?"

"I'm just reporting on a possibility, Harley. I'm not the judge and jury. I have seen Matt going in and out of the building behind the Bayatis' place a number of times, so it figures that he might have been involved with her. I described Matt to Omar, told him about Matt's comings and goings, and suddenly a light bulb went off in Omar's head. He realized that he had seen him behind his house, and now he had a name to go with the face. He became convinced that Matt was Norah's American boyfriend."

"Seems like a stretch to me, Tim."

"Look, Harley, I know that you are friends with Dirk and Matt, so I can understand your reluctance to see it. But Omar seems sold on the idea, and he told me this morning that he was going straight to the Prince William County Police."

"What?" said Harley. "Omar is going to the police?"

"Yes, he went to them with the name and description of his number one suspect."

CHAPTER 16

Youssef Ayad was standing at the front door of the Gold Emporium when Harley stepped on the stoop after the short walk across Washington Street from Riverside Methodist. The day was still very warm, but a front with cooler air was coming in from the west. Youssef welcomed Harley, motioned him to come inside, and then pulled down a shade on the door that said *Closed*. The two of them ascended the creaking wooden stairs, and waiting for them at the top was Sofia.

"We have been looking forward to seeing you, Pastor Camden," she said, grinning broadly. "Welcome to our home." Harley was struck again by how similar they looked to each other. They could have been brother and sister.

"Please, call me Harley," he said, extending his hand.

"And we, of course, want to be Youssef and Sofia to you," she added. "Come, have a seat." She led him into their small living area and motioned for him to take a seat on the couch. Youssef sat next to Harley, and Sofia pulled up a chair so that she could face the pastor. She offered tea and a cucumber sandwich.

As they nibbled and sipped, Sofia told him about the relatives they had visited in London, and Youssef mentioned that they attended the Coptic Church of St. Mark while there—a church with the same name as their Fairfax congregation.

"Of course, that is no big surprise," Yousef added, "since St. Mark founded the Coptic Church."

"We have to get more creative with our names," said Sofia, slyly. "I like your church's name, Riverside."

"It seems to fit the location," Harley said.

"Riverside makes me think of Moses being pulled out of the river in Egypt. And Jesus being baptized in the Jordan River. Rivers carry a message of new life," Sofia said.

"We have an African American spiritual called 'Down in the River to Pray,'" Harley told them. "I like to the think of my church members coming down in the river to pray."

"We like your church members," said Youssef. "Some have been our customers for many years."

"Glad to hear it," Harley replied. "So, how do you feel the Bayatis are doing?"

"I saw Muhammad in jail last week," Youssef said. "He seems to be holding up well, and is eating again—thanks to you." Harley waved away his compliment.

"And Fatima is working to keep the business going, with the help of Sarah and Omar," said Sofia. "The days are long, the work is hard, and she misses Muhammad. But business seems to be back to where it was before the tragedy."

"Yes, they are under a lot of stress," Harley said.

"Indeed they are," said Youssef. "The loss of a child, the jailing of the father, an attack by hoodlums—probably from the Muslim community. Fatima won't talk about that with us, for fear of reprisals. She is worried about us, as well as her own family."

"And she's getting pressure to sell the property as well," added Sofia.

"From Jefferson Jones?" asked Harley.

Sofia nodded. "He's not a bad man, but he always puts business first. Have you met him?"

"No, not personally," said Harley. "But I've gotten to know his daughter, Tawnya." They talked about life in Occoquan for a few more minutes, and then Sofia invited the two of them to move to the dinner table across the room.

As soon as they sat down, Youssef offered a prayer. "Be with us, Lord Jesus, as you were with your first followers in the breaking of the bread. Bless this food to our use and ourselves to your service. Amen."

Sofia passed him a plate of lentils and rice with tomato sauce and said that it was called *kosheri*. She followed that dish with stuffed grape leaves, which she called *warah enab*. Youssef refilled Harley's glass of iced tea and noted that they ate mostly vegetarian meals, which came from the Coptic practice of abstaining from meat during periods of partial fasting. He said that they were allowed to eat fish through most of the year, but the two of them found that they were satisfied with a largely vegan diet. From a spiritual point of view, it took them back to the Garden of Eden, said Youssef, where plants were the only food that humans were permitted to eat. Harley nodded, remembering that according to the Book of Genesis, meat was allowed only after the time of Noah and the ark.

"This food is delicious," said Harley to Sofia. "Thank you very much. It all seems very healthy."

"Food is important to us," Sofia said. "Think of the many times that Jesus sat down to eat with people—even tax collectors and sinners. Christian hospitality is very important to Youssef and me."

"I do appreciate it," Harley added. "Think of how much better the world would be if people actually sat down and ate with each other."

"No doubt about it," agreed Youssef. "The Bayatis have become some of our closest friends here in Occoquan, largely because we have shared so many meals. Back in Egypt, Christians and Muslims are getting together less and less, which has caused the animosity and violence to increase. Did you hear about the attack last December in Cairo?"

"No, I missed that," admitted Harley.

"A suicide bomber attacked St. Mark's Coptic Orthodox

Cathedral. More than two dozen worshipers were killed, including a ten-year-old girl."

"It was horrible," Sofia said, shaking her head. "The worst attack on Copts in years. The Islamic State claimed responsibility."

"How did the Copts respond?" asked Harley.

"With increased security, of course," said Youssef. "But also with prayer—prayers for the victims, and for their attackers."

Harley was impressed that the Coptic community could respond with prayer for such evildoers. Thinking back over the past year, he hadn't said a single prayer for the terrorists who killed Karen and Jessica. And yet he knew that Jesus commanded his followers to pray for the people who persecuted them.

"A Coptic bishop set just the right tone," continued Youssef. "He has a diocese south of Cairo. He challenged us all to love our enemies, to forgive them, and to pray for God to extract evil and darkness from their hearts. This has been my prayer since the bombing, although I admit that it is not easy to do."

"It is the only Christian path," added Sofia. "We need to focus on heaven, and practice heavenly values in this world. After all, our life here is a preparation for heaven."

Harley was aware that the Coptic Orthodox Church, along with most Orthodox churches, had a very heavenly orientation. Their worship was much more otherworldly than Protestant services, which tended to be very orderly and rational, and even more mystical than most Roman Catholic services. He found himself drawn to these two Christians who dared to take the words of Jesus literally and personally, and said to them, "One of our great civil rights leaders had a similar approach. He said, 'Darkness cannot drive out darkness: only light can do that. Hate cannot drive out hate: only love can do that.'"

"Well said," noted Youssef. "Whose words are those?"

"The Rev. Dr. Martin Luther King, Jr."

"He was killed, wasn't he?"

"Yes," said Harley. "Gunned down in 1968."

"Such is the fate of so many Christians who live by their beliefs," said Youssef. "Fortunately, life in heaven is better than life on earth."

Harley felt himself wanting to push back against Youssef's words because he knew that such a focus on heaven had been used to oppress people in the past. Across the South, in the years before the Civil War, plantation owners had told their slaves that Christianity promised a heavenly reward, and that all of their suffering in this life would someday be replaced by a pain-free life in paradise. They would quote the apostle Paul to them, "Slaves, obey your earthly masters with fear and trembling," while assuring them that obedient slaves would receive the gift of eternal life. Harley hated that the Bible had been used to enslave and abuse an entire race of people, but at the same time he realized that Youssef was not speaking out of that particular history. For Coptic Christians, the promise of heaven was not used to oppress people but to strengthen them to endure oppression.

"I heard that when the funeral was held for that ten-year-old," said Sofia, "her mother asked everyone to wear white. She said that black would have made her more depressed."

"In my church, white is the color of resurrection," noted Harley.

"That should always be the color for a funeral," Sofia agreed. "When a person has died, we should always celebrate the resurrection. They have new life in Christ."

For Harley, the conversation began to feel a bit otherworldly, like a waking dream. After the deaths of Jessica and Karen, some of his dreams felt more real than his waking life, and now this wide-awake conversation with the Ayads felt like a vision. He found himself entering a state described by psychologists as "flow," when a person became energized, focused, and fully involved in an activity. For athletes, flow was described as being "in the zone," while musicians called it "getting into the groove."

As Harley talked with Sofia and Youssef, he felt a deep bond to them and to their Christian convictions, a link that he wanted to maintain for as long as he could. As they talked, everything became perfectly clear and deeply connected. Perhaps Youssef's dinner prayer had been answered, and the risen Christ was truly present in the room.

"I feel as though God has been talking to me through dreams," Harley said to them, confessing something that he had not revealed to anyone else.

"Really?" asked Sofia. "There is a long history of that in the Bible."

"I'd be interested in hearing about your dreams," said Youssef. "Such communication has always been fascinating to me."

The name Youssef was the same as the name Joseph. Harley remembered that in the Book of Genesis there was a man named Joseph who had been an interpreter of dreams. The experience of flow between him and Youssef was getting stronger.

"It happened on a Sunday night," Harley explained. "I dreamed I was napping in a student dorm in Israel, the summer I did an archaeological dig there. In my dream I had a dream, and a supernatural messenger told me that my friend Leah was pregnant. I was shocked, since we had not been together in that way. Then the angel said, 'Harley, do not be afraid to take Leah as your wife.'"

"Ah," said Youssef, "the same message that the angel gave Joseph."

"Yes, that's right," agreed Harley. "The New Testament Joseph. Not the Genesis Joseph."

"There are lots of us Youssefs." Harley's host smiled.

"I was stunned," Harley continued. "I couldn't understand why this message was being given to me. I woke from sleep in the dorm, and wondered whether the angel was speaking the truth or not. I tossed and turned, wanting Leah to be held accountable for her unplanned pregnancy, but not wanting to do anything to embarrass her."

"That was Joseph's struggle as well, wasn't it?" said Youssef. "The tension between justice and compassion. He chose compassion, and look what a difference it made."

"So, what is it that God is saying to me?" Harley wondered. "Is he sending another miracle child into the world? How can that be? Leah is still my friend today. She has not had any babies, and she is not having any babies."

"Sometimes God speaks through symbols," Sofia suggested.

"Remember that when Pharaoh dreamed, he saw seven fat cows and seven thin cows. Joseph told him that the fat cows were symbols of seven good years and the thin cows were symbols of seven years of famine. He helped Pharaoh to store up food in the years of plenty to help his people to survive the years of famine."

Sofia's name, like Youssef's, had Biblical significance. It meant "wisdom." Appearing as a character in the Book of Proverbs, Divine Wisdom called the people of the earth to follow Sofia.

"What I am hearing is this," said Youssef. "God is asking you to make a choice between justice and love. You can judge the people around you, or you can show them compassion. Did the friend in your dream deserve to be judged? Yes, probably. But the angel challenged you to make a compassionate choice and marry her."

"Okay," said Harley, "I get it. But Leah is not pregnant and it wouldn't make sense for me to marry her."

"Where else is new life coming into your world?" asked Youssef. "Where else are you challenged to take a chance and show compassion toward someone who deserves judgment?"

One name jumped immediately into his mind: Omar Bayati. But he didn't say anything about him because he didn't want to break his promise of confidentiality.

"Yes, I can think of someone," he replied. It suddenly occurred to Harley that Joseph and Mary had fled to Egypt soon after the birth of Jesus. They found safety in that foreign land before returning to their hometown of Nazareth. *Am I making a similar sojourn in the home of these two Copts?*

"Go to that person," recommended Sofia. "Step out in faith and show them the compassion that Joseph showed to Mary. It is always good to approach people with love, because they have no defense against it."

"You won't regret it," added Youssef. Harley struggled with how to respond, and as he did he felt the feeling of flow dissipate. The presence of Jesus, which had felt so real, was no longer something he could perceive. Suddenly, he was simply sitting in a warm upstairs apartment with two short and heavy Egyptians. He felt a sense of loss and wanted so badly for the flow to return.

"I really want to thank you for the meal and the conversation," said Harley, not wanting to overstay his welcome. "You have shown amazing hospitality, and you have helped me figure some things out."

"You are very welcome," said Sofia, also sensing that a meaningful moment had passed. "We hope that you will return to our home soon."

"Wherever two or three are gathered," Youssef added, quoting scripture, "Jesus promises to be in the midst of them." They walked him down the stairs and through the jewelry shop. Harley said goodbye, stepped into the street, and then turned around to wave. For a split second, they looked like angels. Then they reverted to being a couple of immigrants with light-brown faces and big smiles.

❀

Harley walked north on Washington Street and then west on Mill, enjoying the daylight that continued to illuminate the summer evening. For some reason, the biblical verse "out of Egypt I have called my son" popped into his head. Sure, he had just spent an evening with two Egyptians, but he had no idea who the son in his case was supposed to be. A refreshing breeze blew in his face as he walked along Mill Street, a harbinger of an approaching cool front. He wanted to talk with Omar and hoped that he would be able to find him at home.

The lights were off in the Riverview Bakery, but it appeared that people were moving around in the apartment upstairs. He rang the doorbell at the front door of the bakery and waited for someone to respond. In a minute, a door opened behind the counter and a figure appeared. It was Omar, and he looked surprised to see Harley at the door.

"What's up?" Omar asked, trying to appear cool.

"Can we talk?" Harley asked.

Omar looked out the door to see if anyone else was around, and then gazed behind him into the empty bakery. He finally turned back toward Harley, shrugged and said, "Guess so."

"Let's walk toward the water," suggested Harley.

Omar stepped outside, locked the door behind him, and followed Harley toward the dock where his boat used to reside. He stuffed his hands into the pockets of his blue jeans and kept his head down as he walked.

"I hear you went to the police with your suspicion about Matt Carter."

Omar looked surprised that Harley knew this. "Who told you?" he asked.

"Tim Underwood."

"Well, I think Matt Carter is guilty."

"Any evidence?" asked Harley.

"Tim saw him in the area, going in and out of the building behind our place. And I saw him."

Harley looked at him, hoping that he would have something more solid. "Is that all?" he asked.

"I think that's enough. I went to the police this morning, made my report, and they said they would look into it."

The two of them approached the river, and Harley looked over to the rocks on the other side. The breeze picked up, stirring the water. "I'm glad you made your report. I trust the police to do an investigation. I certainly hope that they find your sister's killer, whether it is Matt or someone else."

"It's got to be him," Omar huffed.

"I want the killer to be found, just as you do, I really do. But when the case is solved, your family will still be in danger. These Woodbridge guys want to do some serious damage, and they will hurt anyone who gets in their way."

Omar looked fearful. "I can slow them down, but I cannot stop them."

"I think you can," said Harley. "I will help you. As soon as the killer is caught and your father is released, we will go to the police, you and me."

As a Christian, Harley had always believed that God took human form in Jesus, and he preached that members of the church had the responsibility to be the hands and feet of Jesus in the world today.

He had accepted this concept in theory for most of his life, but his visit with the Ayads drove the idea from his head to his heart.

"We will say that you were pressured to take the pictures, and we will describe how the Woodbridge guys threatened your family."

"All of that is true."

"When you realized they were terrorists, you came to me," Harley continued. "We will take the pictures to the authorities, and describe their connection to the Belvoir plot."

"But how can I trust the authorities? Look at what they are doing to my father. The system is not fair to people like us. Won't I be accused of participating in the plot?"

"Not with me by your side," promised Harley. "I will do everything I can to protect you. I promise you."

Omar looked at him with confusion. "Why would you to do this for me?"

"Because I want to see justice done," said Harley. "And because I have compassion for you." *Perhaps Omar is my son*, he thought, *called out of Iraq.* The son he never had, and the only child left to him after Jessica's death.

Omar gazed out at the water and then back at Harley. He was defenseless. After taking a deep breath, he said, "I'll do it. I'll turn on the Woodbridge guys—as soon as my father is released."

CHAPTER 17

Dirk and Harley sat on the third-floor porch, drinking coffee and looking down on Mill Street. A slight breeze rustled the dark-green leaves of the trees along the street, and the pedestrians doing Saturday morning shopping moved from one patch of shade to another as they progressed from store to store in the bright sunshine. Dirk had brought his plumber's snake to Harley's townhouse, which he used to clear a drain in the master bathroom. In a matter of minutes, the drain was flowing freely and Harley invited Dirk to join him on the porch for coffee and cinnamon rolls. Sitting in wrought-iron chairs beside a small round table, they sipped their drinks and watched the traffic below.

"Nice view you've got from up here," Dirk said as he took a bite of a roll.

"Great for people-watching," noted Harley. "When I was in Sterling, we lived in a typical suburban cul-de-sac. The only traffic was cars driving in and out of garages, and the occasional dog-walker."

"But here it is people everywhere, constantly out and about."

"Most of the time I like it. Except for maybe late at night, when the drunks are yelling in the street."

As they gazed westward, toward the Riverview Bakery, they saw a woman walking down the street, suspending a child by one arm and spanking her repeatedly. The little girl was shrieking and struggling to break free. Dirk winced.

"I hate to see a mother do that," Harley said.

"You're telling me," Dirk responded.

For a second it looked as though Dirk was going to reprimand the woman over the porch railing, but she stopped hitting the child and the little girl began to trudge along, sobbing instead of screaming.

"Reminds me of my own mother," sighed Dirk, settling back in his chair. "She had a fiery temper and would beat me for minor infractions. One time, when I was probably five or six, I was trying to help her by clearing the table. I knocked a vase off the table and it shattered on the floor. She slapped me hard and knocked me to the ground."

"That's terrible," said Harley. "That would be considered child abuse today."

"Well, it was a different time. Made me feel like I had to walk on eggshells all the time. I never knew what would set her off. She really scared me."

"Where was your dad in all this?"

"He was around, but never intervened. Maybe he was afraid of her temper as well."

"I bet that made you mad at your father."

"I've never really thought about it," admitted Dirk. "Mad? I don't know. Disappointed, yes. He could have stepped in, but he didn't. I always got the feeling that he expected me to take care of myself."

"So, if you needed his help, you were showing weakness?"

"Right. He expected me to be a man, and I didn't want to disappoint him."

"I guess that makes sense at a certain age," said Harley. "But not when you are five or six. I think he should have protected you."

"I guess. But what's the point of being resentful? I can't change the past. He's dead, and has been dead for a long time."

Harley thought about how the dead continued to grab hold of

the living and mess with them, no matter how long they had been in the grave. Dirk was old enough to be a grandfather, but he still winced when he saw a mother beat a child.

"My own parents were kind of the opposite," Harley said. "My dad was the disciplinarian, distant and judgmental. My mother was softhearted and compassionate, which I loved. But as I think back, I really wish she had shielded me more from my dad."

Dirk sipped his coffee and said, "What can you do? They were who they were, for good or bad. They probably thought that if they fed and sheltered us, they were doing their jobs."

"That's true," Harley nodded. "They grew up in the Depression and had fears we never faced. There is a picture of my grandparents from the 1920s, before they had my dad, a couple of hard-scrabble dirt farmers. They look absolutely miserable."

"The good old days," said Dirk with a hint of a smile.

"So, how is Matt doing?" asked Harley, trying to sound as though he were making small talk. In fact, he was intensely curious about whether the police had been in touch with him, but he didn't want to pry. Three days had passed since Omar made his accusation.

"He's been better," Dirk acknowledged, sounding burdened. "As you may have heard, the Prince William Police questioned him about the Bayati killing. I don't know who pointed the finger at him. Maybe Omar. I never liked that kid, from the moment I met him at the American Legion. This is not something that Matt needs to face."

"Did Matt know Norah?" asked Harley.

"Know her?" Dirk asked with an edge in his voice. "Well, I guess so. He was investigating the whole family. Probably because of Omar's suspicious activities."

Harley let this statement stand for a few seconds, trying to be comfortable with awkward silence.

"The FBI has to get close to the people they are investigating," Dirk continued. "Matt was probably poking around in their lives for several months, and then there was a week of surveillance from the property behind their house. But I'm sure you know all this. Tim Underwood has been telling everybody."

"Yes, that matches what I've heard."

"I'm just concerned about what this will do to Matt's career. He is a straight arrow, and his career is on a great path. I don't want anything to derail him."

"Sounds like you are worried."

"Absolutely. It would be wrong for him to be hurt by this. A gross miscarriage of justice."

Harley thought that Dirk's choice of words was a bit odd, but he let it pass. Instead, he asked, "So how is he holding up?"

"Fine, I guess," said Dirk. "You know Matt. He is not exactly one to share his feelings."

"Like father, like son."

"Think so? Compared to Matt, I am an open book."

Harley cleaned up the wrappers from the cinnamon rolls and asked Dirk what he was going to do with the rest of his day. Dirk said that he was going to clean his boat and then take it down the Potomac to a riverfront restaurant where he had a gig at happy hour.

"Want to come along?" asked Dirk.

"No, but thanks anyway," said Harley. "I've got to finish up my sermon for tomorrow."

"I'll sing to the sinners," Dirk joked, "and then you'll preach to the saints."

Dirk gathered up his plumber's snake, thanked Harley for the coffee and the roll, and headed downstairs. Harley followed him into the street and they parted company. As Dirk pulled away, Harley thought of an ossuary from Sepphoris, a Jewish bone box containing a Roman coin that his team had uncovered so many years before. Although he hadn't thought about it since the Duke reunion, that mysterious relic somehow seemed connected to the death of Norah Bayati. But he had no idea how or why.

Harley strolled west toward the River Mill Park. Passing the bakery and the brewpub, he looked to see if the Bayatis were at work and if there were any morning drinkers in the pub. Yes on both counts. Then he approached a vacant lot along the river, one that had been an industrial dock in the days when the mill was active. As he passed the lot, he saw a midnight-blue Mercedes parked on Mill Street. Jefferson and Abdul were nearby. Turning toward the river, he saw them. Jefferson was in a seersucker suit, and Abdul was in a form-fitting T-shirt and warm-up pants. They stood by the water, looking up and down the river.

Not wanting to look like a stalker, Harley stopped to read one of the historical markers placed along Mill Street. He pretended to show interest in the history of the old mill, but after reading the marker three times he was about to give up and continue his walk. Fortunately, the two men headed to their car and Harley was in a good position to intercept them when they reached the sidewalk.

"Good morning," said Harley to Jefferson, extending his hand. "I'm Harley Camden, the new pastor of Riverside Methodist."

"Jefferson Jones," replied the gray-haired real-estate developer. He had a rat-like face, and his eyes narrowed suspiciously. "How are you liking my old church?"

"Very nice," said Harley. He turned to Abdul and shook his hand. It felt like a vise. "Harley Camden," he said.

"Abdul," said the beefy younger man.

"I was just out for a walk," Harley continued. "This is a great walking town."

"Indeed it is," agreed Jefferson. "I am glad we could meet. I heard about you from my daughter."

"Tawnya, yes. I have been happy to get to know her. Lovely woman. Nice husband."

"So how are you settling in?" asked the older man.

"Pretty well," said Harley. "The congregation has been welcoming, as have the people in the town. I have a boat and am enjoying the river. The townhouse provided by the church is beautiful."

"Yes, those are very fine homes."

"Of course, the death of the Bayati girl has been terrible."

"An awful tragedy," agreed Jefferson.

Harley paused to see if Jefferson would say more, but he did not. He glanced at Abdul, but the man was stone-faced.

"It appears that there is potential for additional development here in Occoquan," Harley said.

"Yes, there is," said Jefferson. "My colleague and I are in that business, as you know. We think that this particular parcel has a great deal of potential."

"What are you thinking? A restaurant or a small hotel?"

"It is too early to say," Jefferson replied. "Occoquan could probably support either, if they were done correctly. We are still thinking about how to develop the site if we are successful in acquiring it."

"I wish you luck, Jefferson. It's a great little town." Harvey shifted his gaze. "So, Abdul, I have a question for you. What do you think of the Bayatis?"

The big man seemed shocked. Not only by the question but also by the fact that he was being addressed directly. In the course of their business dealings, Jefferson did most of the talking. He looked at Jefferson, who nodded permission.

"They are good people," Abdul said.

"You share their faith, do you not?" asked Harley.

"Yes, I do," Abdul said.

"As a Muslim, do you believe what people are saying about Norah's death being an honor killing?"

Abdul ran one of his beefy hands across his shaved head and then wiped his mouth. "I do not believe it. Her father would never do such a thing. He is a man of peace."

"Of course, we are not in a position to judge," interrupted Jefferson. "We trust that justice will be done, in a court of law."

Harley looked Jefferson in the eye, wondering if he really believed what he was saying. On the one hand, he was a Republican and a businessman. On the other, he was an African American in the Commonwealth of Virginia, a state historically unkind to its black residents.

Abdul had done time in prison, and Harley wondered what he thought of the potential for true justice in this case.

"We both have deep sympathy for the Bayatis," Jefferson continued. "My colleague Abdul considered Norah to be a friend.

As for myself, I have been concerned about the financial strain that Muhammad's arrest has put on the family. I have offered to help."

Harley wondered what kind of help he had offered, remembering the clear direction that Fatima had given him to get out of the bakery. But he couldn't really assess Jefferson's motives. He had no access to the man's heart. If he had offered to buy the bakery, maybe he considered that proposal to be a sincere offer of help. From years of marriage counseling, Harley knew that there were two sides to every story, and both sides tended to make perfect sense.

"I am sure that they appreciate your concern," said Harley. "And I agree with you that I do not believe the charge of honor killing." Abdul nodded, and Jefferson offered a tight smile.

"Abdul, I think we should be on our way," said Jefferson, pointing to the car. "Reverend Camden, it was a pleasure to meet you. I hope we will see you again."

Harley gave a nod as they drove off, and then continued his walk toward the River Mill Park. He was proud of himself for asking tough questions instead of simply making small talk. The deaths of Jessica and Karen had turned him into a more honest and probing person, even if it made others uncomfortable.

After walking the perimeter of the park, Harley intended to head straight for the church to continue work on his sermon. Dark and angry clouds rolled in from the west, and the wind picked up, transforming what had been a calm and sunny summer day. As he picked up his pace, thoughts about the importance of honesty bounced around his head, and he wondered about including the scripture verse about truth making people free. Then, as he passed the Riverview Bakery, the front door flew open and Omar ran out. Harley tried to intercept him.

"Get out of my way," shouted Omar as he pushed past him.

"Omar, what's going on?" he called out as he followed him toward the dock.

"I don't want to talk."

The young man slowed as he got to the water's edge and then stepped onto his family's dock. Harley followed. They stood for a minute, looking out at the whitecaps stirred up by the wind now snapping at them like a bullwhip.

"Your justice system sucks," said Omar. "The police have found no evidence that Matt Carter was involved in Norah's death. They want to pin it on my father, even though he is innocent. I am furious. Your country hates me, hates my family, hates my religion. We will never be treated fairly here. For us, there can be no justice, no peace."

Tears filled Omar's eyes. As the wind and rain whipped around them, Harley felt a flood of compassion.

CHAPTER 18

The bishop stepped out of her office in Alexandria and greeted Harley. She was nothing if not perfectly punctual and looked as handsome as ever in a light-blue blouse with clerical collar, black skirt, and black heels. Harley stood, shook her hand, noted that her heels gave her a height advantage, and followed her into her fifth-floor office. The bishop sat in the tall executive chair, which made Harley feel as though he were a bank customer asking for a loan. It was his first meeting with the bishop since being assigned to a new church.

"So, you've been in Occoquan for how long," asked the bishop, "about six weeks?"

"Yes, started in mid-June. I'm still unpacking but am pretty well set up in the church and the house."

"How do you like the town?"

"So far, so good. It is small enough to have a Mayberry feel, but so close to DC that it doesn't feel isolated."

"I hear you bought a boat," said the bishop.

"News travels fast. Yes, I've really enjoyed it. Never anticipated getting a boat, but the house has a dock, so why not?"

"You deserve it. Especially with what you've been through."

"I really do enjoy going out on the river. It's very peaceful, very relaxing. And I used it for a church event recently: took a group to Nationals Park."

The bishop smiled. "Let's talk about the church. Did you bring your data sheets?"

Harley pulled out two sets of papers and gave one of them to the bishop. He knew how important metrics were to her. The first page contained numbers for worship attendance, the second was a summary of the church budget, and the third contained information on infant baptisms, adult baptisms, Sunday School attendance, home visits, hospital visits, funerals and weddings. Each page was divided into actuals for the current year and goals for the next year, and at the end was a line for her to sign and date the packet, indicating satisfactory progress by the pastor.

"Okay," she said, looking at the sheets, "walk me through it."

"As you can see," Harley began, "the best worship attendance so far was on my first Sunday—one hundred and five. The church was packed, since everyone wanted to check out the new guy. Since then, we've been fluctuating between sixty and eighty-five. I think a reach-goal for next year would be an average of ninety."

"How many members on the rolls?" asked the bishop.

"Last year, the number reported to your office was one eighty-five," Harley replied. "But I think that the number needs to be revised downward. I saw some people on the list who have died or moved away."

"So, ninety seems attainable?"

"I think so. Might not seem like a huge number, but Occoquan has only a thousand residents."

"Of course, you are the only church."

"True. But some residents go elsewhere, and we draw from outside the town as well."

"How about your budget?" asked the bishop. They flipped to the second page of their packets. "Your total budget is one hundred and ninety-eight thousand per year, with sixty-seven pledging units.

Average pledge of a little under three thousand per year. Not bad for Northern Virginia."

"As you can see, we send twenty thousand a year to the conference."

"Yes, thank you for that. The conference put a lot of money into Riverside when it was first established, so I am glad that your members remember that."

"I think we are tracking pretty well for contributions," noted Harley. "The summer is often a slow period, but we are receiving about what we expected."

"Things will pick up in the fall," said the bishop. "And you'll do your annual stewardship campaign. What will your goal be for 2018?"

"I'd like to have us shoot to surpass two hundred thousand. I think that will be an important barrier to break. I'd like to do an interfaith speakers series in the new year, and put some money in the budget for that."

"Will that inspire giving?" asked the bishop, with skepticism in her voice.

"It is certainly important," Harley replied, "and I think the people of Occoquan feel it very personally. We had the murder of a Muslim woman this summer, and—"

"Yes, I heard about that," interrupted the bishop.

"Still unsolved," added Harley. "Really weighing heavily on the community. So, we have Muslims in the community, Jews as well. I've gotten to know some Copts, who are Christian, of course, but from the Orthodox tradition."

"I can sense your passion," said the bishop, "but I'm not sure you want to base a budget expansion on interfaith relations. People want to get their personal needs met. How about expanding the youth program or doing a series on parenting?"

Harley's heart sank. The bishop was trying to cram Riverside Methodist into a prepackaged program for church growth. *Next thing you know, she's going to ask me about the cleanliness of the bathrooms and the nursery.*

"So, how are your bathrooms?" she asked. "Updated recently? And your nursery? Clean and modern?"

"Not really," Harley admitted. "But I'll take your recommendations back to our church property committee."

Harley had been in a growing church in Sterling, so he knew all about the importance of making a positive impression on families with children and youths. *But how can this be my highest priority with Norah's killer on the loose and a terrorist group preparing to unleash a biological weapon?* Sprucing up the nursery seemed like repainting the Pentagon right before the 9/11 attack.

"Let's look at your last page," suggested the bishop. "One infant baptism, zero adult baptisms, Sunday School off for the summer, eight home visits, five hospital visits, one funeral and zero weddings. You've only been there for six weeks, so those numbers seem about right. What would you say your most significant visit has been since you arrived?"

Here's my chance, thought Harley. "Muhammad Bayati, a prisoner in the Prince William County Jail." The bishop's eyebrows raised. "He is the father of the young woman who was murdered. I was called by a corrections officer to visit him and see if I could convince him to end a hunger strike. The good news is that he is eating again, and since then I have developed a relationship with his teenage son. It started when I saved his life on Gunston Cove—his powerboat caught on fire and I was able to pluck him off before it exploded. So anyway, I have stayed in touch with him and we both hope that the killer of his sister will be arrested soon, so that his father will be released. Although this visit with Muhammad has not led to an adult baptism for my data sheet, I think it fits the category of visiting people in prison and maybe even encountering Jesus."

The bishop sat quietly for a few seconds, then picked up a pen, tapped it on her desk, and signed his packet. "Good work, Harley," she said with a smile. "I think I did the right thing by sending you to Occoquan."

✳

Returning home, Harley replayed the meeting in his mind and thought about his description of the visit to Muhammad. He hadn't told the bishop everything but had given her a fairly accurate account of his involvement with Muhammad and Omar. No doubt she wanted him to focus on his little Methodist flock, but given the chaos in the Occoquan community she had to see that it was appropriate for him to step in as he did. He wondered if she was being sincere when she told him "good work" at the end, and at the same time he thought it was entirely predictable that she would take credit for the decision to send him into that community. If he turned out to be a hero, she would be the first to brag about putting him there. If he turned out to be a disaster, she could go on record saying that he was a troubled pastor who was sent there to heal from a personal trauma and quickly stuck his nose where it didn't belong. The bishop was in a position of complete deniability when it came to Harley's involvement with the Muslims, given the fact that she had done no more than sign a form that contained information about worship attendance, church budget, one baptism and a handful of visits. *She's good at her job*, he admitted.

Glancing out of his car window, he saw dark clouds approaching; another summer thunderstorm was on its way. Powerful gusts came in from the west, sending newspapers and other litter across the travel lanes. Rain fell in waves of such volume that the Passat's windshield wipers couldn't clear it, even at the highest setting. Motorcyclists huddled under overpasses to wait out the storm, and a number of motorists pulled over to the side of the road and put on their emergency flashers. Harley motored at just a few miles an hour, plowing through standing water and trying to stay in line with the taillights in front of him.

And then it was over. The rain stopped and the wind ceased. Shafts of bright sunshine broke through the clouds, causing steam to rise off the wet pavement, and Harley half expected to hear a chorus of angels. The traffic quickly returned to normal speed, although the danger of standing water remained, and a few people performed dangerous evasive maneuvers to dodge puddles at the edges of the highway. Harley marveled at how people seemed to resent any disruptions of their anticipated travel plans, driving with reckless speed to regain any time they felt they had lost because of a storm or a traffic jam. He, on the other hand, had learned to modify his expectations of travel, and to anticipate that there would be disruptions of almost any trip around the Washington area. Clear roads were an anomaly, and he had come to see a smooth and uneventful trip as a gift rather than a right.

Rolling down I-95 toward the Occoquan exit, Harley realized that expectations always caused suffering, whether someone expected to have clear travel lanes or a long and happy life.

Pulling into the parking lot of the Riverside Church, Harley thought that the town looked shiny and new, as though it had been scrubbed clean by the passing thunderstorm, with sunlight sparkling in the puddles in the streets and in the water on the rooftops. He waved to Doris King and Eleanor Buttress, who were across Washington Street in front of the Yarn Shop, picking up a sandwich-board sign that had been blown over by the storm. Harley had been trying to be friendly to them in recent weeks, but the truth was that he was still intimidated by pit bull Doris. He entered his office, checked his messages, and wandered into the sanctuary to straighten things up from Sunday worship. Then he spent a couple of quiet hours at his desk, answering email and planning his work for the week.

The Washington Nationals had a game that night, so Harley ate dinner in front of the television. The Nats and the Braves were tied up in the eighth inning when Harley's doorbell rang. Hating the interruption, he trudged to the door and opened it to see an intense Omar Bayati, standing on the porch in the twilight.

"I need to talk to you," the young man said.

"Come in," said Harley, motioning him to a seat at the kitchen table. The baseball game became distant background noise. "Want anything to drink?"

"No," Omar replied, fidgeting nervously. He swallowed hard and said, "I want you to give me the camera."

Harley didn't reply immediately, but tried to figure out what might be driving this change of plan. After a few seconds, he said, "This is not what we discussed before."

"Things are different now."

"What do you mean?"

"Just different. I really need the camera."

"Omar, this is not what we discussed. We agreed that as soon as Norah's killer was caught and your father was released, we would go to the police. We would turn over the camera and explain the situation."

"But they don't want to catch her killer. They want to pin the killing on my father."

"You don't know that for sure."

"Just give me the camera," Omar insisted. "It belongs to me." He looked around the room, hoping that the camera was sitting in plain sight.

"No, I won't do it. If you give it to the Woodbridge guys, they will use it to kill a lot of people, maybe even your family."

Omar sat for a second, processing Harley's words, and then hissed, "Give me the camera or I will report to the police that you touched me in the park."

Harley felt stung by Omar's words, but he wasn't really surprised. The young man was revealing his desperation.

"Go ahead," Harley responded. "Give it your best shot."

Omar swallowed hard and said, "They are threatening me and my family. If I don't give them the camera, they will go after Sarah and my mother. Worse than what they did before."

Harley sensed that he had an opening, a chance to get Omar back on his side. An image of Youssef and Sofia Ayad popped into his mind, and he heard them saying a single word, "Hospitality." In a bolt of inspiration, he got an idea. "How about if you disappear?"

"What?" asked Omar.

"You disappear. If the Woodbridge guys don't know where you are, they cannot pressure you or threaten your family. Their threats only work if you are around to receive them."

"But how can I disappear?"

"You can live here," Harley offered. "In my guest suite on the top floor. No one will know that you are here. You can hide until your father gets out of jail."

"For how long?"

"As long as it takes. You go gather some clothes, and I'll tell your family that you are going away for a while, for your safety and theirs."

CHAPTER 19

A strong wind began to blow across the Potomac River as the three men fished for catfish in the deep water near the Maryland side. Dirk looked up at the sky and said that the weather was turning and they better head home. Matt gathered up their fishing gear, stowed it away, and moved toward the bow to pull up the anchor. Harley put the key in the ignition and pressed the button to run the blower motor. He heard nothing and pressed it again. Still nothing. Feeling a wave of panic, he asked the more experienced boaters what might be wrong. Dirk opened the engine compartment, poked around for a few seconds, and turned a switch from battery one to battery two. He asked Harley to try again. Still dead. By now, the boat was being battered by the waves and the wind was against them, pushing them toward the Maryland shore. The anchor line was stretched tight, with the anchor just barely maintaining its hold on the sandy river bottom.

Angry clouds rolled in from the west, carried by the fierce wind. The sun was swallowed up and the day turned to night as sheets of rain assaulted them. Matt and Dirk grabbed their raincoats and put up their hoods, but Harley was unprepared and quickly became soaked to the skin. Lightning flashed on the horizon, followed by a crash of thunder. The three of them huddled in the cabin of the boat, hoping that they could ride out the storm and avoid a lightning strike.

Then, out of the darkness, someone came walking toward them on the river.

"Who is that?" asked Dirk. Matt grabbed the boat's spotlight, but its beam couldn't pierce the driving rain. Harley moved toward the bow and squinted. Lightning flashed behind the figure and thunder boomed, explosions louder than the roar of the rain on the water. But then, cutting through the pandemonium, came a voice, "Harley, it is I; do not be afraid."

Harley turned to his companions and shouted, "Did you hear that?" They shook their heads. He looked back toward the figure, who was approaching them but still a good twenty yards away. Harley heard the voice again, and this time it said, "Come."

Harley swung his legs over the bow and put his feet into the churning water. Dirk shouted for him to stop and Matt lunged to grab him, missing him by a foot. Harley was already moving away from the boat, walking on the water. But then, when a gust of strong wind whipped around him, he became frightened and began to sink. Reaching toward the figure, he called out, "Lord, save me!"

❀

Harley awoke with a start, wet with perspiration. His bedroom was as black as the storm on the river, but the air around him was air-conditioned and perfectly calm. His heart settled as he realized that he had been dreaming, but still he felt a sense of dread. No, he was not facing a lightning strike on the river, but he was sleeping one floor below a Muslim teenager who was supporting a plot to unleash a biological weapon. He had invited a potential terrorist to take up residence in his house, a young man who had threatened to accuse him of sexual molestation. *What was I thinking? What am I doing?* He envisioned Dirk shouting for him to stop, and Matt reaching out to grab him.

Staring at the ceiling of his bedroom, Harley thought about the danger he was in. *What if Omar decides to sneak into my bedroom and smother me? Or slit my throat?* Harley listened carefully for footsteps above him but heard nothing. Still, he realized that it would not be difficult for the young man to kill him in his sleep and then recover his camera from the trunk of Harley's car. The terrorist plot would continue and Harley's death would be reported in a small article in the Metro section of *The Washington Post*. Occoquan would gain a reputation as the murder capital of Prince William County, with two unsolved cases in a single summer. He gazed at the ceiling for a few more minutes, knowing that he was not helping himself by going to such dark places in his mind. But then, just to be safe, he got out of bed and locked his bedroom door.

It was five in the morning and Harley sat on the edge of the bed and touched his toes to the floor, thinking about how he had put his feet into the water at the end of his dream. *What would Youssef, the interpreter of dreams, think of my most recent nighttime vision?* The voice in the storm had been so clear when it said, "Do not be afraid."

In time, the first shaft of morning light came through his bedroom window and Harley decided to dress for the day. After showering and putting on his clothes, he went downstairs and made coffee, and a few minutes later he heard footsteps on the staircase. Omar came down in a T-shirt and basketball shorts, looking more uncomfortable than dangerous. Harley gave him some coffee and offered him a bowl of cereal and a banana. The two of them ate breakfast together, beginning to get a feel for what it might be like for them to live together for a while.

"I'm happy to keep you fed and sheltered," offered Harley, "but you are going to have to promise to keep yourself hidden."

"I don't want to see anybody, believe me."

"Just keep the blinds pulled down in the guest suite. I'll keep them down in the rest of the house. You can turn the bed back into a couch, and use the television in the suite. You've got a full bath, of course. I'll put some food and drinks in the wet bar refrigerator so that you can make yourself some lunch. You can text me if you need anything during the day."

"So, how long do you think I'll be here?"

"Hard to say," said Harley, sipping his coffee. "The best case is that your father gets out of jail soon. I can contact the guy at the newspaper, Henry Kim, and see if he can do a follow-up story on your dad."

"But what about the Woodbridge guys?"

"The key there is to stay completely off the grid. Don't be in touch with anyone by email, text, or social media. Just drop completely out of sight. If they cannot find you, they cannot hurt you. And I don't think they'll mess with your family if you are out of contact with them. Not even your mother knows where you are."

"What did you tell her?"

"Just that you are safe. I told her that it is better that she does not know."

"But what if I need to reach her?"

"You can send a message through me."

Omar twirled his spoon in his cereal bowl as he considered Harley's words. He wasn't happy with the plan, but he couldn't think of anything better.

"I just want my father to be released," he said. "But I'm not trusting the system to do the right thing."

"Give it time," said Harley. "The wheels of justice turn slowly."

"Whatever," Omar replied with a sigh.

"Just keep yourself safe and out of sight," Harley recommended. "And as hard as it will be for you, stay off of the internet."

After Omar trudged back upstairs, Harley loaded the dishwasher, grabbed his briefcase, and walked to the church. He scanned the street up and down, looking for anyone who might seem out of place. Everything seemed normal with commuters driving slowly down the street and shopkeepers sweeping the sidewalks in front of their businesses. Youssef Ayad stuck his head out the door as Harley passed the Gold Emporium, and gave him a hearty greeting. The two chatted for a moment and Harley admitted that he had thought of Youssef in the middle of the night, after he awoke from his vivid dream.

"I'll have to get together with you for some interpretation," he said as he broke away and crossed the street.

Entering his office, he saw the light flashing on his answering machine and pressed the button to receive his message.

"Reverend Camden, this is Jefferson Jones. I'd like to have fifteen minutes of your time today, if you can make yourself available." Harley was thrown a little off balance by the request but jotted down the number and immediately returned the call. Jefferson answered his cell phone on the second ring and they arranged to get together at eleven o'clock.

Tuesday mornings were a good time to prepare the Sunday bulletin, so Harley jumped into that task, figuring that it would prevent him from worrying excessively about what Jefferson Jones might be up to. He pulled a hymnal off his bookshelf and picked three hymns for the Sunday service, then booted up his computer and wrote the prayers that would be included in the order of worship. His work was interrupted once by a call from a church member asking Harley to visit her elderly mother in the hospital, but aside from that request he was able to focus on the Sunday bulletin until a knock came at his door.

"Mr. Jones," said Harley to the impeccably-dressed man at the door, "please come in." Although it was a hot July day, Jefferson Jones wore a blue linen suit with a red silk handkerchief in the breast pocket, one that matched his tie.

"Thank you for seeing me, Reverend Camden, especially on such short notice."

"My pleasure. And please call me Harley." He motioned Jefferson to take a seat in a wooden armchair in front of his desk, which the visitor did after taking a few seconds to look around the pastor's office. Harley sat in a similar chair a few feet away from him, feeling terribly underdressed in his short sleeve shirt and casual tie.

"I haven't been in here in years," Jefferson said wistfully.

Tawnya must have gotten her beauty from her mother, thought Harley. Her dad was meticulously groomed, but brutishly unattractive.

"You know my uncle was the pastor of this church, don't you?"

"Yes, I've heard good things about him."

"He was quite a preacher." Then, smiling slightly, he added, "And a rabble-rouser."

"Quite active in the civil rights movement, I understand."

"Yes, indeed. There is a long history of activism here in Occoquan, and my uncle embraced that tradition fully. Did you know that the Underground Railroad ran through here?"

"No, I didn't."

"It's true. A history I am proud of, as a Republican here in Prince William County. There was a cell of abolitionists here in Occoquan, staunch supporters of Abraham Lincoln. They had a warehouse along the river, and it contained a secret storage room that was one of the stations. You know that terminology, don't you?"

"A station was . . . what? A safe house?"

"Exactly. Railroad terminology was used throughout the network. Conductors would move people from station to station as they worked their way from slavery to freedom. From Occoquan, slaves would be put on boats in the middle of the night and taken across the river to the next station in Maryland."

"I had heard about the Republicans in Occoquan, but not the Underground Railroad."

"It has not made it onto the historical markers," Jefferson said. "Maybe because some people still sing Dixie here in Virginia, and the Underground Railroad was a truly subversive organization. But I love to talk about it, because it was dedicated to freedom. The warehouse by the river, if I'm not mistaken, was situated exactly where your house now stands."

Harley couldn't believe it. *The Underground Railroad passed straight through my home? What are the chances that I would learn this at the exact time I've created a safe house for Omar?* He felt the same sense of flow that he had experienced with the Ayads.

"But I'm not here today to talk about Occoquan history," continued Jefferson. "I am concerned that Fatima Bayati does not have the financial resources she needs to mount a robust defense of her husband. I am aware that you visited Muhammad in jail."

"Yes, I did," responded Harley. "Just once, but I had a positive impression of the man."

"Everyone deserves a fair trial," said Jefferson. "Originally, I thought that the Bayatis might be interested in selling their building to me, as part of my plans to redevelop their section of Mill Street." Harley had seen Jefferson and Abdul in the bakery, although he had no idea who they were at the time. "But since then, I have had a number of discussions with my partner, Abdul. We believe the time is right to help create a defense fund for Muhammad."

Harley was impressed. "That is very generous of you, Jefferson."

"This community is important to me. The town and its people." He leaned back in his chair. "But here is the problem. I do not think that Fatima would accept a gift from us. She would think that there were strings attached." He broke into a sly smile and said, "I have a reputation around here."

Yes, you do, thought Harley. "So how can I be of help?"

"My daughter likes you and trusts you," said Jefferson, "and I trust her judgment. I am guessing that you have developed at least the beginning of a relationship with Fatima. In addition, I am guessing that you have some kind of a pastor's discretionary fund here at the church."

"Yes, I do." Last time Harley checked, it had about two hundred dollars in it.

"What I would like to do is this: Write your church a check for ten thousand. Have your treasurer deposit it, and then write Fatima a check for the full amount. You can tell her that it came from an anonymous supporter. Do you see any problem with that?"

Harley thought for a moment about how the church treasurer would respond. She was a CPA in her early fifties and very much by the book. This would be an extraordinary transaction, for sure, but not out of line with the intent of the discretionary fund. When Harley first arrived, the treasurer had told him that members made special donations to the fund to help neighbors in need, and that the pastor had complete control over how the funds were spent, as long as they were used to help the needy. "In other words," she had said with uncharacteristic levity, "you cannot use them to buy yourself a boat."

After reflection, Harley responded to Jefferson. "No, that should work just fine."

The businessman reached into the pocket of his linen jacket and pulled out a checkbook and a fountain pen. *So old-school*, Harley thought. As he wrote the check, Jefferson said, "I want to be clear that this fund is being established by Abdul as well as myself. He may not seem to be a sensitive man, and to be sure he has great value in exuding toughness in our business ventures. But he feels the difficulties of the Bayatis very keenly, and his own early experience with the justice system taught him the importance of quality representation. He shares my commitment to this endeavor."

As Jefferson signed the check, he said, "Ten thousand dollars might not go very far in the world of murder defense, but perhaps it will be a catalyst for other giving."

"This will be a tremendous help," Harley said, holding the check. "What role does Abdul's faith play in this?"

"I hesitate to speak for him," said Jefferson, "but I am sure he is motivated by his Muslim faith. His early years were terribly chaotic, and the Christian church that he grew up in was not a help to him or to the men in his life. That knowledge pains me, because this church, Emanuel Baptist, was always very good for me." He rubbed his fingers along the edge of the old oak desk that was at the center of the office. "This desk was my uncle's. Did you know that?"

"No. I had no idea."

"They didn't move it when the congregation went to its new, modern venue," Jefferson said with a hint of sarcasm. Continuing to caress the desk, he said, "The current pastor of Emanuel has a modern glass and steel desk, which fits the new location, I suppose. But this will always be the pastor's desk to me."

"I like it," Harley said. "Makes me think of Jesus, the carpenter's son."

"Good point," said Jefferson. "My uncle worked as a carpenter's helper when he was a young man. He used to say that he found the work so challenging that he knew why Jesus left his father's shop and entered the ministry." He smiled. "Anyway, back to Abdul. He had already converted to Islam when I met him. It is kind of surprising that we met at all, since I was visiting the jail as part of a ministry group from Emanuel. I was teaching a personal finance class, and he quickly emerged as my star student. We stayed in touch, and I hired him as soon as he was released."

"What was he in for?" asked Harley.

"I'd rather not say," Jefferson replied. "That is information that only he should share. But I want you to know that he is one of the most righteous men I know. His faith is important to him, and he walks the walk."

"That's good enough for me," said Harley. "Please tell him that I will honor his intentions for the gift."

Jefferson stood up and said, "Thank you for your time and for your help." The two men shook hands and Harley showed him to the door. As Jefferson walked across the parking lot to his Mercedes, he turned, looked back, and said, "Take care of this old church building, Pastor."

That afternoon, Harley called the church treasurer and told her about the check. She promised to pick it up after work, deposit it, and then write a check for the same amount to Fatima Bayati. She predicted that it would take a few days for Jefferson's check to clear, but she should be able to have Fatima's check by the end of the week. Harley said that a few days should be no problem, especially since it would come as a surprise.

✺

Not wanting to take the time to shop for groceries, Harley ordered a pizza to be delivered to his house for dinner. Walking home at six o'clock, he met the delivery man at the door, tipped him, and then entered. For a moment he wondered if Omar would even be there. Feeling a wave of panic, he imagined the kid getting second thoughts about the safe house and running off to live with the Woodbridge guys. If that happened, Harley would have no way to find him, and no way to slow their plot. *What if Omar bought a new camera, rented a boat, and resumed his cooperation with the terrorists?* If he left the house, Harley would lose control of him completely, and would have no real evidence to show the authorities. Pictures of the Fort Belvoir shoreline, disconnected from Omar Bayati, would be evidence of nothing.

"Omar?" he called out after closing the front door. He heard some footsteps, and a wave of relief came over him. The young man plodded down the stairs, looking more bored than anything. "I got us a pizza for dinner."

"Cool," said Omar as they sat down at the kitchen table, behind drawn shades.

Harley put two plates on the table and pulled a couple of soft drinks out of the refrigerator. "I got vegetarian because I don't know what kind of meat you eat."

"I don't eat pork, but beef is okay. In my family, we are not strict about the beef being halal."

As they ate, Harley told Omar about the Underground Railroad running through Occoquan, with a station being right underneath them. He talked about the bravery of the conductors who helped slaves to escape, and described the situations in which he thought it was right to commit acts of civil disobedience. Omar gnawed on his pizza and sipped his drink, paying attention but looking fairly unimpressed. Then Harley told him that a defense fund was being established for his father, based on a gift from two anonymous donors. Omar stopped eating when he heard that news. He became animated, and it appeared to Harley that there was hope in his eyes. Omar asked about how the money would get to his family, and how it might be used. For the first time in weeks, he had reason to believe that his father might actually get out of jail.

On the strength of that gift, Harley and Omar lived peacefully in the safe house for the next eleven days. And then Harley received a visit at church from the one man Omar truly despised.

CHAPTER 20

"I've never been very close to my father," said Matt Carter as he sat with Harley in his office at Riverside Methodist Church. The August Saturday was a steam bath, and the window air conditioner was roaring. Matt wore a dark-blue FBI T-shirt and black shorts. Harley was not quite as casual, since he was on duty that day—a golf shirt and long khaki pants. They sat facing each other in a pair of armchairs, their knees almost touching.

"He and my mom divorced when I was three, so I saw him mainly on weekends as I was growing up. They had a bitter breakup, caused largely by one of my dad's affairs. My earliest memories are of the two of them bickering with each other as they would hand me off on Saturday mornings and Sunday afternoons. In fact, some of the transitions happened right here, at this church. It was designated a safe and neutral space. I remember a white-haired African-American man sitting in the social hall, reading a book and giving people a stern look if they started getting worked up."

Harley had only seen the stoic side of this square-jawed FBI agent. "Glad this place was a sanctuary for you, during such a rocky time."

"Anyway, my dad did his best—coaching my Little League team, taking me fishing, and showing me how to use tools and fix a flat on my bike. But my mother complained about him constantly, so I always had a very negative view. Never really trusted him, based on what my mother told me. But once I was in my twenties and the FBI sent me to Quantico, we started meeting in Lake Ridge for dinners once a week. We got to know each other as adults, and I heard his stories about Vietnam and his difficulties in the Marines, especially near the end of his career. You might know that the pipeline for advancement gets more and more narrow as an officer gets older, and I think he was told to retire before he was ready. That left a bitter taste in his mouth. His stories made me feel a compassion for him that I had never felt before."

Still waters run deep. That's what Dirk had said when he introduced Matt, and now the minister understood what he was talking about. "Getting to know our parents as adults can help us to forgive them," said Harley, who wished that his own father had lived long enough for him to reach that point.

Matt nodded. "Since things between us had improved over the last few years, I felt I could talk with him about a tough work situation. I couldn't discuss it with anyone at the Bureau, and I figured he might give me some guidance. We met at his house in early June. I told him about a woman I was attracted to, someone I saw every day. I didn't give her name, but I described her—long black hair, olive skin, really beautiful. Said that we had gotten together once, in the evening, but I immediately regretted it. Told my dad that it would be a disaster, professionally, if I got involved with her."

"How did your father respond?" Harley tried to picture the woman and found himself imagining the gorgeous Norah Bayati.

"He was actually pretty good," said Matt, smiling. "Since he cheated on my mom a few times, I guess he is an expert in inappropriate relationships. He advised me to get a transfer to another case, and I said I had thought of that, but didn't really want to. I told him that I was on the Bayati investigation, which was an unusual assignment— the Bureau usually keeps agents away from communities where they have friends and relatives. Told him we had been given some solid information on the Bayati boy and a terrorist cell, and the case was one that would be good for my career. He asked me if I could arrange my work in such a way that I didn't have to see the woman, and I said no, not really. He admitted that such attractions can be powerful, and he had succumbed to a few himself. But looking back he wished that he had done more to keep from crossing certain lines."

Harley asked how Matt felt about his father's counsel, and he acknowledged that his dad was right to say what he did. He said that he didn't really expect his father to have a quick fix for him, but he was glad that they could talk about it. Matt told Harley that his father had gone on to divulge some of the mistakes he had made, and some of the lines he had crossed, including the affair that had dealt a death blow to his marriage. The conversation opened a door for Matt, helping him to see Dirk as a flesh-and-blood human being for the very first time, not a stereotype of a military man or divorced dad. Dirk had admitted that he was still ashamed of that last affair, in particular, because it had been with the wife of a fellow Marine. Sounding defeated, he confessed that his self-indulgence had cost him his marriage, the friendship of a good man, and the respect of a number of fellow Marines. Matt told Harley that he had never heard his father sound so broken and full of regret.

"Oddly enough, I left the conversation feeling better," said Matt. "I realized that I wasn't facing the situation alone. Once back at work, I did my best to keep boundaries in place. One week was especially tough, because we were doing surveillance here in Occoquan. Long hours very close together. At that point, I figured that the best way out was to get a transfer, even if it hurt my career. Our stakeout ended on a Sunday, and then Tuesday was the killing."

What's Matt saying? He sounds so matter-of-fact. Is he confessing to the killing? If so, he's a complete psychopath, totally cold-blooded.

Matt said he went ahead with the transfer, then called his father to tell him. "I think that was the day you two met, and were having lunch at the American Legion."

"I remember that," said Harley, still trying to figure out the connection between Matt and Norah. "Your dad took your call and bolted."

"His reaction really surprised me," Matt said. "When we got together that Sunday, he seemed agitated. Asked me why I would leave a case that was so good for my career. I reminded him that he had suggested that I pursue a transfer, but he didn't want to hear it. He just kept shaking his head and saying that I was sabotaging my career. I was looking for his approval, but he left me feeling that I had made a huge mistake. We ended up yelling at each other and not talking for almost a week. The next time I saw him is when we took you out on his boat."

"Yes, I sensed that you two were at odds," Harley said.

"We stayed away from the subject for quite a while," Matt continued. "Then, the day before yesterday, things got really weird. I called him after dinner, just to check in on him. Told him that the new assignment was going well, and I had been down at FBI Headquarters that day for a meeting. Said that I ran into the woman that I had been so attracted to on the Bayati case. He didn't respond, and it sounded to me like he was trying to catch his breath. Gasping, almost. Then he barked the words, 'What are you talking about?' I said, 'You know, the black-haired beauty. The one I was obsessed with.' He said, 'That can't be.' And I said, 'Of course it can. She was my partner on the Bayati case, the one I went out with one time, even though I knew it wasn't right. I couldn't stop thinking about her and wanting to be with her.' Next thing I know, he hangs up on me. I try to call him back, but he doesn't answer. It's been two days now, and I haven't heard a thing from him."

After a few moments of silence Harley asked, "Why do you think your dad reacted the way he did?"

Matt shrugged. "I have no idea. Once again, I thought he'd be proud of me. I had drawn a line and stuck to it. I wanted to let him know that I was okay with seeing her at headquarters, that my feelings were not nearly as intense as they had been. But I never got that far—he hung up before I could tell him."

Harley was as mystified as Matt but didn't want to waste time speculating. Trying to be practical, he asked, "What is it that I can do for you?"

"Well, if you see my dad, tell him that I want to talk. And, of course, if he wants to talk with you, that's fine with me."

"Can I share anything that we have discussed today?"

"Sure," said Matt. "Just about everything I've told you has come out of conversations with him. So go ahead, say what you want. I just hope he's okay."

"Thanks, Matt. I appreciate it."

"No, thank you," said Matt, reaching out his hand for a shake. "This has been good. I feel better having gotten this off my chest."

After Matt headed out the door, Harley picked up his phone and placed a call to Dirk. He got no answer, so he left a message asking for a call. Then he sat at his desk and continued to work on his Sunday sermon. He was preaching on a passage from Paul's letter to the Romans: "I do not understand my own actions. For I do not do what I want, but I do the very thing I hate." He leaned back in his chair and looked out his office window, gazing over the parking lot and toward the river, hoping that the flowing water would take all the crap away. The line "O sinners, let's go down, let's go down, come on down" popped into his mind, a line from the song he had mentioned to Sofia and Youssef—"Down in the River to Pray." Harley thought about how hard it was for people to do what they wanted, and how often they ended up doing the things they hated. Dirk wanted to support his son by giving him good advice, but then reacted in ways that drove Matt away. Harley ached for Leah to be a close friend and confidante, but lashed out at her with anger and frustration. Terrorists said they wanted to do the will of God but broke the most foundational laws of their faith with the hope of a heavenly reward.

Harley returned his eyes to the Bible, which said, "But in fact it is no longer I that do it, but sin that dwells within me." *What an odd phrase.* According to Paul, sin was like an alien force that took control of people's wills and directed their actions, a power that corrupted even their best efforts and intentions. He read it again: "Sin that dwells within me." *What a tough concept for the twenty-first century*, thought Harley. *So old-fashioned. Who talks about sin anymore?* And yet, people today knew very well what it felt like to be addicted to alcohol or drugs or social media or pornography. And they knew the deep and lasting scars that were left by childhood neglect or sexual abuse. Whatever dwelled within them—whatever tempted them or tormented them—it was a force that must be acknowledged and addressed and eventually overcome. "I can will what is right, but I cannot do it," wrote Paul in a line that seemed to Harley to be both perceptive and terribly pessimistic. "For I do not do the good I want, but the evil I do not want is what I do."

So, how can this alien force be overcome? How can such deep brokenness be healed?

Harley had to think of something if he was going to preach a decent sermon. He got up and walked around his office, running his fingers along the spines of the books on his shelves. These were the toughest of questions. The problem with sin was that it lived not only inside of people, but also all around them. Dirk struggled with Matt because of his experiences in Vietnam, his failed marriage, and the unsatisfying end to his military career. Harley was frustrated with Leah because of his unresolved issues with Karen, his grief over her death, his anger at the terrorists that killed her, and his own unrealistic expectations of the people around him. Terrorists killed innocent people because they were manipulated by bad preachers, or because they grew up in awful circumstances and blamed foreign powers for their desperate situations. There was no easy solution to sin, no quick fix for the deep brokenness in humanity and in the world. *Or was there?*

Paul certainly thought so. Harley returned to his desk and looked down on the Bible. "Who will rescue me from this body of death?" asked Paul. "Thanks be to God through Jesus Christ our Lord!" The words "rescue me" seemed to be important here, and it occurred to Harley that God had sent Jesus to earth on a rescue mission. His objective was to save people from an alien force that had taken control of their bodies. Suddenly, Paul's letter to the Romans seemed more like the plot of a summer science fiction movie than a passage of holy scripture. Body of death. Rescue mission. Liberation from the alien invader! The wheels turned in Harley's head as he started to think about how to present a message to the congregation.

He tapped on his laptop for an hour, crafting an imaginative sermon that turned Paul's letter into a blockbuster sci-fi adventure. Following the preaching style of Jesus, Harley tried to communicate through parables—stories from everyday life that contained spiritual truths. He liked to hook people with an illustration that grabbed their interest and got them wondering about where he was going with his message, and then end the sermon by pulling practical lessons from the interplay between his story and the Biblical text.

Writing was a pleasure for Harley, an activity that allowed him to escape from the administrative hassles of ministry and create something that had real value for his congregation. He felt good about the approach he was taking, and quickly he had a few pages of text that would help people to understand sin's hold on them in a whole new way. But then he got to the point where he needed to offer a real-world application of his insight, and there he got stuck. *How do I turn the corner from science fiction to daily life, explaining how God really frees us to live a sin-free life?* This was the toughest part of the sermon, comparable to the challenges that a pilot faced when trying to make a difficult landing. After all, flying was easy—it was the landing that was tough. After a few minutes of staring at his computer screen, Harley decided that he needed a coffee.

❋

The day had become only hotter since Harley entered his air-conditioned office, and as he stepped outside he wondered if coffee was the best idea. *Maybe iced coffee*, he thought. He walked up the hill to Auntie's, climbed its creaky wooden stairs, entered the pie shop and ordered his drink. He looked around, wishing he could enjoy it in the cool of the shop, but unfortunately there was no indoor seating. The place was jammed with baked goods and craft beers and wine, with not a single stool or chair. Taking his iced coffee onto the porch, he found a seat on one of the benches running along the front of the building, and as he sat down he saw Tawnya Jones coming up the steps.

"Tawnya," he called out. "How are you doing on this fine Saturday?"

"Reverend Camden," she said with mocking formality. "Look at you, enjoying a cool drink on a hot day." She looked fantastic, as usual. Although in exercise clothes, she was totally made up with nails done and not a hair out of place. "I'm here to get a pie, but it is a sweet treat to see you."

"Please join me," Harley said, motioning to a spot on the bench next to him.

"People will talk," she said with a toothy grin. "But I suppose it's okay, in a public place."

Harley was happy to see her, at least in part because he was working on his sermon and he needed a sounding board. When she sat down, he mentioned that he had been getting to know her father, and she said yes, she had been told all about that. Then he asked how Clyde was doing.

"He is fine. Cutting the grass, although I asked him not to do it in the heat of the day."

"Sounds like he's a man on a mission."

"He is," she admitted. "When he gets a task in his head, he has to conquer it, no matter what."

"I used to be that way, when I had the house up in Sterling. But I have to say, I don't miss it. Living in a townhouse with no yard suits me just fine."

"More time for your boat, right?"

"Absolutely."

"So what are you up to today," asked Tawnya, "besides drinking coffee?"

"Writing my Sunday sermon," he said, taking a sip of his drink. "I'm wrestling with Paul's letter to the Romans."

"The one who is righteous will live by faith?"

"You know your Romans," said Harley, offering his hand for a high five. He liked to talk with Baptists because—unlike more liberal Protestants—they knew their Bibles. "But no, the seventh chapter, all the stuff about sin and doing the things that we hate."

"That is a tough passage," Tawnya admitted. "Tough but true."

Giving him a smile, she said, "You don't go easy on your congregation in the summer, do you?"

Harley shook his head. "No, they need it. They are a sinful bunch. Very wicked people." She laughed and told him to be nice.

"I get what Paul is saying about sin being a controlling force, like an addiction or an obsession," Harley said. "Paul understands human nature, for sure. But how does Jesus actually come in and free us? What does Paul mean when he says, 'Thanks be to God through Jesus Christ our Lord!'"

Tawnya thought for a second. "I guess it has to do with the sacrifice of Jesus on the cross, taking our sins on himself, dying so that we can be forgiven."

Harley nodded. "Yes, I get that, and I believe it. Forgiveness is possible because of the cross. But that doesn't seem to be the same as being freed from sin. After all, we can sin, be forgiven, and then sin again."

"True that," said Tawnya. "Forgiveness is not the same as freedom from sin."

"I'm really struggling with this, because I need my sermon to end with a strong message. I want to be clear about how God frees us."

Tawnya looked out over the parking lot at Riverside Methodist. "I remember that I asked my grandfather about sin after church one Sunday. He showed me a vase that had been in the family for generations, one that he had broken accidentally and then repaired. He said that when we sin, we shatter our relationships with God and each other. Then Jesus comes along and glues us back together through forgiveness. I thought about this for a minute, looked closely at the vase, and then said, 'But Grandpa, I can still see the breaks.'"

"That's it," said Harley. "That's the key question. How do we fix the cracks?"

"I think that comes from the Spirit," Tawnya offered. "Do you have your Bible with you, Pastor?" Harley shook his head. "Well then, give me your phone." She quickly pulled up an internet Bible, and typed in *Romans 8*.

"You know your Bible, Ms. Jones."

"Comes from being in church every Sunday," she said. "Here it is; 'But you are not in the flesh; you are in the Spirit, since the Spirit of God dwells in you.' That's in the chapter right after the one you are preaching on."

"So Jesus rescues us from sin," said Harley, thinking aloud. "And then the Spirit lives in us. The Spirit heals the wounds."

"That's how I understand it," Tawnya agreed, handing Harley's phone back to him. "Paul talks somewhere else about 'the new life of the Spirit.'"

"We Methodists are probably not as tuned into the Spirit as we should be," admitted Harley. "The Spirit is wild and unpredictable, and that makes us uncomfortable. Reminds us of faith-healing and speaking in tongues."

"But that's not all the Spirit does," said Tawnya.

"You're right," said Harley. "I have felt the Spirit. It has calmed me and guided me."

"Amen to that."

"I also believe that the Spirit pulls us together, all of us, and makes us the Body of Christ in the world."

"Sounds like a healing power to me," Tawnya said. "Christ forgives us and the Spirit unites us. And I like what you are saying about the Spirit being active in the community, the church, the Body of Christ."

Suddenly, it hit Harley that he had been fighting too many battles alone. Over the past year, whether he was calling for global justice or nursing his own personal wounds, he acted in isolation. He was a lone voice in the wilderness, a bitter man holding on to his resentments. But these efforts usually ended in frustration and loneliness, because they ignored the presence of something much bigger than himself.

Harley had always believed that God worked most powerfully through communities, but he had been neglecting this truth since the deaths of Jessica and Karen. His pain simply wouldn't allow it. Now, he felt a sudden sense of relief that he didn't have to be alone in his grief and anger and frustration, because the Spirit was with him, really with him. That same Spirit was with Dirk and Matt and Tawnya as well, stirring in them all, offering comfort and healing and help, if only they would let it work through them. Feeling another moment of flow, Harley realized that he needed to switch boats. Instead of doing the exhausting work of rowing all by himself, it was time for him to jump into a sailboat and allow the wind of the Spirit to push him forward.

"Thanks, Tawnya," Harley said. "I think you've given me the end of my sermon."

"Happy to help," she said, giving his hand a squeeze. "Hope it's a good one. Now, I'd better get my pie and head home."

CHAPTER 21

*I*s *it a robber?* That was the first thought that came to Harley as he was pulled out of deep sleep by his doorbell. Pushing aside the curtain of the front door, he saw a young woman in a hijab standing in the early morning light—Sarah Bayati. With her round face and brown eyes, she was a mid-twenties version of her mother, Fatima. Harley invited her in. She apologized for waking him and said that they needed his help.

"About an hour ago, the front window of our bakery was smashed by a rock. We do not know who did it, or why. What should we do?"

"Please sit down," Harley said, pointing her to a seat at the kitchen table. "A rock, you say? A note or anything?"

Sarah shook her head. "No, just a rock. It woke us up, and really scared us. There is a large hole in the window and glass all over the lobby. My mother sent me here to get your advice. You have been so good to us, visiting my father, helping my brother, giving us the donation for the lawyer."

Harley thought immediately of the Woodbridge guys, who might be trying to intimidate the Bayatis or flush Omar out of hiding. But then he realized that there were many residents of the

area with strong anti-Muslim bias who might want to make the
Bayatis miserable.

"Have you called the police?"

"No, not yet," said Sarah. "We wanted to talk with you first.
Would the police be a good idea? After the attack at the farmer's
market, Omar said that we should not press charges."

Sitting back in his chair, Harley thought about the delicate
balance that had been struck between the Bayatis and the
Woodbridge guys, and what the involvement of the police might do
to this equilibrium. But then he remembered his sermon for the day,
and the point he wanted to make about the power of the Spirit in
community. He sensed that it was time to stop working in isolation,
and start reaching out to others.

"Yes, I think you should call the police. You don't know who did
it, so I think they should be allowed to investigate."

Sarah nodded. "Yes, I think you are right. I will recommend that
to my mother."

"Be sure you leave everything as it is," advised Harley. "Don't
touch the rock or the broken window. Let the police do their work."

"We already picked up the rock. We wanted to see what it was."

"Well, put it back where you found it. They will want to see the
whole crime scene."

Sarah thanked Harley and said that she should get back to her
mother. "We are grateful for all of your help, and my mother wants
to ask you to thank the anonymous donor. Their generosity made
our hearts feel very full."

Harley agreed to do so and showed Sarah to the door, secretly
glad that Omar had behaved like a typical teenager and slept through
the whole visit. Realizing that his own sleep was done for the night,
he made a pot of coffee and took a cup upstairs to drink while he
dressed.

As he put on his shirt and tie, he realized that his prepared sermon
would sound shallow and disconnected from reality after the attack
on the Bayati bakery. He decided to abandon his manuscript and
simply speak from his heart. The scripture lesson from Romans was

going to be a tough one to riff on, however, so he thought of another passage on the Spirit that would be easier for him to handle. "There are varieties of gifts, but the same Spirit," said the apostle Paul in his first letter to the Corinthians. "To each is given the manifestation of the Spirit for the common good." *That will challenge the congregation,* thought Harley, *especially in light of the events of the day.*

As Harley left his bedroom, he heard footsteps upstairs. Omar was awake and moving around, so Harley called him down for breakfast. The young man was shocked to hear about the rock attack, and immediately pushed aside the bagel that his host had made for him, wanting to jump into action. But Harley encouraged him to calm down and remain in hiding, saying that the attack might have been done to draw him out.

"The best reaction from you is no reaction," said the pastor. "Don't let anyone know you are still here in town."

"But I'm worried about my mother and sister!"

"They'll be fine. They are calling the police, so nothing bad is going to happen to them."

"Yeah, right," he replied, sarcastically. "The police are always on our side. But I guess you're right. I shouldn't go out. At least not yet."

After Harley said that he would have to leave for church, Omar picked up his bagel and took it to the guest suite upstairs. "If you see my mother," he called over his shoulder, "tell her I am okay."

❀

Standing before the congregation, which was surprisingly large for August, Harley read the scripture verse from First Corinthians and admitted that it was not the passage printed in the bulletin. "I changed my scripture and sermon because of what happened this morning at the Riverview Bakery. As some of you may have heard, our neighbors were attacked once again. The Bayatis had a rock thrown through their window." A murmur went through the congregation, and Harley saw looks of concern. As his eyes went to the back of the church, he was surprised to see Dirk sitting there looking completely drained of life. Harley couldn't tell if his expression was related to the news that had just been shared.

"I have chosen First Corinthians," he continued, "because we are a congregation with 'varieties of gifts.' Some of you are teachers, some are doctors, some are builders, some are analysts, some are caregivers, some are civil servants. There is virtually no challenge in our community that we cannot tackle and overcome, as a group. But I am afraid that we sometimes forget this, or at least I do. We try to face problems as individuals, forgetting that our skills and our strengths are seen most clearly in a united community. That is why the apostle Paul says that there are 'varieties of gifts, but the same Spirit.' Our many different gifts are connected to one united Spirit. I am convinced that we have not yet tapped into the power of this Spirit."

Harley sensed that he had their attention, with many starting to wonder where he was going. Talk of the power of the Spirit was not always welcome in Methodist churches, where people were not comfortable with worship that felt out of control.

"Here is the thing about the gifts of the Spirit," Harley continued. "Although we often think of speaking in tongues or faith-healing, the gifts of the Spirit are much broader. They include any skill or talent that advances Christ's work in the world, and they are given to everyone. Paul says, 'To each is given the manifestation of the Spirit for the common good.'" Harley saw a few nods in the congregation but also some confusion.

"Do you know what 'manifestation' means?" There were a few more nods, but also some blank looks. "I didn't," he admitted, "so I had to look it up this morning. Manifestation means 'an action or fact that clearly shows something.' Each of us is given a gift from God that clearly shows the reality of the Spirit to the world. It is through each of us that people can see the presence and the power of the Spirit. They see it in our teaching, our healing, our building, and our caregiving. They even see it in our civil service—I'm talking about you, Mary Ranger." The postmistress was surprised to be called out, but she smiled. "And here is the most important thing about these gifts: 'to each is given the manifestation of the Spirit for the common good.' Each and every one of these gifts support the common good. If they do not serve all of God's people, they are not true gifts of the Spirit."

Harley went on to say that charismatic leaders had gifts—in fact, the Greek word *charisma* was used in First Corinthians and it meant "gift." But there was a dark side to charismatic leaders, and it usually involved tunnel vision, isolation and arrogance. Such leaders felt that they were above the community and its standards, with freedom to pursue their own agendas, and they rarely pursued the common good. Harley talked about cult leaders who convinced their followers to commit suicide, and terrorists who inspired their underlings to engage in suicide bombings.

"I have felt the consequences of this dark charisma very personally. My wife and daughter were killed by a man who blew himself up in an act that would be considered abhorrent in the wider Muslim community. But because he was influenced by isolated extremists, he destroyed himself and my family."

The congregation sat still and riveted.

"Terrorism is a manifestation of evil," Harley concluded. "It is an act that clearly shows the reality of hatred in the world. I have seen it and felt it. I know it. But fortunately for us, there are gifts available to us that are manifestations of the Spirit, gifts that advance the common good. Two of our neighbors—a Christian and a Muslim—recently gave a monetary gift that will help with Muhammad Bayati's legal defense, a gift that will help him to get a fair trial here in Prince William County. If you want to contribute to this defense fund, I can help you to do that—just let me know. I have found that when we work together as one community, using the full variety of our gifts, we act in ways that show the reality of God's love to the world, a love that drives out darkness, a love that undermines hatred, a love that actually conquers evil."

Harley got an "amen" and a ripple of nervous laughter. Most were not accustomed to call-and-response preaching in their orderly suburban church.

"So here is what I challenge us to do today. After worship, let's walk as a group to the Riverview Bakery. Let's walk as one body, as the Body of Christ, as the physical presence of our Lord in the world today. Let's line up and support this business as a manifestation of the Spirit, as an act that shows the reality of our love."

Looking out over the congregation during the closing hymn, Harley could not see Dirk. He didn't want to lose a friend because of his call to action, but he felt strongly that he was being led by the Spirit of God, with the support of a large number of his church members. In fact, when he gathered with the congregation in the parking lot after the service, he was shocked by the number of people who were interested in walking to the Riverview Bakery. There had been close to a hundred people in worship, and Harley guessed that about seventy-five were ready to march. One white-haired woman even tugged on his sleeve after he gave the benediction, saying that she wanted to participate but couldn't walk that far. She said that she would have her son drive her and drop her off at the bakery. Harley smiled. "Of course," he said, feeling proud to be her pastor.

The group began to walk north on Washington Street, filling the sidewalk and overflowing into the street. As they passed, Doris King popped her head out of the Yarn Shop and asked a church member what was going on. After learning about their destination, she called for her partner, Eleanor, to hold down the fort while she joined the procession. Turning left on Mill Street, they picked up Jessica Simpson, who was on a smoke break in front of the American Legion. And as Harley led the congregation toward the bakery, he was surprised to see Leah Silverman walking directly toward him, carrying a shopping bag. She was clearly amused and perplexed by the sight of her friend Harley leading a parade through the Town of Occoquan.

"Join in," he said. "I'll explain later."

When they reached the Riverview Bakery, Harley was the first through the door. He greeted Fatima and Sarah, and said that his congregation was there to show their support and buy some baked goods. They looked around him at the crowd that was standing in front of the bakery and filling Mill Street.

"I hope we have enough," said Fatima. "You are going to clear our shelves."

"Good," said Harley. "I'll take two blueberry muffins. One for me and one for Ms. Silverman."

The crowd was more than the Bayatis were accustomed to serving at one time, but they handled the group well. Harley and Leah took their muffins out of the shop to make room for others, and ate on the Mill Street sidewalk as the others inched toward the shop with the broken front window. There was police tape in front of the window, indicating that the authorities had responded, but the hole was covered with cardboard and the rock and glass shards were gone. Business was back to normal at the bakery, and with the arrival of the Riverside congregation they were doing better than ever.

Members of the congregation seemed to be enjoying the experience, and most stayed in the area to eat and talk, even the old lady who had been dropped off by her son. The crowd covered the sidewalk in front of the bakery, and most of Mill Street as well. Sunday afternoon traffic was sparse on the one-way street, but the church members stepped aside and opened a space when a car needed to pass. Harley described to Leah what had happened that morning, and how he had been inspired to ditch his prepared sermon and speak from the heart.

"You old bridge-builder, you," she said.

The joy of the moment was interrupted by the revving of a motorcycle approaching on Mill Street. Harley peered over the heads of his church members and saw an unexpected sight—a rider in black leather, with studs and chains. His helmet and dark visor identified him as one of the guys who trashed the farmer's market, and he seemed particularly interested in the damage that had been done to the Riverview Bakery. As he drove slowly along the street, members of the church stepped out of the way. If he wanted to look menacing, he was certainly succeeding.

Harley stepped into the middle of the street, directly in the path of the motorcycle. The biker hit his brakes. Harley stared straight at him, trying to see a face behind the visor. The biker revved his engine as a signal to clear the way. Harley refused to move.

"You will not pass," said Harley gravely.

The cyclist revved even louder. He was clearly getting frustrated and turned to the left to bypass Harley. This time Doris King appeared out of nowhere, blocking his path with her big body. Then he turned right and Will Beckley was there, eyes still sad but standing with the full authority of the US Armed Forces.

One by one, the members of Riverside Methodist Church filled in behind Harley, Doris, and Will, blocking the entire street with their seventy-five bodies. Even the white-haired lady was taking a stand. Although they weren't quite sure what Harley was up to, they trusted their pastor.

"Turn around," said Harley to the motorcyclist. "You shall not pass."

Quickly turning his bike eastward on Mill Street, he roared away with all of the volume he could muster. In a second he turned the corner and disappeared out of sight.

"Nice work, Pastor," said Doris King, looking especially fiery. She was the only one besides Harley who sensed the connection between the biker and the farmer's market attack.

"Thank you, Doris. I appreciate your support."

Then Harley turned toward Will Beckley and thanked him for stepping in. "You are welcome, Pastor," said the young vet. "I saw the crowd and wanted to see what was going on. The Bayatis mean a lot to me."

"I'm glad to hear it."

"I hate that someone put a rock through their window."

"Yes, we all do," agreed Harley. "Maybe it was the guy we just stared down. Hope the police catch him."

Will paused a moment, and then said, "Pastor, would you have a few minutes this afternoon? I need to talk with someone."

"Uh, sure," agreed Harley. "How about if we meet in my office in one hour?"

"Sounds good," Will said. And then, lowering his voice to a whisper, "It has to do with Norah."

CHAPTER 22

The two men sat in the front pew of the sanctuary of Riverside Methodist Church since the air conditioning in Harley's office had unexpectedly broken. The lights were low, the air was cool, and black Jesus looked down on them from the stained-glass window, silently promising to calm Will's storm.

"Norah and I had a relationship," admitted Will, his cheeks looking even more sunken than before. "We met in January and became serious very quickly. It was intense but completely secret."

"Why was that?" asked Harley.

"We knew that neither of our families would approve, so we kept things hidden. Didn't even call each other on cell phones. The only place we would meet publicly was up in Fairfax, on the Mason campus. In Occoquan, I would sometimes sneak into her little apartment late at night, but we had to be very careful."

"Sounds difficult," said Harley, "and frustrating."

"Actually, it was kind of thrilling," Will responded, lightening up for the first time. "We fell hard for each other, and every moment together was amazing. She was such a beauty, with intelligence and passion. She was so feisty—I once gave her a container of pepper spray for self-defense, and she was always threatening to pull it out and use it on me."

"I've heard she had a great spirit. You must really miss her."

"More than you know," Will said, becoming somber. Sitting straight in the pew, he looked to Harley like a classic Roman soldier, embodying discipline, courage, justice. Harley was glad that Will had taken a stand beside him on Mill Street, and that such qualities existed in the Armed Forces. "I still cannot believe she is dead. I walk by her apartment and look up, expecting to see her. My life was terrible after I came back from Iraq; it turned wonderful when I met her, and now it is terrible again."

"I'm sorry. Losing her is awful, and having her die so mysteriously is even worse."

"Yeah, I'm not sleeping well. I cannot stop thinking about her and wondering who killed her."

"So you have no idea who did it?"

"No idea. I know that she and her father had a big fight when he heard the rumor that she was seeing an American. But she didn't seem afraid of him. She always described him as a pretty gentle guy. So I don't think it was an honor killing, like people are saying, unless he really flipped out."

"Did anyone else know about your relationship?"

"Only my father. And that is totally my fault. About a week before her death, I was having dinner with my parents in Arlington. I had bought Norah a gift at a jewelry store up there, and was writing a card to go with it. My parents' dog started barking to be let out, so I left the room to open the door for him. When I came back, my father had seen the card and said, 'Who's Norah?' At first I wasn't going to give him any specifics, but then I figured, why not? I'm a grown man. I can date anyone I want. So I told him all about her."

"How did he take it?"

"He went nuts. Told me I'm better than that, and should only be dating my own kind. Said that Muslims are terrible people, and I should know that after fighting in Iraq. I fired back and said that he didn't know what he was talking about, since she was better than any white girl I had ever dated. He said he didn't want any mixed-race grandchildren, and I told him he better get ready for some. It was a nasty fight. You know, they say that Arlington is such a bleeding-heart, liberal place, but that doesn't include my father."

"Sorry to hear it."

"So, anyway, I told Norah about my argument with him, and she took it well. Said that we were just going to have to be strong for each other. We figured that it was going to be the two of us against the world."

"Will, I don't want to point fingers, but do you think your father could have been involved in her death?"

"I actually wondered that, too. He was so upset at the situation that I could see him coming down to Occoquan to take action. Not that I picture him as a killer, but sometimes arguments get out of control. People go crazy. But after she died, I found out that he was in Philadelphia that night. Some kind of business thing. So my old man is off the hook."

Harley pondered this, and then asked what he could do.

"I'm not exactly sure," said the young man. "I think I just needed to tell someone about Norah and me. There is so much suspicion in this town, so much fear. I was tired of carrying the secret around. So thanks for listening, Pastor."

"Should I keep this confidential?" asked Harley.

"Not necessarily. I'm not talking with anyone about Norah, mainly out of respect for the Bayatis. I thought about going to the police, but then I realized I had nothing to tell them. No suspicions. No ideas about what happened. I was home with my roommates the night she died. But I'm thinking that the story of Norah and me is going to come out eventually. I'm okay with that."

"I'm glad that this has been helpful," said Harley, as the two of them shook hands. "Feel free to stop by any time."

As Will turned and left the sanctuary, Harley suddenly understood the message of the Sepphoris ossuary—Will was a Roman soldier, leaving his coin in the grave of his Jewish lover. *Over the barriers of time and culture and religion, love truly is stronger than death*, thought Harley, *and passion as fierce as the grave.*

❊

Harley had a dream that night that took him back to Sepphoris. He was standing in a field outside the city, and a flock of sheep milled around him in a grove of olive trees. The sun was setting, looking like a huge orange ball in the sky, and the glow of oil lamps began to fill the windows of the houses on the edge of town. A woman came into view, walking along the road toward the main gate. She was wearing robes and a scarf over her head, so he could not see who she was, but she was moving so quickly and gracefully that he assumed she was young. Then, striding out of the main gate was a young man in a tunic, with the distinctive sandals of a Roman soldier. *He must be off duty*, thought Harley, *since he is not wearing a helmet or carrying any weapons.* The two of them saw each other when they were still several hundred yards apart, and at that point they abruptly left the road and walked toward Harley and the flock of sheep. As would be true in any time and place, old Harley was invisible to them.

He could tell that their paths would eventually intersect, but they didn't wave or nod or do anything to acknowledge each other. They passed Harley and the sheep, one on his far left and one on his far right, and he suddenly recognized the soldier to be Will Beckley. The two of them hiked over a ridge and descended into a small valley, still visible to Harley but now hidden from the people of Sepphoris. At that point they turned, ran to each other and embraced, and Harley realized that they were meeting secretly among the olive trees on the outskirts of town. The young woman pushed back her headscarf and Harley fully expected to see the beautiful Norah Bayati. Instead, he saw the face of his daughter, Jessica. For a split second, she turned to Harley and smiled, sending the message that she knew he was there, and was happy about it.

Waking slowly from the dream, Harley felt a sense of peace that he had not known for years. The morning light streamed through his windows, and he stared at his ceiling as he savored the knowledge that Jessica was alive and well—somewhere. Not in this world, of course, but in some eternal City of Peace. He turned over to see if he could sleep again but quickly discovered that he was awake for the day. Rolling out of bed, he dressed and left the townhouse to get an early start on his Monday workday.

He never made it to church, however. While walking up the street, his cell phone rang.

"Harley, it's Dirk. I need to see you. Now. I'm on the pedestrian bridge."

"Where?"

"The pedestrian bridge."

"Okay, Dirk." The location was odd, but Harley sensed that the need was urgent. "I'm on my way."

He quickly turned and walked west on Mill Street. As he strode along, he thought of how Dirk had dropped completely out of sight, except for his ghostlike appearance in the church service.

The August day was heating up and Harley began to perspire as he passed the town museum and turned right on to the pedestrian bridge. A man stood alone in the middle of the bridge, high above the river, but strangely enough he was on the wrong side of the railing, standing on the eastern edge of the bridge and facing west. When Harley quickened his pace, the man turned and faced him. It was Dirk, looking grave.

"Dirk, what are you doing there?" asked Harley as he approached. "Get back on the inside of the railing."

"Don't come any closer," Dirk said when Harley was within a few yards of him. He held on to the railing with his beefy left hand, and his right hand was in the pocket of his light windbreaker. Harley stopped.

"What's wrong?"

"My life is over," said the old Marine. "I have tried to be a good soldier, but I have failed. I need to do the right thing and end this."

"What are you talking about, Dirk?"

"My honor is gone. I have nothing left to live for. I have to rectify my mistake in the Roman way."

Roman way? It took a few seconds for Harley to figure out what he meant. "You want to kill yourself?"

"I must," said Dirk, sounding more decisive than depressed. "I have thought about this for days. Here is what is going to happen. I will tell you the truth about my mistake, so that justice can be done. I will receive whatever absolution you choose to give me. Then I will pull my gun out of my pocket, discharge it into my mouth, and fall into the river."

"Dirk, no!"

"This is the only way. I want no mess for anyone to clean up. The river will do its work. I'm sorry to do this to you, Harley. But it has to end this way."

Harley took deep breaths to calm his pounding heart and quaking voice. "I am your pastor, Dirk. You can give me your confession."

They had the pedestrian bridge to themselves, not uncommon for a Monday morning, and there was not a single boat on the river, as far as the eye could see.

Dirk shifted his grip on the railing and bowed his head. "I have always tried to do my best for my family, my community, and my country. I would do anything to ensure their security. That has always been my commitment." He adjusted his right hand in his pocket, and Harley saw the outline of the handgun. "For the past few years, I have cared about nothing more than Matt and his success at the FBI. My own career was over, but his was not." He lifted his head and looked Harley in the eye. "He told me that he was becoming involved with someone who could jeopardize his career—beautiful, black hair, someone close to him here in Occoquan." He turned his head left, looking toward the Riverview Bakery. "Putting two and two together, I figured that it must be Norah Bayati."

"Oh God," said Harley. "No!"

"I drove over from Lake Ridge and went to her apartment late at night. I knocked on the door, and she opened it a crack. Since she didn't know me, I figured I would scare her—I said that I wanted her to leave my boy alone. She started to close the door, so I stuck my foot in it. Used my shoulder to push it open. She got really nasty, quickly, and told me to get out. I said, 'Not till I have my say.' We were each pushing on opposite sides of the door, and she got mad and said, 'You can't tell me what to do. It's a free country. I'll see anyone I want.' I pushed harder with my shoulder and knocked her away from the door. She spun around and went toward her bed. It looked like she grabbed something off of her nightstand. Then she came right at me and said, 'We love each other. You can't stop us.' And then she blasted me full in the face with pepper spray."

Harley's mouth dropped open. "Dirk, that must have—"

"My eyes burned like fire. I stumbled around, rubbing my eyes, unable to see. I felt like screaming, but didn't dare to. In my blindness I knocked over her nightstand. She gave a little shriek and I told her to shut up. 'Keep quiet,' I said. She called for help and I swung at her, blindly. Hit her across the face and knocked her on her bed. She called out again and I jumped on top of her. My military training kicked in, muscle memory, and I went full force to constrain her. I grabbed a pillow, we struggled on the bed, and I held her down until she was quiet. Finally."

Dirk turned his head toward the ancient rocks on the north side of the river. For a moment the two men said nothing.

"You killed her?"

"She wouldn't shut up. I didn't intend to kill her, but she wouldn't shut up. I left her apartment feeling horrible, but knowing that I had achieved my goal, for Matt."

"But it was a mistake."

"Yes," Dirk said, restraining tears. "Now I know that. When I learned from Matt that he was obsessed with a coworker—not with Norah—I could not believe it. It made no sense to me. But then I saw the truth and realized that my mission was a failure. Instead of helping Matt, I killed an innocent girl. Now the nightmare must end. Right here, right now."

After a few moments, Harley said, "You are living a nightmare, Dirk. And you are right, it must end. But I don't think it has to end with you in the river. You are not a Roman. You are a Christian."

"What difference does it make? I am guilty of murder. An eye for an eye."

"You have your honor, I get that. You want to see justice done. But you are also a sinner. And Christ died for sinners."

"That's why I am confessing, Harley. Give me your absolution and let me go."

"You can be forgiven, Dirk. Christ has taken your sins on himself. But don't add another murder to the murder you have already committed. Suicide is murder," said Harley. "It is the taking of a life. Your life."

Dirk pushed back. "Come on, Harley, you don't believe that. A depressed person who takes his life—he's not a murderer! He's full of despair, mentally ill."

"But that's not you, Dirk. You are the sanest person I know. You are not depressed. You are guilty of hatefulness and a grave mistake. And Christ died to take your guilt on himself. He died so that you could live."

Dirk pushed the handgun deeper into his jacket pocket. "I don't know. I can't live with the shame."

"Matt needs you," Harley pleaded. "You think you've hurt him by doing what you did? You'll hurt him even more by killing yourself. Think about how your own father let you down when you needed him the most. Matt wants you in his life, even if you are guilty of a crime."

"He'll hate me."

"He'll hate your mistake. Hate your action. But not hate you. The truth will come out about what happened. Will Beckley was involved with Norah. His father condemned their relationship, and Norah knew it. You came to confront Norah, and she assumed that you were Will's father. How could she assume otherwise? She didn't know you, and you didn't really know her. It was a tragic mistake."

"Still, I have failed Matt."

"Yes, but you are still his father." Harley didn't know if he was succeeding in talking Dirk off the ledge but figured that he had one more piece of ammunition. "Dirk, there is one more thing I want you to know. If you confess, you can help to stop a terrorist plot."

"What are you talking about?"

"I cannot go into details," Harley said. "But if you go to the police and confess what you have done, you will begin a process that will save many lives. Islamic extremists will be arrested, and an attack will be thwarted."

"How can you be so sure?" Dirk asked. He still looked skeptical, but there was a glimmer of hope in his eyes.

"Trust me," said Harley. "Have I failed you before? I know someone who can expose the plot. I'll have him take the evidence to Matt. Think about it, Dirk. It will be great for Matt's career."

Dirk pondered what his pastor was saying, thinking about the damage he had done to Matt and how he might redeem himself. Quietly, he said, "I do owe him."

"Everything begins with confession," said Harley. "Tell the truth about what you have done. Help the Bayatis to get Muhammad out of jail. Pay your debt in court, not here in the river. Help to make Matt a hero."

Dirk turned to the left, catching sight of two people on the town side of the pedestrian bridge. Harley followed his gaze and saw that it was Youssef and Sofia Ayad, out for their morning walk. Although round and wingless, they looked like a couple of angels walking toward them.

"Here come the Ayads," said Harley. "Coptic Christians. They have seen so many of their brothers and sisters killed by ISIS. Don't make them watch another Christian die."

With that, Dirk pulled his gun out of his jacket pocket, looked at it wistfully, and then handed it to Harley. He knew that he was exchanging a quick fix for a long and painful process. Harley put the handgun in the inner pocket of his sport jacket to hide it from the Ayads. Then Dirk pulled himself up and over the railing of the pedestrian bridge and joined Harley on the walkway.

"And so it begins," said the Marine to his pastor.

CHAPTER 23

"Dirk Carter confessed to the killing of Norah," said Harley to Omar, Sarah, and Fatima Bayati.

He had called the women to his house on Monday afternoon to meet with him and Omar, and the four of them sat in his living room with the blinds drawn. "He has been charged with voluntary manslaughter. That is a homicide that happens in the heat of passion, without a prior intent to kill."

The Bayatis were stunned. "But who is Dirk Carter?" asked Fatima.

"He's a resident of Lake Ridge," Harley replied. "And, I'm sorry to say, a member of my church."

"He must be related to Matt Carter," said Omar, with rising anger.

"Yes, he is," said Harley. "He is Matt's father."

"But why would he kill my daughter?" asked Fatima, choking up.

"As I said, he did not intend to kill her," Harley explained. "He behaved in a reckless and violent manner, but he did not enter her apartment with the desire to kill her. It was a tragic case of mistaken identity."

"What?" asked Omar. "That makes no sense to me."

"Let me explain," said Harley. "Dirk thought that Norah was involved with his son, Matt. He had heard Matt talking about a woman that he was attracted to, someone who looked like Norah. He showed up at Norah's apartment to put an end to her relationship with Matt."

"That would never work," said Sarah quietly, knowing her sister well.

"But it gets even more complicated. Norah thought that Dirk was the father of the young man she was seeing, Will Beckley."

"Norah was involved with Will?" asked Fatima.

"Yes, she was," admitted Sarah. "I knew it, but I never said anything. I knew that you and father would be angry."

"We were very angry when we heard that rumor," said Fatima. "It was not right for her to be involved with an American. But, Sarah, if you knew about Will and Norah, why did you not take that information to the police?"

"Will did not kill her."

"How could you know?" asked Fatima.

"Because I went to him the morning we found her dead. I woke him up and told him. He was stunned. He could not believe it. He was very upset. They really loved each other."

Harley knew that Norah's relationship was still a raw nerve but felt that he had to continue. "When Dirk forced himself into her apartment, she fought back. She shot him with pepper spray. They struggled and he smothered her."

"He should die," hissed Omar.

"Believe me, he wanted to," said Harley. "When he discovered his mistake, he wanted to end his life. But I convinced him to surrender to the police."

The Bayatis sat for a few moments, quietly processing what Harley had told them. Finally, Fatima said, "Nothing is going to bring Norah back, whether her killer is dead or alive. We have to trust that justice will be done. God will help us to get through this."

"You have a good lawyer, right?" asked Harley. He knew that they were using the defense fund to get the best representation they could. "Call him immediately, and tell him about Dirk's confession. He should be able to get Muhammad released right away."

"We are grateful for your support," Fatima said, "and for the generosity of the donors."

"I want you all to have some time together, once Muhammad is released," added Harley. "Omar, I think you can go home tonight, as long as you remain hidden. You and I have some business we still need to take care of."

"What kind of business?" asked Fatima.

"Something that will help you all," replied Harley. "It will make you more secure." Omar just sat in his chair, looking noncommittal. "Get Muhammad and bring him home. Omar, I will see you first thing tomorrow morning. I'll pick you up at nine o'clock."

"Whatever," said Omar.

"Show some respect," said his mother.

"Okay. Nine o'clock."

❋

As the Bayatis left, Harley watched from the window. He hoped that the Woodbridge guys were not in the vicinity, ready to pounce on Omar as soon as he resurfaced. Although solving Norah's killing had been a huge step forward, it did little to change the course of the terrorist plot. Harley worried that the ISIS sympathizers would succeed in finding new photographs and acquiring another boat while he and Omar had their extended slumber party. And he couldn't help but think that his bold stand on Sunday, refusing to let the motorcyclist pass, might have made the entire group angry and even more determined.

Seeing the Bayatis make it safely to their shop, he turned to plan his next step. He wanted to call Matt Carter to set up a meeting but figured that he would still be at the police station with his father, dealing with the shock of Dirk's confession. Dirk had made two phone calls as Harley drove him to the police station that morning: one to Matt and one to his lawyer. When Harley left the station, the lawyer was in conference with Dirk and Matt was on his way from

FBI Headquarters in Washington. Harley wanted to give Matt some time before he asked to meet with him about the terrorist plot. One shocking revelation at a time was probably enough.

Glancing at the clock on the microwave in his kitchen, he saw that it was two o'clock. He figured that he ought to put in a few hours at the church since he was being paid to be a pastor, not a counterterrorism specialist, so he left the air-conditioning of his townhouse and entered the heat and humidity of the August afternoon. He walked up Washington Street past the Gold Emporium, grateful that the Ayads had appeared on the pedestrian bridge. He peeked into the Yarn Shop, saw the red hair of Doris King, and said a silent thanks that she had stepped up and helped him when he took his stand on Mill Street. Whatever happened in the next twenty-four hours, at the very least Harley knew that he was not alone. Then, as he was about to cross Washington Street and enter the church, a green Subaru made the turn from Commerce Street and headed straight for him.

"Harley, get in," said the driver as she pulled quickly to the curb. It was Leah. "I just heard about Dirk from a friend at the police station. Unbelievable."

"You are right about that."

"So, let's go talk someplace."

"Okay," Harley agreed, opening the front door on the passenger side. "Where to?"

"Lake Ridge Coffee. Should be quiet this time of day." They arrived in five minutes and, as predicted, the place was deserted.

Leah bought a couple of iced coffees, and they sat in the back of the café. "Pat and I spent a lot of time here," she said. "She loved it."

"She?" said Harley, bewildered. He didn't think he had heard her right. "Wait a second. Pat was a woman?"

"Of course," said Leah.

Harley stared at her, feeling the ancient rocks under his feet begin to shift. "I assumed Pat was Patrick," he said. And then the movement stopped, the rocks assumed a new configuration, and the puzzle of their perplexing personal history suddenly made sense.

"No, Harley," said Leah. "Pat was Patricia. You know that I am a lesbian, right?"

"Uh, no, I didn't," he said, sheepishly.

Leah laughed. "Harley, how could you not know?"

"I just didn't. Never occurred to me."

"You are so funny," she said, shaking her head. "But look, this is a conversation for another day. Right now, I want to hear about Dirk. Break it down for me. What happened?"

Harley told her the story that he had just told the Bayatis, weaving in elements of his conversation with Dirk on the pedestrian bridge. He ended with a prediction that Muhammad would be out of jail very soon, and said, "I hope the poor guy doesn't have to spend another night in that place."

"What a tragic mix-up," Leah said, shaking her head. "Two young lovers, two angry sets of parents, and one old Marine determined to protect his son. That's a combustible mix."

"You're right," Harley agreed. "It could have been diffused so easily, if people only talked with each other."

"You say that Norah's boyfriend was Will Beckley? I know who he is, but don't really know him. I wouldn't have pictured the two of them together."

"Join the club. I think it was a big surprise to everyone except for Sarah Bayati."

"Yeah, sisters know that kind of stuff. I think I told you that Norah was a patient at our clinic. We knew that she was sexually active, but didn't know the name of her partner. Wish we had known more, and could have done more."

"Don't blame yourself. People deserve their privacy."

Leah sipped her coffee and said, "I give you credit for the relationships you've established, Harley. It's been what? Just two months?"

"Not even."

"You've done some good work, man. You've built a bridge to the Bayatis, and you talked Dirk off a bridge. You had your whole congregation take a stand with you in the street yesterday. Pretty impressive stuff."

Harley felt embarrassed. "Well, that's what being a pastor is all about. Relationships."

"You do well, Harley."

"Although I sure missed the boat on you and Pat."

"Hey, nobody sees everything clearly."

"I know I need to do better," he admitted. "After the deaths of Karen and Jessica, I retreated into myself. Now I see the problem with that."

"What you did was understandable. I was pretty isolated after Pat died. But I'm glad you've come out of your shell. So, what do you think your next move will be?"

"I can't really go into detail," Harley said, "but there is some information that Omar and I need to take to the FBI. I want to call Matt Carter this evening."

"He'll be a mess, won't he?"

"Probably. But part of my persuasion of Dirk included a promise to make Matt a hero."

"Harley," said Leah with a sly smile, "you go big, don't you?"

"Go big or go home."

"I guess that you've got nothing to lose, right? When you are talking a guy off a bridge, you'll promise anything."

"I think Matt can help us. I really do." At that moment, Harley's cell phone rang and he looked at the screen. "Speak of the devil," he said: "Matt Carter. Mind if I take this?" Leah agreed.

❁

"Matt, how are you doing?" Harley said into the phone.

"I've been better. I am still in shock. My father was always impulsive, but this is insane."

"I'm so sorry. Your head must be reeling."

"Well, I'm trying to compartmentalize. We learn how to do that in the bureau. And I guess my dad taught me that as well. I cannot believe he killed that girl and somehow lived a normal life with blood on his hands."

"He felt he was helping you. Crazy, but true."

"This is going to take me a long time to process."

"I'm here to help, you know."

"Speaking of help, I want to thank you for helping my dad on the bridge. I'm upset about what he did, but his suicide would have just made things worse. So whatever you said to him, thanks."

"I just told him the truth, as I understood it."

"Well, it worked. And that's a small miracle in itself, since he isn't very good at listening to anyone."

"I'm glad I could help him."

"I want to let you know that you might be called to testify. He has confessed to manslaughter, but you might be needed to speak, especially at the penalty phase. There is still a lot that lies ahead. I just wanted to call and thank you, and give you a heads-up."

"I appreciate it, Matt. And while you are on the phone, there is something I need to ask of you. Maybe your father mentioned this, but maybe not. I have some information on a terrorist cell in Woodbridge, a group of Islamic extremists who have their sights on Fort Belvoir."

"Stop. Don't say another word."

"Okay."

"The phone is not good for this. Can you talk with one of our people?"

"Yes. When?"

"Now."

"Okay, but I need to bring someone."

"Meet me at your church. I'm still in Manassas, but I'll meet you at your church and lead you to our Washington field office. I can be there in thirty minutes."

"I'll see you then."

"Harley, your timing is good for our investigation. But bad for me."

"Sorry, Matt," he apologized, hanging up the phone.

"Sounds like you have to go," said Leah.

"Yes, let's go straight to the Bayatis, and then to the church."

Although events were moving quickly, Harley was glad that Omar would be put in front of the FBI before he could get cold feet. Within five minutes, they were at the Riverview Bakery, where the Bayatis were getting ready to drive to the jail. Omar protested when Harley said he would have to come with him, complaining that Harley had told him that they would meet in the morning. Harley told him that the schedule had changed and promised that he would be home to see his father that night. Fatima and Sarah said that there was nothing that Omar could do at the jail, so he should keep his promise and go with Harley. Reluctantly, the young man got in Leah's car.

They picked up Harley's car on the way to church, and Leah sat with Omar while Harley retrieved the camera from the trunk. Within a few minutes Matt pulled into the parking lot beside them. "Not him!" Omar hissed.

"He is our best connection," said Harley.

"But his father killed my sister."

"And his father is now in jail."

Omar looked at Matt with loathing, and for a minute Harley wondered if he would be able to get the young man to go to the FBI. But then he asked Leah to step out of the car so that he could talk with Omar alone.

"Let me tell you how this can go. You can come with me and tell your story, which will keep you and your family safe and secure. Or I can go alone to the FBI, tell your story, and then you'll be under investigation right along with the Woodbridge guys. Either way, these pictures are going to the authorities."

Omar's anger was now directed at both Matt and Harley. But he opened the door and walked over to Harley's car.

"I guess he's going," said Harley to Leah and Matt.

Matt called ahead to his colleague Bianca Augustino, who was heading up the Prince William counterterrorism investigation. She met them at the Washington Field Office and thanked them for coming in. As soon as Harley saw her, he knew exactly who she was—the beauty with long black hair and olive skin who had been the object off Matt's obsession.

"Reverend Camden and Mr. Bayati, Agent Carter tells me that you have information about an alleged terrorist cell in Woodbridge."

Bianca Augustino was articulate and quite intimidating. Harley understood why Matt had fallen for her.

"I am in charge of an ongoing investigation in that area, so I am interested in what you know. Although Agent Carter is no longer part of my team, I would like him to sit in on this conversation. Is that acceptable to you?"

Harley nodded, while Omar just looked at his feet. He was still not happy to be anywhere near Matt Carter. But Harley elbowed him, and he said, grudgingly, "Okay."

"What have you observed?" inquired Bianca.

"Omar, would you like me to do the talking?" Harley asked. The young man nodded and Harley continued. "In Omar's circle of acquaintances is a group of six young men in Woodbridge. They are angry at the United States and are plotting an act of violence. When Omar first met them, they talked about blowing something up as a sign of their strength. They knew that Omar was a good photographer, so they asked him to take pictures of some targets at Fort Belvoir. Omar made it clear that he did not want to be involved in killing, and they assured him that their target would not be occupied by people. So he took some pictures from his boat."

"What did you photograph?" asked Bianca.

"Mostly old landing craft," admitted Omar. "If they blew up, no one would be hurt."

"But then the target changed," said Harley. "As you may know, Fort Belvoir is home to a stockpile of biological weapons. The group asked Omar to photograph these new targets, and he objected. But then they started to terrorize his family."

Harley held up Omar's camera. "In this camera are surveillance photos of the biological weapons site. They have never been turned over to the terrorist cell. We want you to have them as evidence of their intentions."

"Do you know where these men live?" Bianca inquired.

"Yes," said Omar.

"Omar is willing to cooperate completely with your investigation," said Harley, "in exchange for immunity from prosecution. He wants this plot to be halted, and for his family to be safe."

"Only a prosecutor can grant witness immunity," said Bianca. "But I think that your cooperation will be very valuable to us, and that you will be able to avoid prosecution. Omar, I would like to take your camera into evidence, and have you write a statement, including everything you know about this group of six men. Include their addresses, phone numbers, and any other contact information that you have. We want to stop them and keep both you and your family safe."

Omar found Bianca to be every bit as intimidating as Harley did, and he agreed to her request. While he wrote his statement, Harley stepped outside the office with Matt, and the two of them talked for a few minutes.

"What a day," observed Harley.

"Probably the worst of my life," said Matt. "I'm glad Bianca did all of the talking tonight. I'm a mess. Can't stop thinking about my father."

"Understandable."

"I cannot believe he is in jail."

"He'll need you, now more than ever."

Matt shook his head. "Just think of it, an FBI agent making regular visits to see his father in jail."

"But look at it this way: His action is breaking this terrorism case wide open."

"Yeah, but we would have caught them eventually."

"Maybe not before they struck."

"True," admitted Matt. "Omar's decision to come forward is going to help a great deal."

"Do you know the story of Joseph in the Bible?" asked Harley.

"Joseph, the father of Jesus?" guessed Matt.

"No, the Old Testament Joseph," explained Harley. "His brothers hated him and sold him into slavery. A terrible thing. He was taken down to Egypt and there he worked his way up in the Pharaoh's administration. Finally, he was in charge of all of the food in the land, which became incredibly valuable during a time of famine. His brothers were starving and they traveled to Egypt to get food. He could have punished them for their evil, but he saved them. And then he said to them, 'Even though you intended to do harm to me, God intended it for good, in order to preserve a numerous people.'"

"Interesting," said Matt. "I've never heard that."

"Your father's intentions were not good. He did a terrible thing. But God has been working through this whole mess to save a lot of people."

At that moment, Omar walked out the office door and said that he was ready to go home. Harley said goodbye to Matt and Bianca, and then drove Omar back to Occoquan. As they pulled up to the bakery, Muhammad Bayati was getting out of the family car, free at last.

CHAPTER 24

"I live in the apartments by the marina," said the stranger to Harley. "I walked over here on Monday but the church was locked."

Harley put his key in the front door and said, "Are you the only one around here who doesn't know what happened this week?" The man shrugged. "Well, it's been something. Come on in." Harley flipped on lights in the narthex and then the sanctuary, and the stranger trudged along behind him. "What is it I can do for you?"

"I've been out of work for a month, and money is real tight. I could really use some food."

"We've got a food pantry, and you are welcome to a bag of groceries." Short and thin with a stubble of beard, the middle-aged man looked to be a smoker and a heavy drinker. "I'll open the pantry for you, and you can fill a bag with what you want." The stranger said thanks and followed Harley to the pantry on the lower level, next to the social hall. Harley had a lot to do before the worship service that Sunday morning, and felt mildly annoyed that the stranger had ambushed him when he arrived. But he had been in the business long enough to know that ministry happened in and through interruptions, so he decided to try to be patient.

"I was delivering pizzas, but I wrecked my car," said the man as he started to examine the shelves of canned food and dry goods. "They couldn't keep me on without a car. I've been looking ever since, but it seems like nobody's hiring."

Harley stood nearby as the stranger slowly filled his bag, examining each food label. "Sorry to hear it," he replied, wishing that the guy would make his selections a little faster.

"So, what happened this week in Occoquan?" asked the man.

"On Monday, a man from Lake Ridge confessed to the killing of Norah Bayati."

"The Iraqi girl?"

"Yes, exactly."

"I thought her father did it," he said, looking up from his bag of groceries.

"Many people did," Harley acknowledged, "but he's innocent. Then, on Wednesday, a team from the FBI raided three apartments in Woodbridge. They arrested six men and found a cache of weapons and bomb-making chemicals and equipment. It seems like they were planning a terrorist attack."

"Muslims?"

"Well, yes, but not good ones. Islamic extremists."

"I'm suspicious of them all."

"You might want to rethink that," cautioned Harley. "They were turned in by a young Muslim man right here in Occoquan."

"Well, that's good."

"He saved a lot of lives, maybe even yours and mine."

The man continued to fill his bag and Harley checked the time. He still needed to straighten up the sanctuary since the events of the past week had thrown his normal routine into chaos.

"That should do it," said the man as he put a box of cereal in the top of the bag. "But I was wondering, pastor, do you have any money to help with a three-hundred-dollar electric bill?"

"No, I'm afraid I don't," Harley replied. "But you could check back next week. I might have something then."

The Bayatis had told Harley that they wanted to return the bulk of the money that had been given to them for Muhammad's defense, once they settled their account with their attorney. Harley told them that it wasn't necessary, but they insisted—they wanted it to be used to help others. He had a sense that his pastor's discretionary fund would be in good shape for the next few years.

"You know, I'm a pretty spiritual guy," said the man as he stood in front of Harley with his bag of groceries. "I can feel things. People say I have a sixth sense. I knew the exact moment my brother died, even though he was all the way over in Manassas. I feel the Spirit is here, right here in this church."

"Really?" replied Harley, surprised. "Thank you."

"No, thank you," said the man. "I appreciate the groceries." And then he slipped out the back door of the lower level.

Harley walked up the stairs to the sanctuary level, wondering what the man had actually been feeling. Over the years, he had met a number of people with keen spiritual sensitivity, folks with built-in radios that could pick up stations no one else could hear. In his very first church, he had a member, an eighty-eight-year-old woman, who told him, "I've got the sight," even though she was as blind as a bat. Given that she had incredible intuition and the ability to sense Harley's fears and insecurities as a young pastor, he had no doubt that she was absolutely right. *Bertha Washington. I wonder what happened to her? She was so good to me.*

Bertha had told Harley, "You were born with a veil over your face," which he never understood but assumed to be some kind of good omen. Enjoying the memory of her blessing, he turned on the lights of his office and picked up a stack of Sunday bulletins. The air conditioner had been fixed, so he cranked it up to cool the room. As he reentered the sanctuary, he looked up at black Jesus, whose stained-glass clothing glowed in the sunlight flooding in from the east. The window had never looked so radiant, and he wondered if it was the time or the fact that it was shaping up to be a cloudless day. Dropping the bulletins on the ushers' table near the entrance, he moved through the pews to pick up leftovers from the previous Sunday.

Harley's days had been filled with a steady stream of people wanting to talk about Dirk and the Bayatis and the Woodbridge terrorists. Harley spent most of the time listening as church members expressed shock that Dirk, a lifelong Methodist, could commit such an act of brutal violence. Most were glad that Muhammad had been released, although they questioned his condemnation of Norah's relationship with an American, a judgment that they felt laid the groundwork for the tragedy. Some wondered why Will had remained silent, and how Dirk and Matt could have miscommunicated so badly. And all were grateful to Omar for coming forward and making his statement, exposing the terrorist plot and sparing the region from a devastating calamity. Deep relief was just one of the many emotions expressed that week, as people unburdened themselves and found ways to understand what had happened.

On Friday night, Omar came to Harley's house to pick up some clothes he had left in the guest suite. He told Harley about his father's transition from jail back to home, and how something as simple as having the freedom to go outside for a walk, at any hour of the day, was a major adjustment for him. Fatima was happy, he reported, smiling and laughing more than she had since the day of Norah's death. Omar admitted that he felt kind of guilty when the Woodbridge guys were arrested on Wednesday, but the burden was eased when it immediately took away the cloud of fear hanging over his family. He said that he had been hungry for the acceptance and support of the guys when he first met them, but he quickly discovered that they were using him for his boat and for his skill with a camera. And then, when they began to terrorize his family as a way of manipulating and controlling him, he saw how unprincipled they really were. By the time he wrote his statement for the FBI, he had concluded that they were Muslim in name only, with no respect for people or reverence for God.

"Still, I have some guilt," Omar confessed to Harley. "Is that the right thing to feel?"

"It's not right or wrong," Harley told him. "It is just the thing you are feeling. Given the fact that you had a connection to these guys, I think it makes perfect sense."

"But they were evil guys."

"Yes, they were plotting something evil. But they were still people, capable of doing good. Your guilt tells me that you knew that."

"I wish I could feel just one thing—relief."

"Don't we all?" Harley said to him. "It's just not always possible."

After passing through a half dozen pews, Harley glanced up at the stained-glass window and saw the deep blues and greens of the water, along with the frothing white caps of the waves. The sun brought the panes of glass to life in a new way. He had never noticed the colors of the storm before, focusing always on the faces of Jesus and his frightened disciples. He realized that the tempest was a major character in the story, threatening the lives of everyone in the boat until Jesus exerted his influence and calmed the wind and the waves. What blew across the Sea of Galilee was a very different wind from the Spirit of God; it was a chaotic and destructive force much more like the violent energy that drove Dirk and the Woodbridge terrorists to take the actions they did. Harley had felt that evil wind himself, every bit as much as he had felt the breath of God. He knew now that both forces were present and real, in Occoquan and around the world, and that they could blow up again in unexpected ways.

At that point, the front door opened and a figure appeared. "Good morning, Harley," said Mary Ranger as she entered the church. Walking down the center aisle, she asked, "Do you have a minute?"

He sighed. "Sure. Can we talk right here while I am straightening up?"

"Sure," she replied. "May I help you?"

As the two of them moved through the pews, the postmistress admitted, "I'm terribly upset about Dirk. He's all I can think about, ever since Monday." She wiped away tears. "We have sat together in this church for years. We just had such a good time going in your boat to the baseball game. How could he kill that young woman?"

Harley paused and looked at her. "He thought he was helping Matt."

"But how can that be?"

"For Dirk, nothing mattered more than protecting his family, his community, his country. He was taking action to do that, or so he thought."

"But he was wrong to go after Norah."

"Yes, it was a mistake. A terrible mistake."

"What did Matt tell him that would send him after her?"

Harley thought for a second about what had been told to him in confidence, and what had not. Even though the details of the killing had emerged, he wanted to keep his promises.

"They weren't communicating well," he offered. "They were talking past each other. Assumptions were made."

"Deadly assumptions."

"Yes, indeed. People have got to communicate well, and really talk to each other. Horrible things happen when they fail to do so."

Mary shook her head sadly, and the two of them returned to the work of straightening up the sanctuary. As they made their way through the last of the pews, Harley asked her, "Have I preached here about the power of words?"

"No, I don't think so," she replied.

"I'm convinced that words create reality," Harley explained. "It's a very biblical idea. Think of God creating the world in Genesis, saying 'Let there be light,' and there was light. Jesus is described in the New Testament as 'the Word.' When Martin Luther King, Jr., said, 'I have a dream,' people began to see a vision of a new world of equality. Words create reality."

"That makes sense, I guess."

"So the words we use are terribly important," he continued. "Whether we say 'I love you' or 'I hate you' makes a huge difference. If I say to a friend, 'I forgive you,' it actually changes our relationship. The words that Matt and Dirk spoke were misleading words. The words that Muhammad spoke to Norah were harsh words. The words that Omar wrote in his statement to the FBI were lifesaving words."

"Huh," said Mary, getting his point. "That makes me think about my work at the post office in a new way. I'm in the business of delivering words."

"Yes, you are. So often we disparage words today, saying 'talk is cheap' or 'that's just words.' But the truth is that words create reality."

"I guess that's why you're here," Mary said as they finished their work in the sanctuary. "Preacher, give us some words."

❋

The congregation that gathered on that second Sunday in August was again a bit larger than usual. Harley knew that times of turmoil and tragedy were actually a good time to be the church, because people were looking for a firm foundation to stand on. The pews were almost filled, and then Harley saw two visitors appear, Fatima and Sarah Bayati, covered with their usual colorful headscarves, and take a seat in the back row. A few church members looked surprised, but Harley noticed that a couple of others welcomed them with smiles.

For the scripture that day, Harley read from the fourth chapter of the Gospel of Matthew. "Now when Jesus heard that John had been arrested, he withdrew to Galilee. He left Nazareth and made his home in Capernaum by the sea," he intoned, pointing up to the stained-glass window behind him. "Our window shows the sea that Matthew is talking about," he said as an aside, "the Sea of Galilee." Then, returning to the reading, "He left Nazareth and made his home in Capernaum by the sea, in the territory of Zebulun and Naphtali, so that what had been spoken through the prophet Isaiah might be fulfilled: 'Land of Zebulun, land of Naphtali, on the road by the sea, across the Jordan, Galilee of the Gentiles—the people who sat in darkness have seen a great light, and for those who sat in the region and shadow of death light has dawned.' From that time Jesus began to proclaim, 'Repent, for the kingdom of heaven has come near.'"

Harley closed the Bible and looked out over the faces in the congregation, people that had been strangers to him just two months before. They looked eager, maybe even anxious, to hear what he had to say. Words created reality.

"Galilee of the Gentiles," said Harley, beginning his sermon. "That's how Matthew describes the place where Jesus lived and worked. He doesn't describe it as 'Galilee of the Jews,' even though Jesus and his disciples were all Jews. No, it is Galilee of the Gentiles. The region was full of Romans and other non-Jews, people called Gentiles. It was a very multicultural place." He gazed to the back row and caught the eye of Fatima Bayati. "It was a place in which people had to talk to one another, really communicate with one another, if they were going to live in peace. They had to be willing to do business with each other and be neighbors to each other, if they were going to avoid fighting over culture and religion and politics."

At that moment, the door of the sanctuary opened and Youssef and Sofia Ayad slipped in. They quietly entered and took a seat next to the Bayatis.

"When I was a divinity school student," Harley continued, "I spent a summer doing an archaeological dig in Galilee. I worked in a town called Sepphoris, which is next door to Nazareth. We found a mosaic of a beautiful woman that has come to be known as the Mona Lisa of the Galilee." As Harley pictured the mosaic, he thought of Norah Bayati—maybe she was the Mona Lisa of Occoquan. Shaking off the thought, he returned to his sermon.

"The important thing about Sepphoris is that it was a community in which Jews and Romans lived together in peace. They didn't fight one another, even though Jews in other parts of the country had been involved in violent revolts against the Roman Empire for many years. Instead, Jews and Romans lived as neighbors and did business together. Some may have even had romantic relationships—we found some evidence of that in Sepphoris. They did so well that it became known as Eirenopolis, 'City of Peace.'"

Sofia Ayad leaned over and whispered something to Fatima Bayati. Harley wondered what it was but kept going. "Here in Occoquan, we live in a multicultural place as well: We have Christians, Jews and Muslims, representing different cultures, races and nationalities. We live next to a river, not a sea, but it would be fair to call us 'Occoquan of the Gentiles.' The question for us is the same one that faced the people of the Galilee. Will we fight over our differences, or will we live together in peace? Will we accept each other and communicate with each other, or will we live in the kind of isolation that leads to violence? I am convinced that isolation is a major problem for us today—just think of those terrorists in Woodbridge, cut off from the larger community and stewing in their resentments, plotting an act of violence that could have killed us all. This could have been a City of Violence! A City of Jihad!" Harley felt his passion rising as he departed from his manuscript. "We can all thank God that Omar Bayati stayed connected to our community and helped the authorities to prevent this disaster." A number of people turned around to look at the Bayatis, and the two seemed embarrassed—but maybe also a little pleased—by the attention.

"My professor on the archaeological dig was a Jew," Harley said, returning to his text. "He has worked hard over the years to support peace efforts in Israel. He sees the history of Sepphoris as a model for us today, and I remember him saying to us: 'You should all be Galileans. Learn to live together as the people of Galilee did in Sepphoris. Galilee can be a model for Jews and Palestinians in Israel, and for Jews, Christians and Muslims in the United States.'" Harley saw a few nods through the congregation, and a smile from Youssef Ayad.

"I agree with my professor," Harley continued. "Occoquan has not been a City of Peace, but it can be. We should all be Galileans here, whatever our religion. We should work together and be good neighbors to each other. Isolation breeds violence, while communication and community lead to peace. Do you remember what I said last week? The Spirit of God gives us gifts to advance the common good. We've seen the Spirit at work this week, helping ordinary people to do extraordinary things, including the foiling of a terrorist plot. We should be using these gifts every day here in Occoquan. God's Spirit is present when people work and live together as one people, but terrible things happen when communities become fractured and polarized. We need to be Galileans!"

More people were now nodding, but he knew he couldn't end there. There was still the elephant in the room—Dirk Carter.

"Hear the words of scripture," he said. "'Galilee of the Gentiles—the people who sat in darkness have seen a great light, and for those who sat in the region and shadow of death light has dawned.' Here in Occoquan, we have sat in darkness, in the region and shadow of death. One of our own members has committed a terrible crime. He will pay for this crime for many years. But the promise of our faith is that God's light shines in the darkness, and the darkness cannot overcome it. Our challenge today is to be light—be light to each other, be light to this community, be light to the Bayatis, be light even to Dirk Carter." That last phrase created a hush in the congregation. "Yes, be light . . . even to Dirk. He needs it."

Looking back at the stained-glass window, Harley said, "Look at the face of Jesus in our window. Such calm in the middle of a storm. Jesus says in today's scripture that 'the kingdom of heaven has come near.' I believe that: The kingdom of heaven has come near, right here in Occoquan. It isn't fully present, but it has come near. We have seen it in the events of the past week, and we have seen it in the bonds that are uniting us ever more strongly each day." Looking around the sanctuary, Harley felt a rush of affection for the people sitting in its well-worn old pews. They didn't have to be there, but they showed up again and again.

As he looked around, he remembered what the church had been named before it became Riverside Methodist. It was called Emanuel Baptist, and the name Emanuel meant "God is with us." He suddenly realized that God was truly with them.

Harley glanced again at the stained-glass window. Something jumped out at him from the face of Jesus—the eyes. They were the eyes of Norah Bayati, the exact same eyes that had peered out at him from the family photo at Riverview Bakery. They were eyes that looked at him and through him, seeing all. Eyes that knew suffering and sacrifice. Eyes with a life that could survive even death.

"Look at the face of Jesus," Harley whispered to his congregation. "Look at the eyes. They'll continue to watch us, here in the City of Peace."

ACKNOWLEDGMENTS

My college roommate, Jay Tharp, brought a brochure home from his religion class, advertising the 1980 Duke Summer Semester in Israel. He decided not to go, but I jumped in—a decision that changed my life. Thanks, Jay, for decades of friendship, as well as for the brochure.

My love for the wisdom of the ancient world began that summer on an archaeological dig in the Galilee region of Israel, led by professors Eric and Carol Meyers. I realized then that all of the stories of the Bible were based on something real: soil, water, stones, olives trees, coins, sheep, goats, flesh-and-blood human beings. Working on a team of Jews and Christians, I also felt drawn to the interfaith community and made the decision to return to college as a religion major.

Several months later, I gave a presentation on my summer in Israel to the people of my home church, and sitting in the front row was Nancy Freeborne. She sensed my excitement about the discoveries I had made—about both religion and myself—and we began to date. Although her focus was biology, she supported me as I went to Yale Divinity School and prepared to work as a

Presbyterian pastor. We married while I was a student, moved from Connecticut to Virginia, and along the way our family grew to include two children, Sadie and Sam, who are now young adults in New York City and Washington, DC. Nancy and our children have been constant supports to me, as a pastor and a writer.

I am also grateful for the encouragement offered by members of the churches I have served since 1986: First United Church of Christ of Milford, Connecticut; Calvary Presbyterian Church of Alexandria, Virginia; and Fairfax Presbyterian Church of Fairfax, Virginia. The work of ministry has always been attractive to me because it puts me in touch with stories that are real: people in homes, offices, and schools who struggle to overcome challenges with relationships, jobs, money, spirituality, and the chaos of current events. I love trying to make sense of it all through writing, whether I am crafting a sermon or a lesson or a church newsletter article. I have also been fortunate to write for a community far broader than the congregations I have served, through essays on religion and culture for *The New York Times*, *The Washington Post*, *USA Today*, and *Huffington Post*.

One conviction that has become stronger for me over the years is the importance of Christian hospitality, which is embedded deep in the wisdom of the ancient world. I am convinced that the key to overcoming divisions in church and society is to find ways to welcome and include people, just as Jesus did, around shared meals and community experiences. Not that hospitality is limited to Christianity—the practice is central to Judaism and Islam as well, and has potential to break down barriers between people around the world. After visiting a number of congregations that do a particularly good job of welcoming people, I wrote the book *The Welcoming Congregation: Roots and Fruits of Christian Hospitality*, and subsequently wove the practice of hospitality into the fictional story of Harley Camden and the people of Occoquan, Virginia.

Thanks to John Koehler, Joe Coccaro and Hannah Woodlan of Koehler Books, who have been a tremendous help in turning my manuscript into a book. Linda Carlton has done a terrific job with my author's website, and Shari Stauch has been excellent in the marketing arena. I hope this novel will be the first in a series of "Mill Street Mysteries," a name suggested by my daughter's friend Kerry Connelly-Wojay, based on the address of Harley Camden. I dedicate this novel to family members Sadie, Sam and Nancy Freeborne Brinton, my fellow lovers of Occoquan, as well as to professors Eric and Carol Meyers, who introduced me to Sepphoris and started me on the road to the City of Peace.

CPSIA information can be obtained
at www.ICGtesting.com
Printed in the USA
LVHW110347130319
610189LV00031B/248/P